CASH MONEY CONTENT

BLOOD, SWEAT &
PAYBACK

Wahida Clark

CASH MONEY CONTENT

First Edition: April 2014

Book Layout: Jacquelynne Hudson
Cover Design: Nuance Art*

www.CashMoneyContent.com

Library of Congress Control Number: 2013957300

ISBN: 978-1-936399-50-5 hd
ISBN: 978-1-936399-42-0 ebook

10   9   8   7   6   5   4   3   2   1

Printed in the United States

To all of the Wahida Clark Readers and Supporters around the globe.

Prologue

He awoke in darkness, a dark, dank basement, fighting to adjust his swollen eyes. The ropes were so tight, they had cut off the circulation in his hands and feet. He couldn't feel them at all. If he didn't know better, he'd think they had cut them off after everything else they had done to him. Being numb was a welcomed blessing because he felt no pain. His face was swollen from the beating, and he slumped in the chair they had tied him to. He knew he would die. They wouldn't be dumb enough to let him go. But he prided himself on taking it like a G. Knowing that death was near, he was determined not to let his killers think they had won.

Soon, he heard footsteps coming down the stairs and realized he had lost track of time. How long had he been tied down? Hours? Days? Weeks? It didn't matter, because he knew it was over. In fact, he welcomed it.

When he saw the man approach, it all made sense. "You!" he growled, hating to acknowledge he had lost.

The man chuckled. "Surprised? Not surprised? I gotta admit, I still can't read you. But I won, and that's all that matters," the man gloated.

"Nigga, suck my dick! Do what you came to do. Get this shit over with because I got some bad bitches in hell waiting for me," he spat.

"In due time, my nigga. I wanna savor this moment," the man answered, walking around him, circling him like predators circle wounded prey. He rubbed his hands together in anticipation. "You know it's over, right? The Consortium is a thing of the past. Now I run the show . . . solo."

The man stopped in front of him and looked him in the eyes. Despite the beating, he still had that fire in them.

"You wanna know how I did it, don't you? How I played all you dumb muhfuckas!" the man laughed. "Don't you?"

"Fuck you."

"Well, I'ma tell you anyway 'cause the shit is just so fuckin' gangsta, you gonna love it!"

"Bitch, you disgust me," Sharia spat, her tongue dripping with contempt.

"You don't understand, Sharia," Demetria sobbed. "I love Briggen! I can't do no shit like that."

Sharia looked at the phone like it had shit oozing out of it. She didn't know which fact made her sicker—that her baby sister had fallen for the same bullshit game she had fallen for, or the visions of Demetria and Briggen fucking. Her stomach turned. She wanted to vomit. She took a deep breath to steady herself as she stood gazing out at the icy Detroit River from the living-room window of her eighteenth-floor apartment. The Lafayette Lofts remained one of Detroit's prominent waterfront residences. And thanks to her new sponsors, paying the $2,500 monthly lease was not a problem. Sharia then walked over to her kitchen window where she saw remnants of a fire blazing in the city. *Stick to the plan,* she told herself. *Stick to the plan.*

"Look . . . Demetria, I know we've had our differences, but despite all that, you're my sister, and I love you," she lied.

"I love you too," Demetria replied, feeling vulnerable.

Sharia had to catch herself from checking Demetria. The words of her grandmother resounded in her ears. "Never show another bitch how good your man treats you. She'll want him for herself."

"So true, Grandmother. So true," Sharia whispered. *Ever since I can remember, this bitch always wanted my spot.* "Be serious, Demetria. This nigga would not be sittin' in jail for one minute for you. Especially not on no dope charge." She let her words sink in. "So, what the fuck is wrong with you? This is your second time. And this time he is going to leave you for dead. Arkansas is not playing with yo' black ass!" Sharia hoped her words scared Demetria enough to cooperate against Briggen.

This was the second time Demetria got busted in Arkansas, carrying dope for Briggen. The first time she kept her mouth shut, thanks to Sharia being the captain of Briggen's street soldiers. But this time, the captain needed her to flip over on Briggen. The line was silent for a moment. Sharia really needed her sister to do this. She needed her to help make Briggen suffer.

"Demetria!"

"I-I don't know. Prob-probably not."

"You have thirty seconds," the automated operator interrupted their mental tug-of-war that Sharia was winning.

"Demetria, that nigga don't care about you," Sharia said, talking fast. "Do what's best for you, you hear me?"

"Uh-I—" Demetria mumbled.

"Demetria!"

"I hear you," she confirmed.

Sharia started to say something else, but the phone cut off. She went back into her bedroom. "Shit!" she cursed, tossing her phone on the bed.

"So what you think?" he asked, as he kicked back naked on the bed.

"She will," she replied, crawling up on the bed, and straddling him Sharia eased down onto his dick as if her pussy could do all of the convincing. "She better."

Detroit. The city that is now bankrupt. With crime at an all-time high and the lack of consistent police presence, The Consortium felt this was the perfect place to take the game to the next level. The Motor City was in need of a modern-day Robin Hood crew. A crew that would take their ill-gotten gains and pump the monies back into the lifeless city. Dark was especially excited. He wanted to get his Nino Brown on, and Detroit was up for grabs.

Benny Thrillz. Dark was right back at the place where he got his start. And being one of the youngest and newest members of The Consortium, he arranged a meeting, anxious to get things poppin'. As he and a few members of The Consortium sat in the back of the restaurant, he could smell the spaghetti sauce from across the room. The waiter brought over stuffed flounder for Born, spaghetti and meatballs for Six-Nine, and Cornish game hen and a salad for Crystal.

The waiter made sure everyone had their entrées. Dark held his glass above his seafood and pasta dish and proposed a toast. Just as the waiter filled their crystal champagne flutes and they clinked, Dark's cell phone vibrated. Since it was *that* 757 area code he answered it.

"I heard you were doing real well for yourself, so I wanted to send you a gift."

Fuck. He loved and hated the sexy, chilling, overconfident voice. "Bitch, don't call my fuckin' ph—" Dark started to say, but his words were cut off by screams. The restaurant erupted into chaos.

Suddenly, three masked gunmen burst through the door and let loose with semiautomatic weapons, emptying their clips in the direction of Dark's table. Stunned and slow to react, Dark's eyes fell on Born and Six-Nine, who were still grinning over the proposed toast.

And then . . . Six-Nine died stuck with his last expression, a grin. One shot blew through the back of his head, and true to the nature of a dum-dum bullet, ripped open the side of his face. Born moved as if he had a sixth sense, diving to the floor an instant before Dark. They looked at each other as they lay flat on the tiled floor, their eyes both asking, *What the fuck?*

Dark looked up at Crystal who sat frozen in place with terror. Blank face and eyes void she obviously wasn't ready for this part of the game. If it hadn't been for the fact that someone behind her tried to duck away, but instead ducked into the bullet, it would've blown her wig back.

"Yo!" he yelled out, shocked to see her not taking cover. He reached up and snatched her under the table as a barrage of shots exploded exactly where she just was.

"Go! Go!" one of the gunmen barked, and then they all ran out the door.

And just like that . . . It was over.

Dark and Born remained still for several moments after the gunshots stopped to be sure they were clear. Then they slowly got up. Dark snatched Crystal up and surveyed the scene. Several innocent bystanders had been hit, including a small boy. What most likely were the screams of his mother could be heard as she kneeled down, cradling her son. Dark was ready to move. His gaze fell on Six-Nine laid out on his back, faceless. Born's eyes fell on him too, then they looked at each other.

"So this is how niggas wanna play?" Born seethed, ready to blaze the entire city. He especially wanted to go to war with whoever was responsible for this.

"This wasn't a nigga," Dark replied, thinking of the call that came seconds before the hit.

Born started to ask what he was talking about, but sirens wailed in the distance.

"We gotta go," Dark spoke up first out of reflex he grabbed Crystal with his cast-clad arm, and then winced in pain. She was still in a daze. *This bitch ain't nothing like her sister Janay,* Dark thought as they all made their getaway.

He remembered when he first met Janay. Right here in Benny Thrillz, his first Consortium meeting. She had recognized Melky, who sat in a wheelchair, as one of the lames who had come to her house and tried to kidnap and rob her and Crystal. She grabbed a bottle of Grey Goose and smashed the nigga across the head. Then she stabbed him in the throat twice. No one could stop the blood from gushing out of his neck. Yeah. Janay had heart. She was made for the game. And from that moment he was very impressed with her gangsta. Crystal, on the other hand . . . well, he would have to see.

> *My Dearest Nyla,*
> *Baby, if you are reading this note then things are going exactly*
> *as I predicted they would. I need you to do this for me; go into*
> *the basement. You know that old sofa you kept trying to get me*
> *to throw out? Give it to my baby girl and tell her daddy loves*
> *her. And then that picture frame of that $2 bill on the wall in the*
> *bedroom, open it. That's a gift from me to you.*

Nyla was confused. Forever was dead. *Who had sent the note? What's going on?* She made her way into the basement and approached the worn-out old sofa. She had promised herself she'd throw it out a thousand times.

Give it to my baby girl.

Why on earth would he want our daughter to have a sofa? It . . . made no sense. She looked at the couch. Still, it made no sense. Raggedy as it was, it needed to get thrown into a dumpster. Out of anger and confusion, she grabbed one of the cushions and unthinkingly ripping it. She now knew why it was so heavy.

It was filled with money!

Nyla frantically ripped away the rest of the cushion, revealing the neatly stacked and plastic-wrapped money. She could hardly catch her breath, not believing her eyes.

"Oh my God, oh my God, oh my God!" she gasped, tears of joy clouding her eyes. "Thank you, baby."

"You're welcome."

Hearing the familiar voice froze her to the bone.

It can't be! Can it? She spun around and came face-to-face with Forever. He was standing, smiling unwittingly.

Nyla backed away.

"It . . . It can't be," she gasped. "I-I-I must be dreaming!"

"No, bitch, I'm your nightmare!"

Nyla spun back around and came face-to-face with Shan holding a pistol aimed at her face.

"I win, bitch," Shan hissed, and then pulled the trigger.

Nyla woke up in a cold sweat. It was the third time she had had that dream. She couldn't get Shan out of her head. Her obsession with payback was so ingrained in her mind, even her subconscious was getting in on the game.

Nyla had to have hers. She couldn't stand the thought of Shan being somewhere happy, while she continued to struggle with the loss of her soulmate. Yes, Forever brought this fate on himself, but she still loved him. Therefore, she was the only one suffering. But she vowed it wouldn't be that way for long. Whatever she had to do, wherever she had to go, she vowed to Forever and to herself that she would put in the sweat, she would draw first blood, and she would get her payback.

Part I

THE BEGINNING
AND THE END

Chapter One

"Push!"

"I . . . am!"

"Come on, baby. You can do it," Nick urged Shan as he stood by the hospital bed, dabbing her forehead with a wet, cool cloth.

"Uuugh, Nick . . . Nick, please," Shan panted, "I can't . . . take this."

"We're almost there, baby. You can do it," he hoped to encourage her.

Weak to the point of exhaustion, Shan found strength in Nick's presence and assurance in the sound of his voice. Since leaving Briggen, Nick had been her rock. He had moved her to New York and bought her one of Harlem's newly renovated brownstones in a section called Sugar Hill. He also bought her a brand-new navy blue Audi A-5, even though driving in New York was a headache, she appreciated all of his kind gestures. And he did everything with no strings attached, because she had told him as soon as they got to New York, "Listen, Nick, I truly, truly appreciate what you're doing for me and my kids. But I'm not ready for anything serious. I've always had a man to take care of me, but I need to get myself together before getting into anything serious. Plus, you are like family. So I'd understand if you want to . . . fall back."

Nick smiled knowingly. He then gave her a tender but passionate kiss, and replied, "I understand, Shan. Believe me, I do. And I'ma ignore that *like family* comment. But I did promise Peanut and now myself that I would be there for you, and I'm a man of my word. But don't worry. No strings attached. No expectations. Wherever destiny leads, I'll follow."

With one final push, the baby slid out. And at 4:43 a.m. January 19th, she announced herself to the world with a strong wail.

"Congratulations, Mrs. Thompson, it's a big baby girl," the doctor announced.

After the baby was handed to her mother, Nick looked on happily as Shan held her daughter for the first time. Even though deep down he wished the baby was his, in the back of his mind, he couldn't help but think of Briggen, his enemy. He couldn't help but notice how much the baby looked like her father.

Am I really gonna play daddy to this nigga's kids? he thought, then his mind started fucking with him. When he looked at the baby again she looked just like his ex-love Brianna. Nick ran his hands over his face in an attempt to clear his head. *Briggen and Brianna? I'm trippin'.* He pushed the crazy thoughts out of his mind and asked, "What are you gonna name her?"

Almost without hesitation, she answered, "Brianna." Brianna was her best friend, her confidante, her sister from another mother. She was her everything. But the streets ate her up and spat her out. She blew her own brains out.

Nick's eyes widened. He had to get up outta there for a few minutes. "I'ma go by the house and pick up Li'l Nut." He kissed her gently on the forehead and left abruptly.

A few hours later, Nick entered the hospital room with Li'l Peanut and a fistful of flowers and balloons. It saddened Shan to see Nick walk in. She secretly wished it was Briggen coming through the door instead.

"Mommyyyyy!" Li'l Peanut squealed. "Can I see the baby?" he asked dashing over to her bed and clumsily scaling the side until he was safe in her arms. He had been hanging out with Nick, and when he wasn't with Nick, he was stuck in the house with Ms. Josie, the nanny.

Nick laughed. "Damn, Li'l Nut, you must be part monkey!"

Shan giggled. "No, my baby ain't no monkey. He misses his mommy. Don't you, baby?"

Li'l Nut nodded vigorously. "Say hello to your little sister, Brianna. Brianna, meet your big brother, Peanut." Shan kissed him on the cheek.

"Can I take the baby's hat off?" Li'l Peanut asked.

"No, baby. You don't want her to catch a cold, do you?"

He shook his head no.

Nick handed her the flowers and balloons with a smile.

"Thank you, Nick, but why the big smile? What are you up to? Why the flowers?" she teased.

"What? I can't get my favorite lady some flowers? And I'm smiling because you are glowing." He winked. "So how you feelin'? And stop being all skeptical and shit."

"I'm feeling as tired as you look." She snickered, letting out a sigh that she hoped he didn't catch. Again she felt guilty seeing him walk in holding Li'l Peanut's hand. Deep down inside, she knew it should have been Briggen walking into her hospital room holding her son's hand and bringing her flowers. But Shan had made her choice. The choice to leave him high, dry, and alone.

"I almost missed the birth. They had to de-ice the wings on the plane and some other shit."

"Yeah, well, the red-eye from Detroit'll do that to you," she tried to joke. "You almost missed it but you better be glad you didn't."

She could tell Nick was worried. He still had that pending case. Since moving to New York, he had spent a fortune flying back and forth every few days, and he flew back and forth between New York and Detroit almost weekly. He was facing some serious charges that held a lot of time, dinosaur numbers. Not to mention the streets that he still had to run without a right hand man, or someone to be out front in his stead. All the while trying to play house with Shan. It was taking a toll on him.

"How's it looking?" she questioned with genuine concern.

He shrugged. "Shit, ma, I ain't gonna stunt. Shit lookin' fucked up. Bottom line is, I'm working on some things, and the show must go on, and that's what I want to talk to you about."

"What?"

"Not now. When you get home. Just know it'll put you in a position where you can eat for life," he promised.

"Nick, you don't mean—"

"Not now, but just do me and you a favor. Keep an open mind. I gotta go." He gave her another kiss, pried Li'l Peanut away from her, then left her with the nagging feeling that shit was about to get hectic.

The man watched Nick putting Peanut in his car seat and then walk around to the driver's side of his platinum Range Rover. It would've been easy to have put a bullet in Nick's head; he was that close. But that wasn't the assignment. He had instructions to simply watch so that's what he did. Still, surveillance was boring. Killing is what got his blood going. He told himself . . . *Soon.*

Nick smiled as he pulled off looking straight-ahead. "Fuckin' amateur." He chuckled, thinking that whoever had put a tail on him hired the worst.

He had been aware of the tail every time they tried to follow him. He gripped his .40 cal, resting it in his lap. He wouldn't flip the script yet. Not just yet.

Briggen sat on the other side of the glass holding the phone while his lawyer Rudy Harrington explained the situation. Rudy had fought every one of Briggen's cases. From the early days of him catching petty drug charges to the more serious crimes like attempted murder to murder. And each one of them he won. He was more like family than his attorney.

"So basically you're tellin' me that this whole case rests on that bitch Demetria," Briggen summed it up.

"Minus the legal jargon, more or less," Rudy affirmed. "Everything comes down to her."

Briggen ran his hand over his face in frustration. To be so close yet so far away. Pushing a button on that bitch Demetria should be so easy, but he had burnt one too many bridges. He no longer had a decent team or decent money, especially after paying Rudy so much for his case. The Feds already confiscated his home, a few cars, and two bank accounts. He had to face reality. Things weren't like they were back in the day.

His money was running low, his crew had been dismantled, and the clock was ticking.

"A'iight, look . . . I need you to—" Briggen finished the statement on paper, writing. *Find my man Silk.*

Rudy looked at the paper, then back at Briggen. "Calvin, I'm an attorney, not a private detective, okay? I do not—cannot—I will not be involved with anything—"

"Fuck that!" Briggen growled, cutting Rudy off. "For the kind of money I'm payin' you, you should be sending me thong shots! Make some fuckin' calls, and if you don't get him, find him!"

From the look in Briggen's eyes, Rudy knew it was best to appease him. "I'll do what I can," Rudy answered, jotting down the number.

"Yeah, you do that."

Rudy stood up, but before he hung up, he said, "Listen, Calvin, how long have I been your lawyer? Have I ever failed you? Then give me a little credit, okay? I'm on the case," Rudy assured him with a cocky grin.

Briggen sighed and let off a little steam. "Yeah, man, I hear you. I'm stressed the fuck out."

They both hung up. Rudy left, and then the officer on duty came to escort Briggen back to his unit. When he got back, his celly was asleep. Briggen woke him up.

"What up, though?" his celly groggily asked.

"Lemme hold that Jack," Briggen told him.

His celly reached in his stash spot and pulled out a small flip phone and handed it to Briggen. With one ear listening out for the guards, Briggen dialed a number by heart.

"Speak on it," Keeta, his first cousin, answered. Since he could remember she had always been closer to his brother Forever.

"Yo, Keeta, what up? This Brig," he whispered, looking over his shoulder.

Keeta sucked her teeth. "Boy, you know I know who the hell this is. What you hidin' under your bunk?"

Briggen chuckled. "Man, fuck you. What up, though? You find Silk?"

"Naw, baby. Niggas all sayin' he went back to New York."

Briggen shook his head. "Goddamn, Keeta. We gotta find this nigga, ASAP!"

"I hope you don't think I'ma go lookin' for his ass, not with this stomach," she snapped, rubbing her baby bump.

Briggen shook his head. Now it came down to Wise. He was his only hope. He couldn't trust anybody else to take care of Demetria, or anyone else who would do it, for that matter.

"A'iight, yo," he said, not waiting for a reply before breaking the connection.

Keeta felt for her cousin, but what could she do? She was four months pregnant, and she wasn't a killer. She was simply the cousin of two kingpins. She couldn't help who she was related to. Her baby daddy, Mo'Betta, rubbed her naked back, as he reclined on the two pillows behind his neck. He was basking in the afterglow of good sex.

"Who was that? Briggen?"

"How you know my cousin?" she asked.

"Shit, ma, who don't know yo' cousin? I was at his brother Forever's funeral," Mo'Betta explained.

Mo'Betta was an up-and-coming hustla, born and bred in Detroit. Hearing Briggen's name made his ears perk up because he was looking for a come up.

"Oh," was all she said as she got down onto the floor where he was. They were in the living room of his unfurnished house. She went to straddle him again. "Now . . . where were we?"

Goddamn, this bitch is a nympho, he thought. Playing it off, he pushed her off him. "Goddamn, li'l mama, let a nigga catch his breath." *Pregnant pussy may've been good, but goddamn!* "Naw, I'm sayin', what's good wit' cuz?" he questioned.

As soon as he asked, Keeta was hipped to what Mo'Betta was fishing for. She didn't want to expose too much, but she knew if Mo'Betta could help solve Briggen's problems, he'd put him in a better position. And being his baby mama, she stood to eat too. They both were plotting.

"Ain't too much, he just lookin' for his man. He holdin' some money for him," she lied.

"His man who?" he probed.

"Damn, nigga. Nosy, ain't you?" Keeta was just testing where his head was before she brought him up to speed.

He palmed and caressed her soft, ample ass in an attempt to soothe the answer out of her. Little did he know, she was only looking for a reason to give it up.

Angles.

"Listen, ma, we 'bout to start a family, and your cuz yo', he family. So therefore, his beef is mine. So let a nigga know what's good, and I'll handle it," he assured her.

She looked at him a few moments and then said, "Silk."

"Silk?" he echoed. "Silk, Silk, the cat own Full City? That whole strip is rakin' in the dough."

She nodded.

"Shit, since them indictments started droppin', niggas been gettin' ghost. He might be in goddamn Mexico speakin' Spanish." Mo' chuckled. "Naw, but on the real, let me see what I can do," he said, as if it was going to be difficult. Deep down he was amped because he knew exactly where to find him. Silk had been fucking his little sister Tee-Tee.

"Uh-huh. Well, now that we got that straight, you think I could get some of my dick now?" Keeta purred.

He gave her the sexy gaze she loved so much. "You can always get it, li'l mama."

She massaged the base of his half-hard dick until it stood up fully, and then she slid it up inside her. "Ssssss," she sucked her breath in, feeling him fill her up. Her pussy walls twitched with each stroke.

Her pussy was sloppy wet. Mo'Betta gripped her by her hips and pumped himself in and out, longer and harder.

"Ohhh, yess, big daddy. *That's* what I'm talkin' about," Keeta groaned, playing with her own clit while Mo'Betta long dicked the pussy.

"Cock your leg up," he growled at her.

He grabbed her left knee and pulled it forward, positioning her where she was half-squatting on his dick. The angle had her leaning to the side, so he lifted his hips and began to pound away, his dick hitting her spot every time.

"No . . . no . . . no. Oh yeah," she gasped, scared of how good it felt from that angle. It made her feel like she had to pee, and she tingled all over.

Her squeals got louder as Mo'Betta went into a line, beating the pussy with the stamina of a nigga working on a second nut.

"Oh my God! Mo! I'm squirtin'! I'm squirtin'!" Keeta squealed as the clear, juicy liquid shot in spurts from her pussy. She had never squirted before.

Mo'Betta pushed himself as deep as he could go and came hard and long, his body jerked three times before his seed was spent.

Keeta collapsed on his chest and covered his face with kisses. "Goddamn, I love you, baby," she barely got out in between breaths.

"I love you too," he replied, but his mind was on other things. Because the whole time he was digging up in Keeta's guts, he was putting together a plan to dig in Briggen's pockets.

Chapter Two

"Yo, Kay-Gee, man. Please, yo. Tell this nigga it wasn't me," Silk begged, banged up in the middle of his own garage. "I don't know nothing about no restaurant shooting." Silk was one of Briggen's most trusted soldiers but now his loyalty was being tested.

He lay in a pool of his own blood, his ribs broken and several teeth gone. Born, Kay-Gee, Slim, JoJo, and Teraney surrounded him. Born held a golf club while everyone else had guns.

"If he don't believe you, fuck make you think he gonna believe me?" Kay-Gee joked, and the rest of the crew laughed.

"Gee, I told you I've been practicing my swing, yo. You can't be a corporate nigga if you don't play golf," Born explained in a maniacal tone that Silk feared more than the pain. "But it's all in the *swing*!" Born grunted as he swung the G iron club dead into Silk's nuts.

Silk let out a sick moan, his eyes rolled up in his head, and his whole body shuddered right before he threw up.

"Ooooh!" The crew collectively cried, all of them grabbing their nuts.

"Goddamn!"

"Now *that* hurt!"

"You wrong for that, dawg!"

Silk tried to speak, but it was so low the words came out in a hoarse whisper.

"What was that? Speak up," Born taunted. He crouched down and leaned into Silk.

"I . . . didn't . . . set you . . . up," Silk swore with all the strength left in his body.

"Then why you ain't show, huh? You was 'posed to be there, then at the last minute you don't show? Really? Now you wanna play with the God's intelligence? Huh?"

"It wasn't—"

"Man, this fuckin' fag sound like a broken record," Born spat. Then without hesitation he stood up, rearing the golf club back and commenced to beating Silk's head into a bloody pulp. Gray matter oozed from his eye sockets.

"Goddamn, Born! If he ain't dead by now, you can't kill 'im," JoJo cracked, looking down at the bloody mess that used to be Silk's head. "Born. Born. He done, God!"

The sound of JoJo's voice brought Born out of his zone.

"Fuck that, maine. Niggas tried to body me, so nobody in this city sleeps until I find out who," he vowed. He looked at Teraney and said, "Burn this muthafuckin' house down to the ground."

As soon as Dark walked through Crystal's front door, she was all over him. "It's almost ten and you ain't even dressed. I thought we were goin' out," he asked, while at the same time enjoying her raging hormones.

"Mmmmm, I want you in—" she shot back, kissing and sucking his bottom lip. "My mouth, my pussy . . . my ass," she added, yanking off his coat.

Crystal looked at Dark as her knight in shining armor. She couldn't get enough of him ever since he had pulled her to safety in the hit attempt at Benny Thrillz. That same night she didn't want to be alone and found herself bent over Dark's couch getting fucked like never before. The two of them had been inseparable, and Dark had been fucking her ever since. He was her new addiction. For Dark, it was a win-win, fucking his connect who had a killer head game.

Crystal dropped to her knees as she pushed him back against the front door and lowered his True Religion jeans. His dick popped straight out. She wasted no time running her tongue around the head, giving it a firm squeeze so she could taste his precum. Then she ran her tongue tantalizingly along the shaft until she reached his nuts. She sucked from one nut to the other, her right hand jacking his shaft and never losing eye contact.

"Put it in your mouth," Dark demanded, his voice raspy with lust.

She didn't hesitate to please him. Crystal slid his dick inside her warm, wet mouth and began to greedily slurp him, like she knew he loved. He placed his hands on the back of her head, and he began fucking her face as she deep-throated him with no hands.

"Stand up and bend over," Dark told her. He knew he was about to come, but he wanted to fuck that tight pussy first.

Crystal crawled seductively to the stairs and planted her knees on the fourth stair. Leaning upward, she braced her hands on the sixth step as Dark plowed into her, spreading her ass cheeks so he could watch himself beat that pussy.

"Fuck me, Dark! Fuck your pussy!" she urged him, bucking back to meet him thrust for thrust.

Not only did she have killer head, but Crystal had to have one of the tightest pussies Dark had ever had. If he wasn't all about *money over bitches*, he could've easily fallen in love.

"Oh, Daddy, I'm comin', I'm comin', I—" Crystal gushed as she creamed all over his dick, making her pussy that much juicier and causing Dark to explode inside of her.

He sat down on the stairs, pulled her onto his lap, and kissed her passionately as he caught his breath.

"You tryin' to turn a nigga out or something?" Dark teased with a skeptical grin on his face.

"Ummmm. Nigga, you know you already open!" Crystal giggled. She was definitely feeling Dark. Not only was his dick game on one thousand, he was so fucking gangsta that she always felt secure around him. A part of her had been traumatized by the hit attempt. She still had nightmares about it. But she had Dark, and psychologically, he calmed her fears. Besides, she used his team for the muscle, so all she had to do was keep him supplied and sit back counting money. Fair exchange was no robbery.

"So, I guess dinner and a movie is out, huh? What we gonna eat, 'cause you damn sure ain't cookin'." He chuckled, remembering the last time she tried.

Crystal playfully hit him. "Boy, I can cook!"

"Yeah, just not in the kitchen!"

They both laughed.

"I talked to Daddy today," she told him on a more somber note.

"How is he?"

"Not good," she answered, holding back tears as she once again pictured the frail figure that was now her father.

Dark shook his head. He really didn't give a fuck about Big Choppa. He just wanted to make sure the dope would keep pumping even after Big Choppa's heart didn't. "Wheneva you talk about Big Chop, it always makes me think, you know. Like . . . this life is all we got, and it ain't long, you know? So when you find happiness . . . you gotta hold on to it," Dark remarked, running game like a pro.

The way he said it and the words he used made Crystal's heart jump. Her heart knew what he was trying to say. He was going to ask her to be his wife, but her mind wanted to be sure. "Wh-what are you saying, Dark?" she asked, looking into his eyes tenderly.

He looked back, softening his gaze as best he could without laughing at how truly easy it was to lie to someone who wanted to believe. "You know what I'm sayin', baby. Even though I have a son and a baby mama, I don't want you to ever trip about that or feel threatened. It ain't about her. It's all about him. I have to do right by him. But now . . . this ain't planned or rehearsed. I'm sayin'," he paused, putting her hand in his. "I've never met someone who was so much like me. I know you not like the rest of these chicks tryin' to come up off of my money. You really fuck wit' me, and I really fuck wit' you. But I'm trying to take shit to another level. I do a lot of dirt in these streets, and I need somebody stable in my corner. Crystal, I want you to be my wife," he announced as he gazed into her eyes.

Crystal didn't respond.

Fearing she was going to reject him, he said, "I'm sorry. I know I don't have a ring, and I will get you one. But shit, you got a thousand rings upstairs, and I know and you know that you don't need a ring to be my wife."

Crystal's whole body trembled, and she covered her mouth with her hand as tears welled up in her eyes. "Oh my God, baby, yes! Yes! Yes!

Yes!" She squealed, wrapping him up in a big hug and almost knocking them both down the stairs.

They laughed as Dark pushed off the wall to right their balance.

"I love you, Crystal."

"I love you, Jerome," she responded, calling him by his government name. She gave him a quick kiss. "Love and all, I still want my ring!"

They were both ecstatic, but for different reasons. Because for Dark, the only thing better than fucking the connect was being married to his daughter.

"Janaaayyyy!" Crystal screamed into the phone. "He went there! My baby went there!"

"Crystal, who went where and why are you screaming?" Janay peered over at the clock on the nightstand. 3:12am.

"Jerome, girl! Jerome! He proposed to me, Nay. He really proposed. I am getting married!" She squealed out in excitement.

"Who is Jerome?"

"My man, silly. Dark. Jerome is his government name."

There was silence on the phone.

"Nay, he's my man. And he proposed to me. Can't you be happy for me? Damn. Say something."

"You don't want to hear what I have to say, Crystal, and you know it."

"What do you mean I don't want to hear it? What can you possibly say? You don't even know Jerome like that."

"Exactly. And you don't either. But even a blind man can see that the nigga has motive and is just going through the motions. He's not going to marry you, Crystal. He's just using you. And that's all I have to say because you're going to do you anyway. So, congratulations." Janay hung up, leaving a stunned Crystal on the other end.

The next day when Choppa called Crystal he got more than he antici-pated. "Married!"

"Daddy, don't start."

"No! *You* don't start," Choppa shot right back, breaking into a coughing fit. He may not have had his health, but he still had his fire. "That boy in love with me, more than he is you, Crystal! I know you ain't that goddamn stupid!"

Hearing her daddy's objection only made her resent him and want to marry Dark even more. She wanted to spaz, but she remembered who she was talking to, took a deep breath, and replied, "Daddy . . . This is my life. I'm not asking you for permission to live it, but it would be nice if you could be happy for me."

Choppa grumbled something under his breath. "Look, bring the boy to see me. I wanna look him in the eyes before I welcome him into this family. Can you at least do that?"

Crystal's heart leapt. She had always been spoiled, so she thought she had won out on will. "Yes, Daddy, of course. We'll be up there next weekend. I love you!"

"Yeah," Choppa grumbled. He hung up, hoping he had bought himself enough time to do something about the situation.

Thinking about Crystal only made him madder at Janay for walking away from the family business. After getting shot, Janay went on some holy roller, straight and narrow, want-to-live-my-life-right type shit. And went as far as packing up and moving away. She was adamant about being out of the game, but more so, not being her father's puppet. With Janay out, he had to put Crystal in charge, but seeing her falling weak for this nigga, Dark, made him regret the day he made that decision. He didn't like Dark, and he damn sure didn't trust him.

"It ain't over, baby girl," he vowed, searching his mind for a way to get Janay back in the game.

Joy was the quintessential bad bitch. From the Kewpie doll nose to her dimpled smile, her hazel bedroom eyes to her pouty lips, she looked like Halle Berry in her prime. Her style of dress only spoke Italian and French. She rocked every designer from Dolce & Gabbana, Versace, Valentino, Christian Lacroix, and Jean Paul Gaultier, just to name a few. Her strut was so fierce, her Red Bottoms looked like the blood of the broken hearts she had trampled on. She wasn't ghetto thick or corporate petite. Her body was perfectly proportioned and turned heads wherever she went. Now that her husband Cisco was gone, all she wanted was more money, power and lots of respect.

As she walked along the halls of Congress, she was doing just that . . . turning heads. But she remained strictly business and focused on her alligator skin briefcase in her right hand. She knew exactly where she was going, literally and figuratively. Being that she used to be Congressman Duffy's chief of staff, that last fact was a given. She went directly to his office, knocked, and then politely entered.

The office consisted of only two rooms, the office of the chief of staff and Duffy's secretary. Because he wasn't a ranking member in the House, his accommodations were less than ideal. But thanks to gerrymandering, he now had a district that was 90 percent African American, which all but ensured him reelection for life. A politician with that kind of job security could amass a lot of power, and Joy planned on using it to her advantage.

When she walked in, she was met by the polite smile of the new secretary, who, to Joy's amusement, was a cheap knockoff of herself.

It was obvious Duffy had had Joy in mind when he selected her replacement after she resigned. Seeing the new hire was like seeing a fake Gucci handbag. Joy could tell the woman saw it too, because even though her smile was polite, it was plastic, trying to mask the resentment in her eyes.

"Can I help you?"

"I'm here to see Maurice."

"Do you have an appointment with Congressman Duffy?" She asked as if she was correcting her.

"No, but he'll see me. Tell him it's Joy Parker. You have my old job."

"I'm sorry, but the congressman doesn't see anyone without an appointment," she said, happy to find something to deny Joy and acting as if she didn't know who she was.

Joy smirked, hit speed dial, and put the phone on speaker.

"Yeah?" Duffy's voice came through loud and clear.

"It's me, I'm coming in," Joy announced, more for the girl's benefit than his.

"About time." Duffy chuckled.

Joy hung up, sashayed over to his office door, and cracked it. She swung her bag over her shoulder, stopped and then told the secretary, "Hold his calls. And I'll have a bottled water."

She closed the door, leaving her knockoff to stew in her own resentment. "Bitch," Joy hissed.

When Joy waltzed toward Duffy, he rose from his seat. She smiled at the fine figure he cut. He was only thirty-two, looked like a young Will Smith, and had the charm to match. He was a hell of a politician, and if he could keep his dick in his pants, Joy could see him as the next black president.

He rounded the desk to give her a warm hug and a warm kiss on the cheek.

"Joy, Joy," he said, hitting her with his dimples, "your mother named you well. Are you back for your position? Go ahead, tell Simone she can leave now."

Joy snickered. "Flattery will get you everywhere, Maurice."

"And with you, everywhere is where I wanna be," he shot back smoothly and kissed her hand.

They both laughed.

"Still the smoothest politician inside the Beltline, I see," Joy remarked as she walked around the desk and sat in his swivel seat.

"And you still look better in my seat than I do. What can I do for you?" he asked, propping up *GQ* style on the edge of the desk.

She crossed her long sexy legs and let her Red Bottom dangle delicately from her right foot. "It's what we can do for each other," she corrected.

"Reciprocity." Duffy smiled evilly as the word rolled off his tongue. "The grease that makes this country spin. Better yet, I rub your back and you can massage mine," he flirted.

Joy set her briefcase in her lap, faced him, and then popped the clasps. She lifted the lid to reveal seventy-five thousand dollars neatly filling it.

Duffy ran his eyes over the money but kept it poker. "And that would be . . ?"

"A campaign contribution . . . the first of many, we'll call it." She smirked.

"Which of my . . . *policies* are you interested in? Immigration reform, foreign affairs . . ."

"Law enforcement. Federal jurisdiction. Nicholas Powell," she told him. Nicholas "Nick" Powell. The number one drug supplier to the city of Detroit.

Duffy nodded, pinching his lip pensively. "I see . . . Sounds to me like you need a lawyer more than a congressman."

Joy saw the game he was playing so she decided to jump right to the point. "There are several vacant federal judgeships. One in your district. The road to confirmation may end in the Senate, but it runs through your office. Nicholas Powell doesn't go to jail. He doesn't even go to court. Make it happen. The number is five hundred grand. Do we have a deal?"

Duffy liked the way she ran it down. She knew politics cold. He had taught her well . . . maybe *too* well.

"Leave the briefcase and a number."

"Here's the number," she answered, handing him a business card. "Our man is one Detective Sherman of the Detroit Police Department. He calls all of the shots for their Drug Task Force. But as for the brief-case . . ." Joy stood up and dumped the money out on the desk before closing and retaining it, "—it was the only mauve one in Milan."

He chuckled at her femininity as she headed for the door.

"Oh, and, Maurice, I ask only one thing of the politicians I buy." She had his undivided attention as she placed one hand on the doorknob.

"What's that?"

"That they stay bought," she responded, blew him a kiss, and then she was gone.

Chapter Three

I Miss You . . .

What was it about those three little words that could so easily tug on the heart-strings? They weren't like the words 'I love you' that were in the present and always seemed like something to be desired. Love was so big . . . so vague . . . so all-encompassing. But *miss* was a word that said despite time, distance, and circumstance, *I am thinking of you.* It was the one word that let her see beyond those rose-colored memories.

When her phone chimed, Shan was sitting in the den playing with Li'l Peanut. She picked it up. She didn't recognize the number, but her heart said it was Briggen. She stared at the screen before opening the text. Her hands were trembling. She knew. She rushed to her bedroom and sat in the recliner next to the window. She opened the text and there they were. Those three words . . . *I miss you.* Her heart skipped a beat. She closed her eyes and placed the phone to her heart. "I miss you too," she whispered.

Shan acknowledged that she did him dirty. Yes, she took his money, refused to help him out while he did his bid. She ran off with his kids. And then there was Nick. She *thought* that 'for better or worse' meant everything to her. *And then there was Nick.* She felt guilty because she still loved Briggen. In spite of everything that went down, Briggen was her husband. The father of her children. And now it took everything inside her not to call the number attached to the text.

All throughout the day those three little words interrupted her. At the stoplight, while getting her hair done, or sitting on the couch with her feet curled up under her, while the rain beat a soft pattern on the window. Especially as she sat holding their daughter. She couldn't help opening the text over and over again, hoping the phone would ring. That's one of the reasons she never changed her number . . . just in case.

Then it happened. Another chime. She grabbed her phone, and the next text warmed her up.

No matter what I'll always love you. I need you and my kids.

She rubbed the screen of her iPhone as if touching his face. She knew this wasn't a good idea, but it did wonders for the guilt she was carrying. Maybe it had something to do with just having the baby. Now she wanted to text back but knew she shouldn't. Especially after getting a text from Nick not too long ago that read: **Be home soon—I love you.**

The guilt. She went to delete Briggen's text, but couldn't, and then, as if he were reading her mind, he sent another one.

Tell me about our little girl.

Briggen sat back on his bunk waiting for Shan's reply. It didn't bother him that she didn't text back after the first one. In fact, it was a good sign. After all the fly shit she popped about taking the money. If she was still on some bullshit, she would've used his emotions to twist the knife.

Because she hadn't he knew he had her stuck. Deliberately, he waited a long time to text again, allowing her to stew in her own juices. He knew he had to be extra gentle so he could rock her to sleep and get close enough to do what he needed to do.

Her name is Brianna Michelle.

She texted back and included a picture, the one she felt showed that she had Briggen's eyes and her nose. A perfect combination, she thought like a blending of their best features. The best of them, to make her. Before she knew it, they were texting back and forth about the baby's weight, her birthday, her ways, and joking about who she got them from.

The baby broke the ice and helped to melt the tension. She knew she took her anger against him too far. The guilt had been eating her up. Hell, it still was. What did he do to her that justified her to turn all the way against him? *How angry was he at her? Did he hate her?* She had to know. But the elephant in the room went unacknowledged until Briggen's next text:

Can I call?

Before she knew it she had sent him a text right back:

Yes

She loved the way the recoil of the 9 millimeter Beretta felt whenever she let it blow. The way it created the tension in her grip, then spit whizzed through the air, matrix-like, until it found the soft flesh of the target. Running her eyes over her vic, she got excited. He stood naked before her, raw fear in his eyes.

"You bitch!" he gritted through clenched teeth. The vic moved his head away from the gun, attempting to show bravery in front of his homeboys.

"Bitch, huh?" She gripped the pistol tighter and squeezed the trigger. Like a bolt of lightning, the bullet lodged into his shoulder, instantly dropping him to his knees. He wailed in pain, realizing that she was not playing.

"Nigga, shut your bitch ass up. It was only your shoulder," she taunted him. She used to be timid. Shy even, especially around dudes. But it was hard to be scared of niggas when she had seen the look in their eyes when she gripped the steel and aimed it sideways at their dome.

Fear. And she was addicted to its scent.

The nigga lay on the floor trembling, screaming out in pain, blood oozing from his wound. "Nigga, you ain't slick. You think somebody gonna hear you!" The shooter's partner chuckled, standing over him with a gun in her hand as well. "Scream out one more time, and I promise you, it'll be the last time."

His two friends remained still, barely breathing. Both glad that it was his house and not theirs. What they thought was about to be a freak fest turned into a jacking. Now the only thing on their minds was how to get out alive. The third girl lay naked on the bed, scared out of her mind. She was certain that since it was almost three in the morning Valentine's Day, someone heard the gunshots. It was obvious these two chicks were not here to play games. Their names were Courtney and Michelle, but tonight they had been Lisa and Monet . . . until the guns came out.

"Now, I'ma ask you again," Michelle hissed, squatting down next to dude. He still couldn't believe she had shot him. She looked way too fine to be so cold, but he learned quickly that looks were deceiving.

Before she could get the rest out, Courtney spat, "Shit, I ain't even askin' no more." Then *Boom!* She shot him in the thigh.

"Aarrrghh, fuck!" the dude bellowed.

Courtney hit him in the other thigh.

"Please!" he yelled.

She took aim at his nuts.

"Okay!" he agreed with quickness; it was clear these bitches didn't want to talk. "Okay!"

"Okay what!" Courtney snapped.

"My stash is under the floor, in the kitchen. You have to move the refrigerator. I ain't trying to die for you bitches." He snitched himself out, almost paralyzed with pain. Three bitches, three niggas. What started out as a night of flossin' and gettin' freaky ended up with him and his boys stripped of all of their jewelry, pockets emptied, stripped down to their boxers, and now on the floor kissing the carpet. A bad ending.

"Lisa, check it out," Courtney ordered using the alias of her partner in crime.

Courtney and Michelle had been partners in crime for the last six years. Friends since high school, the two grew up in the same hood. They hit their first lick after some baller talked them into a threesome with a promise of a thousand apiece. After they fulfilled their part of the deal, he refused to give them their pay. Michelle wasn't having it, and she started calling him all kinds of names: "bitch-ass nigga, broke-dick nigga, bitch-ass nigga," again and again. After that third bitch-ass nigga he wasn't having it either, and he smacked the shit out of her. Courtney, the hothead of the two, always carried a pistol. She didn't hesitate shooting the nigga. And she was a good shot because the bullet caught him right between the eyes. It was Michelle's idea to ransack the apartment, and they came up with forty-seven thousand dollars and a shitload of jewelry. Their new hustle was found, thus, bringing them into the present.

Courtney wasn't actually the leader of the two. She was just the thinker. Darker than Michelle, the Nubian black cat-eyed diva was more ruthless than the average nigga.

Michelle stood up and waved her gun at the naked chick. "You. Bitch. Come with me," Michelle ordered, and the girl named Stephanie quickly complied. She was the one who put them onto the pussy lovin', flossin' ballers.

Once they were in the kitchen, Michelle whispered, "Yo, you doin' good. These niggas dumb as fuck."

"Let's just get this gwap and go," Stephanie urged nervously, "and please don't kill these niggas 'cause I ain't tryin' to catch no bodies."

"I got you." Michelle winked. "Just help me move this shit."

The two of them pushed and pulled until they saw the stash spot hollowed out in the floor. Michelle bent down, ran her fingers over the loot, her heart dropping when she saw the short-ass stacks in the stash. It couldn't have been any more than twenty grand.

"Jackpot!" the chick whispered excitedly, eyes filled with greed.

Michelle looked at her like she had two heads. If that short money excited her, she *definitely* was in over her head. Michelle grabbed a shopping bag and put the money inside.

When they got back in the bedroom, Michelle kicked the nigga dead in the ass. "Nigga, you made me move a refrigerator for *this?*" She spat, holding up the bag with disgust. "You coulda' kept that short-ass shit in a shoe box!"

Courtney peeked in the bag, looked at Michelle, and shook her head like *god . . . damn.*

"Fuck it. It is what it is," Courtney summed it up.

They quickly filled the bag with the niggas' chains, rings, watches, and earrings. Now, it was time to go . . . almost.

"Y'all niggas believe in God?" Courtney smirked.

The words sent a chill through the air that they all felt instantly.

"Come on, ma. You got that. Shit ain't that serious," one of the dudes tried to reason, while keeping the tremor out of his voice.

"I ain't ask all that. I just asked do . . . you . . . believe . . . in . . . God?"

"Yeah, man, yeah," the bleeding dude answered.

"He just never around when you need 'im, huh?" She chuckled, letting her snubnose bark.

Michelle let loose at the same time, and nine shots later, the three dudes lay twitching and lifeless, brains splattered and guts leaking at their feet.

"You killed them! You killed them! Oh my God, I told you not to kill them!" Stephanie sobbed while out of her mind with fear.

Courtney and Michelle looked at each other. They hadn't planned to, but . . .

"Stephanie, Stephanie, chill, yo, chill." Michelle tried to calm her. "Relax. You not goin' to jail, okay?"

"And neither are we," Courtney concluded as she put the gun to the back of the chick's head and relaxed her forever.

After dumping the guns in the Delaware River, they headed over the Ben Franklin Bridge into Camden. The little rented Ford Prius rocked to the old school sounds of Bone Crushers, "Never Scared."

"I ain't nevah scared," Michelle rapped as she counted the money.

"How much?"

"I ain't finish. I ain't *nevah* scared," Michelle continued to rap.

Courtney sucked her teeth when she realized Michelle was just being funny. "Bitch, stop playin'."

Michelle laughed. They were tighter than wolf pussy.

"Like twenty-three, twenty-four grand."

"What about the jewels?"

"Jewels? Man, between these cheap-ass black diamonds, and these fuckin' chips, we'll be lucky to get fifteen stacks for all of it."

Courtney was vexed. "We coulda stayed in Newark for that. God-damn!"

"I know, right?"

"These short-ass niggas out here, man. Where all the real ballas, yo?" Courtney vented.

"Wit' long dicks and long money!" Michelle chimed in.

"Exactly!" Courtney agreed.

"We need a fuckin' . . . heist, yo. Word up."

Several moments later, Michelle's phone rang with a text. She looked at it, frowning up. "Yo, who the fuck is Shan? And why is she texting me at five in the morning?"

"Shan?" Courtney echoed. "Dude or chick?"

"Oh snap! Shan! Remember ol' girl from Detroit that we met in Vegas? At the Mayweather fight."

"Hmph, Mayweather," Michelle remarked. "Now that nigga! We need to be doin' some serious fuckin' with his fine and very rich ass. He would be more than a heist."

"You remember?"

"Yeah, yeah, I remember. Ol' girl was kinda cool."

"And you know them bitches from there, real slick and they 'bout that gwap."

"No doubt," Michelle agreed, "and the way she was slingin' that paper, I know she could turn us on! Her text say she just moved to New York and she just had a baby. Aww! Look at her. Baby girl cute, too!"

"New baby, new city, new life . . . shit, I smell a lick up in this mix," Courtney snickered.

"You already know!" Michelle chimed in, texting Shan back.

Even though Sharia wasn't really into anal sex, she was so gone off Fat Rich's dick that in the heat of passion, he was able to slide it straight in her ass, making her pussy quiver and come with a quickness.

"Oh fuck, Rich, take it out!" she squealed, but it was a curious type of pain that made her beg for more.

"You know you like it," he grunted, spreading her ass cheeks so he could watch his dick disappear between her juicy, round, phat ass cheeks.

"Y-yesss," she melted as the pain went away and turned into pure unadulterated pleasure.

She began to throw it back, timidly at first, but when he reached around and started playing with her clit, the sensation drove her wild, and she started to take the ass fucking like porn star Janet Jacme.

"Oh shit, daddy, my ass feel so good just like my pussy," she purred as he pounded away on her back door until it smacked wet like her pussy.

"Tell daddy who his nasty bitch is," he demanded, pulling her hair.

"I am! I'm your nasty bitch, daddy! Ooooh, put it back in my pussy. I'm about to explode!" Sharia performed like a seasoned pro.

Fat Rich slid out of her ass and back up in her pussy without missing a stroke. Her pussy was now super wet. Just the feel of her tight, hot wetness sent him over the edge a stroke before Sharia followed him.

The two of them lay spent until he got up to go take a shower.

Sharia watched him disappear inside the hotel bathroom. Fat Rich was a gettin-money-ass nigga, but he was also a new member of The Consortium. That fact alone made up for his overweight ass and average dick game. Sharia was simply in search of another sponsor, and Fat Rich fit the bill.

Her phone rang. She looked. It was *him*. She always took his calls.

"If you wanted to listen, you're too late," Sharia joked.

"Did he beat it up like me?"

"Nobody beats it like you, daddy," she cooed, wishing he was there right then.

He chuckled. "I know that's right. You hear about ol' boy Silk?"

"Yeah, somebody did him dirty. You think it was—"

"Naw, but whoever it was, they did us a favor. He could've been Briggen's legs on the street, and we gotta make sure that nigga stay crippled. We almost there. You got Demetria?"

"She good. I got her layin' low."

"Make sure she stay that way," he warned. "And find out about some cat named Mo'Betta."

She lowered her voice hearing the shower turn off. "I gotta go."

"Remember, keep that dumb bitch low."

"I got you, nigga." She hung up.

Fat Rich came out, still wet with a towel around his shoulders. "So what you tell 'em? You with your girlfriend? At the mall?" He chuckled.

"No, I told him I'm suckin' the next nigga," she shot back sarcastically.

"And what he say?" Fat Rich asked, playing along.

"Get yo' money up front."

Fat Rich laughed. "I know that's right. I like you, li'l mama. You real as fuck. Real talk, I ain't tryin' to wife you, but you break me off a li'l sumthin', I break you off a li'l sumthin'. You feel me?"

"I'm cool wit' that."

"That's what it is then."

Later as she drove off, she couldn't help but laugh at her own frustration. The nigga broke her off a little something all right, in both ways. But her main man needed to hurry up with his plan, because she was tired of tricking with ballers.

The minute Big Choppa entered the visiting room, Dark knew the old man was living on borrowed time. There was no longer anything big about the old man besides his ego and his rep. He had shrunken in weight and shriveled in height so much that the wheelchair he sat in seemed to swallow him. The inmate pushing him brought him to the table. Choppa's eyes had never left Dark's from the moment he spotted them from across the visitation room. So by the time they actually spoke, their eyes had already had a long, heated conversation.

"So I hear tell you think you gonna marry my daughter," Choppa began, skipping the small talk, handshakes, and hello kisses.

"I—Daddy. He is—" Crystal started, but Choppa raised his hand to silence her.

"A man don't need a woman to speak for him. You a man, ain't you?"

"One hundred percent," Dark countered, not feeling the way Choppa was testing his gangsta.

"Then, goddammit, answer the question!"

"I have every intention of doing so. I love your daughter so—"

Choppa laughed. "Love my daughter? Youngin', please. You don't even know my daughter. What's her favorite color? When's her birthday? And where'd that scar on her right leg come from?"

"Daddy, none of those—"

This time it was Dark who raised his hand, but when he spoke, he looked at her.

"Purple's her favorite color, or fuchsia, to be exact. Her birthday is in seven months and eleven days, and the scar . . . we never discussed it, but I guarantee she wouldn't have got it if I had been there," he answered smoothly.

If he didn't already have her heart, she would've given it to him on the spot.

Choppa could see from the look on Crystal's puppy dog, I'm-in-love face, his tactics had backfired. He had to admit, the boy had more game than he gave him credit for. Disappointment was written all over his face.

"Nigga, you may be nickel slick, but you a dollar short wit' me. You ain't nothin' but a two-bit hustler tryna come up off the love of a good woman from the right family. That's the type of shit you burn in hell fo', and nigga, I'll burn in hell befo' you marry her!" Choppa grumbled.

Crystal couldn't contain herself any longer. She kept her voice low, but her tone was unmistakable. "Daddy, you will not control my life! We love each other, and we're getting married, and ain't a goddamn thing you can do about it!"

Choppa could tell she was adamant about it, because she looked just like her mother when she put her foot down. For a moment his heart ached, missing her, but the rage quickly engulfed the sensation.

"Crystal, I swear fo' God and fo' mo' white folk, if you so much as set foot in that church with the intention of givin' this nigga your hand, you play your hand with me! I'll strip you of that connect and toss it to hell fo' I see him with it!" Choppa's voice turned deep.

Crystal laughed. "Really, Daddy? Really? You think I care about your precious connect? I don't give a damn about that! We'll survive, and we will thrive, so you can keep your goddamn connect!"

Dark thought, *Hold up, bitch. You goin' too goddamn far,* but he held his tongue.

Crystal wasn't looking at Dark, but Choppa was and he could see it in Dark's eyes. He smiled at the irony. *You got the goose, but the bitch ain't golden!* "Well, in that case, congratulations." Choppa looked over his shoulder and got the attention of his inmate attendant. "Nigga, come on here."

Before he was wheeled away, he said, "Baby girl, I love you. Never forget that. But you about to make one of the biggest mistakes in your life, and I just can't be a part of that."

With tears in her eyes and a catch in her throat, she replied, "I love you, Daddy, but I love Jerome too."

Choppa nodded grimly. He knew once a woman's heart was committed, the situation would have to play itself out. Once more he eyed Dark who had a smirk on his face, and Choppa accepted the silent challenge.

"Get me outta here," he told his attendant, who wheeled him away from more than the table. Choppa was wheeled away from his baby.

As Dark and Crystal rode away from the Memphis FCI, both were locked in their own thoughts hypnotized by the sound of the windshield wipers sliding back and forth. Dark knew he had to move carefully, but there was no way in hell he was going to get married if she was out of a connect.

"Listen, Crystal, I hate seeing you caught up like this. I know that's your father and all—"

"Baby, he'll always be my father, but I choose you. Therefore, the rest is irrelevant," she replied.

"Naw, I'm just sayin', this shit could get . . . ugly. I know your father. You know your father. He ain't gonna just lie down and roll over if he feel a way about shit, you know that," Dark said, choosing his words carefully. He hadn't expected Big Choppa to be so stubborn but was glad that he was. He just made it easier for him to make his next move.

Crystal looked over at him. "What do you mean, Jerome?"

He glanced at her as he handled the steering wheel. "Your father's a very powerful man with long arms. And I damn sure ain't the type to let a nigga move on me. I don't give a fuck who it is," he emphasized, putting his cards on the table.

Crystal glanced out of the window. Torn. She knew Dark was right, but Choppa was her father. Still, there was no mistaking the situation. Somebody would be the winner. Somebody would have to die.

"Jerome, that's my father. But . . . I trust you. I have to if you're about to be my husband, and I stand behind you."

"So what you want me to do?"

She looked him dead in his eyes, and replied, "Let the cards fall where they may, baby. Play the hand you've been dealt. I will arrange for you to meet the connect."

That was all the confirmation Dark needed. Love was a powerful force, but his dick was even more powerful. It took everything in him to contain his composure. He wanted to pump the air with his fist.

"Yo, Brig, I know you heard about Silk."

"Yeah . . . I heard."

"I tried to get at the nigga for you, yo," Mo'Betta said as he drove along Nine Mile Road.

Briggen pinched his nose as he kept one eye open for the police. He was crouched in his cell on a cell. "Yeah, fam', Keeta told me. Good look."

"That's nothin'! I know you a good nigga', you just in a bad situation. But what up, doe? Tell me what you need. Say the word and it's done. Keeta said ol' boy owed you some bread, but I feel like it's more to it than that. Not tryin' to pry or nothin', but I'm here, nigga. One hundred," Mo'Betta vowed.

Briggen contemplated the situation. It was like all day he could hear the loud *tick . . . tock* of the clock ticking loud in his ear. Time was running out. He never wanted to move out of desperation, but it was now or never, and he knew he had to make a move.

"Peep game. Go cop a TracFone and hit me back from that ASAP," Briggen instructed.

"I got you, dawg," Mo'Betta answered. He hung up, charged. He was down for whatever because he knew if Briggen got out, his come up was in stone.

Mo'Betta was so caught up he didn't recognize he was being followed. When he stopped at the Chinese spot on Six Mile, *she* stopped too. When he went in, she was right behind him. And when he ordered beef and broccoli, three egg rolls, and a bottled water, she remarked, "Hmmmm, I like a man with an appetite."

He turned and liked what he saw. A brown-skinned bombshell that reminded him of Kerry Washington with her pouty lips and aggressive stance. A bombshell that he wouldn't mind fucking.

"Sheeeit . . . dependin' on the dish, I might lick the plate," he replied, looking her up and down, taking in her thick hips and thighs. "Can I get a name?"

She stood with her hand on her hip, making sure his eyes drank her all in.

"Shayla," she lied, not wanting to say Sharia.

Mo'Betta licked his lips. "Shay-Shay," he joked.

"Uh-uh." She wagged her finger back and forth. "Only my Daddy calls me Shay-Shay."

"I could be your Daddy," Mo'Betta flirted.

"Yeah, well, you gonna spoil me, *Daddy?*"

"Then you must be a good girl, then, huh?"

"Even when I'm bad."

They both laughed.

"Eleven nine-nine," the Chinese lady cackled, holding his order. "Eleven nine-nine you pay."

Mo'Betta pulled out his money and then looked at Sharia. "Anything you want, ma, is on me," he offered.

"Save that thought, playa." She winked and giggled.

After exchanging numbers, he continued on his mission. He went to Walmart and copped the TracFone and some minutes, then sent Briggen a text. A few minutes later, Briggen called back.

"Yo, Br—"

"No names," Briggen cut him short. "I'ma text you the problem, but not the solution. I already talked to our people, feel me?"

"Yeah."

"You sure?"

"Yeah, yeah, our people."

"She gonna school you to the situation. You handle this li'l bruh, and you'll be a made man with me," Briggen assured him.

"That's a bet."

"Hit me after you got the whole picture."

They hung up. Briggen texted him one word to the TracFone:

Demetria

Chapter Four

They finally made their move, and despite his attentiveness, they had almost caught Nick slipping. Nick felt a little more relaxed in Detroit than he did in New York. He was always on point driving around New York, and he always lost his tail who was sloppy, almost laughable, so it was easy to detect and even easier to evade. He always slipped them before arriving at Shan's spot or his spot. But he wasn't aware of their presence in Detroit, which almost cost him his life.

Lesson number one: *gangstas don't use drive-thru*. Why? Because you're boxed in and a sitting duck for a hit, and Nick violated that rule. He had been shooting moves all day and ended up on the East Side of Detroit on an empty stomach. Not really having the time to sit down and eat a meal, he stopped at McDonald's on Gratiot sat trying to decide whether to use the drive-thru or go inside. He felt safer in his car, plus the line was short.

Nick was driving a rented Lincoln MKZ. Two cars were ahead of him and one car behind him. An old gray Taurus hooptie pulled into the parking lot while he placed his order. By the time he looked up, the Taurus was in his blind spot, idling . . . waiting.

The Taurus lurched forward. The sound of the sudden acceleration caught Nick's attention, and he saw the blur from his peripheral. They skidded up and opened fire with semiautomatic AR-15s.

"Goddamn!" Nick bellowed as he ducked and was sprayed with shattered glass. He yanked out his .40 caliber from his waistband and let off several shots blindly, only trying to buy time as he stomped on the gas and rammed the car in front of him. Wasting no time, he yanked the steering wheel hard right and peeled out of the tight space before the Taurus tried to ram him and keep him pinned in. Through the sounds of metal on metal, sparks flying and filling the air, Nick managed to pull free. The Taurus was dead on his ass.

He tried to hop the curb in hopes of merging into traffic, but an oncoming SUV sideswiped his rear-passenger side, bending it until the rear left tire was totally flattened.

Recognizing their opportunity, the shooters in the backseat hopped out and moved in, but Nick dived across the seat and crawled out the passenger door. When he hopped up to return fire, he used the jet black Lincoln as cover, but the two shooters were in the open. He let off two shots. Both hit the shooter closest to him, once in the chest and the second in the neck. Blood squirted and he dropped, lifeless. The second shooter dived behind the Taurus seconds before Nick sent a barrage of bullets his way.

Nick ducked, his gun empty, but lucky for him the sound of approaching sirens signaled the end of round one. The Taurus hopped the curb and sped off in one direction while Nick sprinted away from the scene in the other.

He said fuck all his appointments and headed straight back to New York. This chick named Debra rented the car for him, so she would have to deal with that drama. He promised himself that he was going to pull that tail and find out who the fuck it was and who sent them. And then cut that tail right off—literally. His instincts said it was Mr. G, but he couldn't be sure. The media did report that they were partners. They had collaborated on a few deals, including conspiring to squeeze The Consortium from both ends, but they were still competition. But now that Nick had been indicted, was Mr. G trying to clip the loose ends?

Then he thought of Janay and Big Choppa. Had they figured out the relationship between him and Mr. G, or somehow learned it was his shooters that had carried out the hit attempt on Janay and Boomer for Mr. G? Big Choppa was no one's fool, and his daughter was just as sharp. But finding that out would be impossible. He and Mr. G would have to tell on themselves. And then it hit him.

Briggen.

Had he sent the team at him because he had taken Shan from him? Because he had betrayed him? He may've been locked up, but he knew Briggen's reach was long and real. All three were valid choices, so he knew he needed to lay low until he could figure out his next move.

Nick headed straight to Shan's once he was back in the city. He needed to see her and tell her what was on his mind. Besides, he missed her. He knew Shan was a good girl and wifey material, and he wanted her in his corner. Especially if she agreed to his proposal. When he got to her place, he noticed a mint green BMW 650 with Jersey license plates parked behind her Infiniti. His first thought was, it's a nigga—his blood pressure heated up his ears. She said she needed space, but he'd be damned if that included space enough for a nigga to be laying up in a place that he kept up.

Nick rang the doorbell, and when it wasn't answered instantly, he rang it again. He started to ring it a third time, but Shan peeked out, saw him, and opened the door.

"Nick, what's wrong?"

"Nothin'," he replied, moving past her with swiftness and entering the living room.

Instead of a nigga, he was met by two sexy pairs of eyes looking back at him. One chick had Brianna lying across her lap, and the other was holding a rattle. The floor was strewn with torn wrapping paper and ribbons, as if presents had been opened. Shan came around the corner and sat back down.

"Nick, these are my peoples, Courtney and Michelle. Y'all, this is Nick!"

They all exchanged pleasantries, but remembering the look on Nick's face before he saw the females, Courtney remarked, "Don't worry, Nick. That's me out front."

When Shan caught on, they laughed, and even Nick had to join in. "Naw, yo, I wasn't on it like that. I'm just sayin'," Nick smirked sheepishly.

"Oh, we know *exactly* what you was 'just sayin','" Courtney snickered.

Nick liked the two chicks' swagger. They definitely didn't have a dyke vibe, but their vibe said they weren't on some gold-digging shit either. They struck him as straight-up go-getters; he just didn't know how right he was.

After they left, and she put the kids to bed, Nick and Shan kicked back on the couch, her feet up in his lap as he massaged them gently.

"Nick . . . Did you really think I had someone up in here . . . like that?" Shan asked, but her expression stated the real deal. *Nigga, come on. Be for real.*

"No, I'm just leery of strange cars," he said.

"Yeah right."

He started to tell her about the shoot-out, but something told him not to. Instead, he began with the subject that was really on his mind.

"So, did you think about what I said about making some moves with me?"

"Yeah, but you didn't go into detail. You just said you thought it was time that I made some moves with you. And then you said, keep an open mind."

"Well? Did you?"

"Nick, just tell me what you need me to do," she replied with a hint of impatience.

"Look, with this fuckin' case I'm under, I can't move like I need to. But shit still gotta flow. I need somebody I can trust to hold shit down for a while," he explained.

"Hold what down?"

"My connect," he answered, getting straight to the point.

Shan looked at him. "You mean—"

"Ma, believe me. It will be free money for you. I've got everything in place, so you ain't gotta ever touch nothin' but money. It's just that. I ain't tryin' to introduce nobody to my connect. Believe me, Shan, in six months, you'll see more money than you've ever seen in your life," he emphasized, needing to seal the deal.

He definitely had her attention. Shan knew her little stash wouldn't last much longer. She needed a source of income. But . . . drugs? And he trusted her enough to turn her on to his connect? She now had a whole new respect for Nick.

Shan took her legs out of his lap and sat up. "But . . . Nick, I don't know anything about moving weight," she protested weakly.

He slid closer to her.

"You don't have to, baby. I'll be right there, just in the shadows. I got you. By the time I'm finished with you, they'll call you the Doña," he joked, making her giggle.

"Why me, Nick?"

"Because I trust you," he replied, caressing her cheek. "You are all I got. And like it or not I'm all you got. Period. Real talk, I want to spend my life with you, Shan, and I'm starting here and now. It's no coincidence how we were brought together. And look at all we've been through. We can continue to build this together, baby. All you gotta do is say yes."

"Nick . . ." she whispered as he kissed her neck.

He playfully mimicked the duo Floetry. "All you gotta do is say yes," and continued his soft kisses down into the V of her cleavage as he slid her blouse off her shoulders, and then down over her breasts. He then began to lick and tease each nipple.

"Don't," she whimpered, but her body was singing another song. "You said not until I was ready."

He ran his tongue ticklishly along the length of her torso until he met the fabric of her jeans. He unbuttoned them, unzipped the zipper and slid them down along with her thong as he continued his full-body tongue massage.

"Oh, Nick, that feels so good. I—" Her voice caught in her throat when he began to lick and suck on her clit.

Shan instantly arched her back to meet his tongue, putting her hands on his head and gripping his head.

"Oh my God! What are you doing to me?" She gasped as his tongue unleashed all of her pent-up passions, passions she was scared to release because she didn't know where they would lead her.

Nick sucked her pussy until she melted in his mouth and screamed his name.

"Fuck me," she panted. Her pussy was on fire.

He couldn't get his pants off fast enough, so she helped him, using her feet to take his pants down. He plunged into her wetness, and the first thing she felt was that delicious curve in his dick. She wrapped her legs around his waist, urging him deeper.

"Oh, baby, I missed you, I missed you," she groaned, gone in a zone as he stroked her spot over and over. They had only fucked once before back when she was a teenager. And then as if they had an unspoken agreement, they fell back after she had the baby. Nick told her nothing else would happen until she felt ready.

Part of her held back, the part that felt guilty, the part that still loved Briggen. But the part that craved Nick, that wanted to embrace all that he had to offer, opened up wide and welcomed him inside. When he did explode inside of her, and she lay content in his arms, she knew only one thing . . . she was caught up. What if Briggen found them? What if she got pregnant by Nick? Who would she choose? Was Nick right when he said they were destined to be together?

Janay let the music wash over her, totally immersing her body in it. She swayed gently and sang along from the depths of her heart.

"Never could have made it, without you."

The large North Carolina Apostolic church was packed with worshippers who felt the same way, but for different reasons. Janay squeezed her eyes tight and thought about her whole life, from Shadee, to finding him with a man, the attempt Skye made to kidnap her, her prison stint, to getting shot.

"I could've lost it all. But now I see how you were there for me."

Tears ran down her cheeks as she remembered the searing pain of the bullets that just missed her spine and could have paralyzed her for life. Her first thought had been revenge. War. Bloodshed. But something inside her stood up and said, "No!" A no that reverberated like the horns of Jericho inside her soul and brought down her gangsta walls. She attributed the transformation to Jesus, and she planned on spending the rest of her life thanking him.

The services concluded, and she led Marquis out of the church. She didn't interact with too many people. She may've loved the Lord, but she hated the fakeness and hypocrisy of many churchgoers. Outside, she headed to her Lexus until Marquis yelled, "Uncle Born!" He let go of her hand and dashed off toward him.

Born grabbed Marquis and put him up in a playful chokehold. "What's good, nephew?" Born smiled. Even though they were really cousins, Marquis had always called him Uncle Born, and he enjoyed it. "Dang, you're getting tall. How old are you, fifteen?" Born joked.

"I'm eight. So you takin' me to play basketball?" Marquis eagerly inquired.

Born chuckled. "We'll see," he said, putting him down.

When Janay approached, Born gave her a hug. The minute she saw him she knew what it was about.

"Hello, Born. How are you?"

"Hot," he joked. "This Carolina weather is too humid for me."

"You get used to it."

"Either that or leave."

Janay chuckled. "That too."

"I went by the house. Boomer said you were in church."

"And?"

"And what? I just came to check on you," Born replied.

"Is that right?" Her left eyebrow rose.

"Besides, I could smell Boomer's famous fried chicken."

"All the way in Detroit?" She twisted her mouth playfully, and then they both laughed.

But the innuendo was clear: *What are you doing here?*

When they got back to Janay's house on the outskirts of Charlotte, Boomer had the place smelling like a soul food restaurant. He had made fried chicken, candied yams, glazed ham, macaroni and cheese, greens, corn bread, and mashed potatoes. He did this every week at the behest of Janay, because all that they didn't eat went to a nearby shelter.

After dinner, Janay and Born went out by the pool to relax on the patio. He saw an ivory chessboard with the pieces arranged as if a game was in progress.

"You play?" he asked with a hint of surprise in his voice.

"You wanna find out?" Janay teased, good-naturedly.

They sat down and set the board up.

"So what brings you to Charlotte, Born?" Janay probed.

"Business."

"Thinkin' about expanding?"

He shrugged. "Just curious," he smirked.

"Well, whatever business you have, I wish you the best," she told him.

He decided to play a queen's pawn opening, and she adopted the queen's Indian defense.

"Who taught you to play?" Born asked.

"Which game?" Janay joked.

"Both."

"Then you already know the answer."

"He definitely taught you well. That's why I came to see you before I made a move out here. I needed to see if I'd be steppin' on any toes." Born attempted to bait a trap, offering her a piece which would've given him a strong positional advantage.

"If you are, they won't be mine," she told him.

He respected her game. "Come on, Janay. This Born. I know that bullet won't keep you down. You go too hard."

He made a careless move with his knight and left his queen's side vulnerable. She made the most of it and pinned his knight and queen with her black bishop.

"Listen, Born, this ain't because of fear of a bullet. This is real with me. The Lord is real to me. When I walked away, I didn't look back. Period. Now, I go hard for the Lord," Janay broke it down to him.

Before he could respond, her phone rang. She looked at it. Prison call.

"Excuse me," she said, getting up and walking toward the pool.

She pressed five and the automated system put Choppa through.

"Hey, baby. How are you?"

"I'm good, Daddy. How are you?"

"Your ol' daddy is hangin' in here. You just comin' back from church?"

"Yep," she told him.

"Did you pray for me?" He chuckled.

She smiled, knowing it was his way of asking, did she still love him. "Always, Daddy."

"Yeah, well, you need to pray for that sister of yours. She gettin' married."

"She told me. But you say it like that's a bad thing."

"That's because it's to Dark."

Janay stopped walking around the pool. She had peeped game as soon as Crystal told her the news.

"Well . . . if that's what she wants to do, to each his own," Janay remarked, but she couldn't keep the hint of worry out of her voice.

"She needs you, 'Nay."

"She needs Jesus, like we all do," Janay shot back.

Man, fuck Jesus, Choppa started to say, but instead, he said, "Your sister needs you, 'Nay. I need you, the family needs you."

Janay sighed hard. "Really, Daddy? You're going to try to use her marriage to convince me to change my mind? Wow!" She shook her head. "Unbelievable."

"Baby, I'm just sayin'—"

"I *know* what you're sayin', but if that's all you have to say, then ain't no need to continue this call."

For a moment neither said anything because they both were stubborn, locked into their own sense of right.

"Let me speak to Boomer," Choppa grumbled.

Janay took the phone over to the driveway where Marquis had taken Born to shoot basketball.

"Marquis, here. Take the phone to Boomer," she instructed him, and Marquis ran it inside.

"Listen, I can see you have a lot on your mind. Just know I'll be around a lot more, so if you change your mind—"

"I won't!" She snapped, a little sharper than she should have.

Born held up his hands in mock surrender.

"Don't shoot." He chuckled, and then gave her a kiss and a hug. Before he walked away, he turned back and said, "I left you in check. We'll finish the game soon."

"I bet we will," she remarked. Janay turned and headed in the house, mumbling, "Lord, give me the strength!"

It was February and snowing but the sun was shining. All of the Saturday afternoon lovers were out and about where Dark and Mook met in Campus Martius Park. Mook had been one of Cisco's top soldiers, but once Dark made his move, he had been treating Mook as his lead-ing right-hand man. He was young, ambitious, and dangerous, but now Dark wanted to be absolutely sure of his loyalty.

"Yo, maine, shit 'bout to get real deep. I'ma 'bout to take this whole shit to the next level. But I need good muhfuckas around me, muhfuckas I can trust. Feel me?" Dark explained.

Mook nodded. "No doubt, I feel that."

"And real talk, I fuck wit' you because you saw the situation. You knew I had to do what I had to do and you rolled wit' me," Dark remarked, referring to the Cisco murder.

"Yeah, yo, fuck that nigga. Nigga was pussy. He was holdin' us back."

"Indeed, but now, some mo' shit holdin' us back, and I need you to handle that."

"What up, though?"

"The Oak Ridge Crew," Dark replied, looking at Mook to see how he would react. "I'm talkin' about all them Tennessee muhfuckas—Rob, Mac, Darnell, Reggie, and Cisco's two cousins Dana and Wes. They gotta go. Every one of 'em. They fucked wit' Cisco, so one day, if they get the chance, they might wanna even the score. Fuck that! So I'm cleanin' house. Startin' a whole new family, and you the foundation. Tell me what's good."

Mook knew exactly why Dark was coming at him with the move. Mook had come up with Cisco's people. He wasn't related to any of them, but they had been a crew longer than he and Dark. Dark was an outsider, and even though he was the boss, the crew wasn't really his. Dark wanted to know where Mook's loyalties lay, and he wanted blood to prove it.

"Yo, Dark, I fuck wit' you too. You a real muhfucka, and what you askin,' it's a done deal, but—"

"Everything after *but* is bullshit," Dark jeweled him. "You either wit' me 110 percent or against me 110 percent. No buts, no fence-walking. So what's good? You still got some buts?"

"Naw. I'm good," Mook said without hesitation. Then he got straight down to business. "Now, real talk, hear me out. Them other niggas can eat a dick, but Mac is a muhfuckin' soldier. We gonna need somebody out in Oak Ridge that understands how shit run. So leave Mac in place.

I'm vouchin' for the nigga. And since I feel like you respect my G, respect my judgment," Mook proposed.

Dark thought about what Mook said. It made sense, but he didn't want to leave loose ends. A few moments later, he came up with the solution.

"I'll tell you what. If Mac wanna fuck wit' me, then bring him the move I'm bringin' you. You handle half them niggas, and Mac handle the other half. He gotta get his hands dirty too. Feel me?"

"Fair enough."

"And remember, Mook. You vouched for the nigga, so he your responsibility," Dark warned him, looking him straight in the eyes.

Mook met his gaze and nodded, but in his heart, he felt like he had just made a deal with the devil.

Dark's phone chirped with a text. He checked it and smiled. It read: **Mission accomplished. You owe me big.**

Choppa sat in the back of the gym in his wheelchair, watching the young men go hard on the court. They were going so hard that some were shirtless and still their bodies glistened with sweat. A couple of players were extremely talented. Even LeBron James talented. The only difference was they had made a bad decision, and now they were stuck behind bars for the decades they should've been making a name for themselves in the NBA. Subtly, he shook his head. Life rarely played fair. So a man had to make his own luck. Choppa had done that, but now looking death in the face he wondered what it all meant.

Choppa could literally feel the cancer eating up his body. He could feel himself getting smaller. Weaker. Frailer. His mind was still as sharp as ever, but his body was rotting away, like a man trapped on the top floor of a burning building just waiting for the fire to totally consume him.

His inmate attendant rolled him back to his cell. They usually played cards and talked, but his attendant said, "Unc, I'll be right back. I gotta handle something."

It wasn't what he said or the way he said it. It was simply that Choppa had been around so long, he had developed a sixth sense for the game.

"Yeah, young buck, you take care of yourself," Choppa responded.

The remark caught the young man off guard. He looked back over his shoulder, and the look in his eyes said, "I'm sorry."

Choppa didn't blame him. He had to live in that prison too. He wondered if he was down with the move, paid to get out of the way, or simply scared. It didn't matter. Nothing mattered anymore. He was tired. They were doing him a favor. Still, when they came, he wished they would've tried this shit when he was still at full strength.

Three of them. All cowards individually, but together, they *almost* added up to a man. They moved swiftly, all armed with shiny six-inch blades, long and slender like ice picks, but actually made of metal that was filed to a dangerous point.

"Dark says he'll see you in hell, old coon," one of the killers taunted.

"And as soon as I get there, I'ma stick my dick in that sorry bitch's mouth that you call your mama," Choppa retorted coldly.

The three of them swarmed and began plunging the blades in Choppa from every direction. Blood spurted from his neck, chest, and stomach all at once, but he never once cried out. He had been living with pain for so long, a few more minutes didn't make any difference.

After the frenzied attack, the killers dispersed as quickly as they had come. Choppa slumped to the floor with a sickening slap as he fell face-first into his own blood. His last mental image was of Janay, and his last thought was, *Maybe now, she'll understand.*

When the killer told Shokkah, he waited for the coast to clear before pulling out his cell phone and sending Dark the text:

Mission accomplished. You owe me big!

Chapter Five

Dear citizens of Detroit, we face a grim problem. A problem that has plagued our community for too long . . . black-on-black violence. But as terrible as it is when another black child is gunned down, this violence is not the cause. It is an effect. Just one of the many effects of an even bigger problem . . . poverty." Congressman Duffy orated as he stood on the podium addressing the large rally right on the front steps of downtown Detroit city hall. It was March and the gusty winds had already knocked a few hats off heads.

The crowd applauded as there was continuous flashing from the cameras. Duffy played to the crowd, delivering his speech with reverend-like cadence and played to the cameras with subtle postures and well-timed smiles and scowls. He was one smooth politician. Born to do this.

"The war on poverty has become the Republican's war on people. Not just blacks, but *especially* blacks, if y'all can read between the lines!"

"Amen!"

"Poverty, joblessness, hopelessness, despair. This is why we kill; this is why we get killed! But a new day is coming!"

"Preach it!"

"A better day!"

"Yes, Lawd!"

"And all I ask is that you walk with me. Walk with me and together, we will bring this city back from its ashes to stand in the full light of the sun!" Duffy called out, dabbing at his brow with a handkerchief.

"Congressman Duffy for president!" Someone yelled out, and the crowd cheered.

Duffy put on his humble smile and said, "They'll never let me be president, because I'll truly be the black people's president." He remarked, taking a jab at Obama. "In conclusion, I say, some people look at the way things are and ask why. I look at the way things could be and ask . . . why not? Let's find out together!"

The crowd erupted in thunderous applause. As he left the podium, he was swarmed by well-wishers and engulfed in a standing ovation. Supporters wanted to shake his hand and take pictures, women wanted to flirt, and babies needed to be kissed. He moved swiftly through the crowd, never stopping for too long but never neglecting an outstretched hand. It could be a potential vote.

His handlers got him to the limo. He waved once more, and then disappeared inside. Waiting for him in the limo was Detective Sherman and his own trusted chief of staff, the sexy and long-legged Simone. Sherman pulled his eyes away from her long legs to shake Duffy's hand. She handed him a bottle of water as he loosened his tie.

"Great speech, Congressman." Simone smiled.

"Thank you, Simone. What's next?"

She checked her iPad for his itinerary. "A luncheon with the mayor and the Black Businessman's Council."

"Call the mayor. Tell him I'll be about ten minutes late. Get Mike on the phone and tell the driver to take the scenic route so I can speak with the detective," Duffy ordered, and then turned to Sherman.

"Sooo our mutual friend says we need to talk," Sherman began.

"Nicholas Powell. That's what he said."

Sherman whistled. "Big fish on a federal hook."

Duffy waved it off dismissively. "Feds mean nothing in Detroit. This is my city. I'll handle that. But I'm asking you to keep Powell on a leash . . . a very *short* leash. Can you?"

Sherman smiled. "Detroit may be *your* city, but these are *my* streets. That's no problem."

Both men laughed and shook hands. Just like that, Nick went from having a case to being one.

When Nick first laid eyes on her, he thought she was the most beautiful woman he had ever seen. He'd jump over seventy Shans to get to one of her. She was the type of woman you worshipped. His attraction and obsession was instant. He *had* to have her.

"Let me introduce you two. Nick, this is Joy Parker. Joy, this is Nick," Rudy, Nick's attorney, introduced them.

Nick had hired Rudy, Briggen's lawyer, because he knew he was one of the best in Detroit, if not the country. They were seated around the rectangular dark brown conference table surrounded by matching book shelves crammed with law books.

Nick took her hand and kissed it, fighting the urge to suck each finger. Her soft skin alone had his dick close to a total erection.

"The pleasure is all mine," he charmed.

"Yes, but mine is all business," she replied without sounding cold. Joy snatched her hand away getting her point across just the same.

Rudy cleared his throat. "Excellent, excellent. So, Ms. Parker, if you would be so kind as to tell us what this is about," he suggested.

"Certainly, Mr. Harrington," Joy replied, and then looked at Nick. "I deliberately didn't tell your lawyer the nature of my business so you wouldn't have any preconceived notions. Besides, I didn't know if I'd even be in the position to offer what I'm about to offer."

Nick was all ears, but her demeanor raised one red flag. "Before you do, answer one thing. Are you a law enforcement agent of any kind?" Nick questioned.

She smiled. "No, Nick, I'm not."

"Then, by all means what's the offer?"

"As we speak, your indictment is conveniently disappearing. It isn't lost, it isn't being destroyed, but it will disappear. Now I assure you, it *can* reappear at any time if you do not agree 100 percent with my terms," she explained.

Nick couldn't help but feel her no-nonsense attitude. She definitely had his attention. "I'm listening."

"Number one is that you do things my way. Period. This is nonnegotiable. Any discrepancies, I throw you to the wolves, and I promise you, there will be nothing Mr. Harrington can do to save you," she told him with a dead-ass expression.

"What's number two?"

"There is no number two."

Nick sat back and contemplated her offer, which was more of an ultimatum. He looked at Rudy. Rudy looked at him. "Suppose I say no?"

She shrugged. "Then I'll remove my influence, and you'll never see me again."

Not seeing her again was reason enough to contemplate her offer. Not to mention his freedom from indictment. "What do you want me to do?" he asked.

"Whatever I say."

"I mean *specifically*."

"I mean *totally*," she replied with a hint of impatience. "Believe me, Nick, I can make you untouchable, but as the Greek myth Achilles will tell you, invincibility comes with a price. Do we have a deal?"

"Ms. Parker, my client—" Rudy tried to interrupt.

Joy turned her swanlike neck in Rudy's direction and said, "Mr. Harrington, Nick's a big boy. Aren't you, Nick?"

Untouchable. He thought about the word and his chest swelled. It was an offer he couldn't refuse. "You got a deal."

Joy rose from her seat as she extended her hand. Nick shook it. "My people will be in touch. You will deal with them," she informed him.

"Why can't I deal with you?" he flirted.

Her smile turned all sass. "Because I don't fuck with the help."

Nick acted like he was bending down to pick up his face. A hint of a smile showed on her lips. "You deserved that. Next time, be more direct. With me, you only get one chance to make a first impression." She started to walk away.

Nick held her forearm to get her attention. "I wanna lay you across this table and fuck the shit outta your pussy. How's that for a first impression? Is that direct enough?" He said aggressively. Nick really wanted to choke the shit out of her and take the pussy. For some reason she was making him feel out of his element.

Joy laughed as she searched his eyes. As if reading his mind she said, "But you don't have the heart."

She walked out of the office and shut the door behind her.

Sharia was feeling the young boy Mo'Betta, and this was only their second date. The first one, he took her shopping and out to dinner. She stopped counting when the tab for those two dates reached four stacks. He was worth her time, and he had so much swag, her pussy got wet just watching him. Even though she knew she was supposed to just keep an eye on him, tonight she planned on doing more to him than that.

I'ma turn this young nigga inside out, she thought while looking at him as he drove.

This bitch 'bout to get it, Mo'Betta thought when he glanced over at Sharia.

She bit her bottom lip in a sexy way. He couldn't wait to get her to his spot. Just the thought about what he was going to do to her had his dick rock hard in anticipation. He had taken her out to dinner and a movie, his smooth gentlemanly way of winning her over. Now he was about to give her what she really needed. A good thuggin'.

"I didn't know you were from the West Side," Sharia remarked.

"Born and raised, li'l mama," he replied proudly.

He pulled up to a two-story house in the middle of the block. From the outside, it looked run-down and dreary. But then, so did half of Detroit.

Sharia looked at the house disapprovingly. Reading her expression, Mo'Betta said, "It's a foreclosure. I copped it straight from the bank. I'ma fix it up and flip it real quick."

"Not in this market," Sharia replied, knowing a thing or two about real estate.

"You think I should rent it out? The shit was a fuckin' steal. I had to cop it."

"Nope. Use it for Section Eight. That way, your money is guaranteed," Sharia schooled him.

He pulled her close and kissed her neck as they walked up to the door. "Shit, li'l mama, why don't you handle that for me? We'll split the money."

"We can work out the details."

Mo'Betta opened the door, and they went in. The glare from the streetlight outside cast long shadows as she stepped inside. Sharia looked around in disgust. The place was a mess and an eyesore. It looked abandoned. Garbage and debris were all over the floor. A refrigerator lay on its side and a broken down couch with no legs furnished the room.

With a twist of her neck, Sharia snapped, "Nigga, what—" She turned to Mo'Betta and was met with a vicious left hook that hit her so hard she was off her feet and on the floor.

Mo'Betta was all over her. He reared back and kicked her in the stomach, knocking the wind and the fight out of her. He was in a zone. Secretly, he got off on shit like this. He was a sadistic motherfucker that loved to give women pain. Her moans and pleas had his dick harder than it was in the car.

"Wh-wh-why?" Sharia moaned pathetically.

Mo'Betta ignored her and instead, calmly slid on his racing gloves. He then got down on top of her, pinning her shoulders with his knees and then proceeded to beat her face like a jackhammer. Sharia blanked in and out of consciousness.

"Yeah, bitch, you ain't so pretty now, huh?" Mo'Betta huffed out of breath.

Her entire face was now swollen and disfigured. Blood leaked from her lips and nose. Her whole body hurt. Her mind couldn't wrap itself around what was happening. *Why is he doing this?*

Mo'Betta pulled off one glove and pulled out the TracFone. He hit speed dial. Briggen answered on the other end. "I got her."

"Let me speak to her," Briggen fumed, feeling the rising sensation of payback in his chest.

He had told Mo'Betta if he found Sharia he could find Demetria.

"You got a picture of her?" Mo'Betta had requested.

"Yeah, have my fam' show her to you."

When Keeta first showed him the picture of Sharia, she burst out laughing because all the while he was looking for her, she fell right into his lap. "Shayla," he said, thumping the picture. "Bitch was all on my dick at the Chinese spot and didn't even know she was writing her obituary."

Now, here she was totally at his mercy. Her short skirt had slid up around her waist, revealing her thick honey-colored thighs, her panties hugging that juicy-looking camel toe.

"Yeah, bitch, who's laughing now?" Briggen laughed.

Briggen! Her mind screamed in the midst of her lazy haze. At that moment, she knew she was about to die.

"Br-Br-Br-" she stuttered, her jaw broken; slobber ran down her chin.

"You thought it was a game? Bitch, I'm God! You fuck-ass ho! Now, how much pain I have to put on yo' ass is up to you. Where the fuck is Demetria?"

Sharia wasted no time in trying to form the words. She just wanted it to be over, even if it meant giving her sister up.

"Oaf . . . oaf . . . oaf . . ." she mumbled.

"Oaf?" Mo'Better echoed in confusion.

"Oak Reee," she stressed.

It took him several seconds until Mo'Betta blurted out, "Oak Ridge?"

She nodded. Mo'Betta put the phone to his ear.

"Oak Ridge, maine. The bitch said Oak Ridge."

Briggen wondered why that place sounded familiar, but he brushed it off. "Get the number."

Mo'Betta reached in her purse and grabbed her phone. He found two and he handed her one. She shook her head. He handed her the other one and with a trembling hand, she went through her contact list. She gave it to Mo'Betta.

Demetria 555-3997

Mo'Betta smiled. "Bingo, my nigga!" Mo'Betta told Briggen and then put the phone to her ear to give Briggen the last word.

When Briggen heard labored breathing, he knew who it was. "Stupid bitch, you was wit' the juice! All you had to do was ride, but now, all you can do is die. Don't worry though. Your triflin'-ass sister'll be joinin' you soon!" he ranted.

Mo'Betta took the phone hearing every word.

"Make her suffer," Briggen instructed him before hanging up.

She then grabbed at his pant leg and stabbed a shard of glass into his flesh, pressing it in with all the strength she could muster.

"You fuckin' cunt!" Mo'Betta gritted as he snatched the stabbed leg back and began stomping her with his other one. He stomped her until he couldn't feel anymore pain in his wounded leg.

Mo'Betta leered over Sharia's broken body.

In the dark, her eyes found his. "Peeessee," she tried to beg, her mind screaming, "Peeeesse . . . just kill me!"

Mo'Betta knew he had been in the house long enough. He couldn't do her like he really wanted to, but when his eyes fell on the refrigerator, he knew what would be his next move.

He grabbed her by the ankles and dragged her over to the refrigerator. Once he opened it, he snatched out all the racks, and he then lifted her up and began to stuff her inside. Where she didn't fit, he pummeled her body and forced it in. The last blow he landed broke her nose, and she went limp. Sharia was fully conscious, but no longer had the will to live. The last thing she saw before he shut the refrigerator door was him blowing her a kiss. And then, everything went dark. With her broken nose she could barely breathe, so it didn't matter that she would suffocate. She forced her mind to take her back to her favorite spot in her apartment looking out of the window onto the Detroit River. Her thoughts then went to Briggen. She was lying next to him looking into his eyes and professing her love. He kissed her sweetly on the lips. She went back to her apartment when she was last on the phone with Demetria. She wanted to hurt Briggen. Make him suffer. But now who was suffering? She wished for death.

Demetria was out of jail and snuck away from the "D," leaving behind everything she owned. As her sister was being tortured, she was entering a club in Oak Ridge. It was a ghetto hole-in-the-wall, but she had to get out of that apartment. She needed to breathe. She just didn't know her sister did too—literally. As she sashayed across the floor in her fuck-me pumps and little dress, she had no clue that Sharia was gasping, clawing with all the strength she could muster to open the refrigerator door. How much torture it was to suffocate to death.

All Demetria knew was, she needed a drink, some dick, and not necessarily in that order. But looking around, she didn't see much of either. The drinks, she was sure were watered down, and so were the niggas. When she walked in, the men all paused, but they were all such . . . lames. The only reason she came to this club was because it was close to her apartment. And for the end of March, Oak Ridge was boasting a beautiful and record breaking seventy-five degrees. But after twenty minutes of weak-ass game and lame-ass music, Demetria was ready to try her hand at another club . . . until *he* walked in.

He wasn't that tall, five-eight at the most, but with his curly hair, ebony tone, and gangsta swagger, she knew she was fucking him tonight. Not to mention his True Religion jeans, diamond earrings, and platinum grill made her know that he was ballin'. She decided to make herself known by using the most ancient form of communication.

Dance.

But in this day and time it was her . . . twerk game.

She made her way on to the small dance floor and proceeded to dance as if she was back on the pole at All-Stars. Niggas that tried to dance with her she moved away or totally ignored them. She wanted him to know this was all for him. When he did notice, he couldn't take his eyes off her. He was one of the hustlers that ran Oak Ridge, so he was used to that kind of treatment. However, he had never seen Demetria before, and he was intrigued, to say the least. She was a stallion. Her breasts sat up as if they were full of saline, nevertheless, they were all natural, and she had an ass and aura like Pinky the Porn Star. Her butt shots were complements of Big T.

He bought two Cirocs with cranberry juice and then made his way onto the dance floor and handed her one as he got closer to look at her skills.

"The way you workin' it, li'l mama, I thought you might be thirsty."

Demetria sipped and giggled, turning to face him. "Mmmmm, a mind reader. What else do you read?" She flirted hard.

"Body language."

"Oh yeah? Well, what's my body sayin'?" she quizzed, turning and putting her ass on him, grinding provocatively.

"It's sayin', let's go!" he said, dick on sprung.

She gave him her phony sexy laugh. "Slow down. You read my body right, but what's your name, baby?" she remarked, giving him the innocent eyes.

Thick as she was, he was ready to rock.

"Rob, li'l mama, what's yours?"

"Deme—"

"Huh?" Rob strained to hear over the music.

"Dee-Dee," she replied.

He got up close in her ear and said, "Ma, I'm a man of few words, little patience, and no games. I'm sayin', what you tryin' to do? Because it's a million other places we could be."

Grinding up against him, she already knew he had a decent-sized dick, and his swag was definitely a turn-on, so why play hard to get when she wanted the same thing?

"So what you tryna do? And where you from, Dee-Dee?"

"That's irrelevant. The point is, where we goin'? Or, did you change your mind?" she challenged.

"I like that aggressive shit. It turns me on," he told her as he led her to the door.

With her face down and ass up, all Rob could think about was Jell-O, watching her ass bounce and roll with every stroke. Demetria's pussy was so wet it started to talk to him from the first stroke.

"Ohhh, fuck, yeah, daddy. She is talkin' to you," she moaned, gripping the sheets.

Rob spread her ass cheeks and slid his thumb deep in her ass. She released a sexy squeal and started to throw it back harder and harder the more he thumb-fucked her.

"Mmmmm. Put-put it in my-my ass, daddy," she begged.

Rob didn't hesitate. He slid in her ass with a full stroke and instantly fell in love. She began playing with her clit. The way she was moaning, coupled with his grunting, it sounded as if they were filming a porno. Rob was in a zone listening to the wet smack of every stroke.

"Oh God! Fuck this ass, fuck . . . this . . . assss," she squealed, feeling like her pussy was about to explode. "Oh, Rob, I'm about to come, baby!"

Rob had been doing his best to hold back, but with Demetria's ass muscles squeezing his dick, he couldn't help but bust off right behind her.

Exhausted but satisfied, Demetria knew how she'd pass her days in Oak Ridge until the trial. When the Feds gave her a temporary get out of jail free card, she knew she had to get out of the "D". If Briggen discovered that she'd turned and was cooperating, her ass would have been cooked.

While they both lay there half-asleep, Rob received a text from Mook: **I'm here. We need to powwow.**

Big Choppa's funeral was packed. They say the size of a gangsta's respect can be measured by the size of his funeral. If that was true, then Big Choppa had to be one of the most respected gangstas from Memphis to Detroit. Old players came out of the shadows long enough to pay their respect while young players got a lesson in how it was to be done. Everybody was there in full force, on this dreary Friday morning, including the law.

Detective Sherman and a surveillance unit sat in a van across the street watching the cameras that had been strategically set up to photograph the guests going in and out of the funeral home.

"Now him right there, that's Fat Rich from Zone 8. He's also a new Consortium member," Sherman boasted, proud that he knew the who's who of the streets. He waited as pictures were snapped before he continued.

"Next up getting out of the Aston Martin is Kay-Gee and JoJo. Behind them, Slim and Teraney. Their crew is dangerous."

"Who's that behind them?" One of the officers asked as several important looking men filed out of the Mercedes stretch limousine. He held his camera steady as Sherman shuffled his mental rolodex.

"I don't know," Sherman replied. "Probably an out-of-towner. Make sure you get some pictures."

Unbeknownst to Detective Sherman, the small framed, Italian gentleman flanked by four men was Big Choppa's connect. Victor Conti. Once Victor heard from Boomer that Choppa was gone, he made it his business to pay his respects.

"Oh, here comes Choppa's daughter Janay and his right-hand man, Boomer. Janay is supposed to be out of the business end of the family and moving into the legitimate end. Go figure. I heard several different versions as to why Janay walked away from the family business. I'm really not sure if that was before I was on the clock or not. She moved to North Carolina, so she's somebody else's headache now."

Behind Janay and Boomer's limo were Dark and Crystal. Dark helped her out of the car. She began to walk slowly and couldn't stop crying. He put his arm around her as she clung to him.

"That is the man to watch. His name's Dark, and he could very well be the next kingpin of Detroit. Yeah, Dark." He leered at him as Dark looked back before entering the church. "I've got my eye on you," Sherman promised.

The next person made Sherman chuckle.

"Who's that?" The technician was curious.

"Nobody," Sherman remarked, watching Nick and Shan get out of his Silver Range Rover and go inside.

"Hmmmmm, Mo'Betta. You must be movin' up in the world. Guess I'm gonna have to watch you too," Sherman remarked, seeing Mo'Betta arrive with Keeta.

"Why do you say that, Detective?" another officer asked.

"That's Calvin Thompson aka Briggen's cousin. She must be pregnant by Maurice Young, or like I said, Mo'Betta. But if she is, you can bet Thompson is keepin' him close and probably using him as legs, ears, and eyes while he's inside," Sherman surmised correctly, then added, "Yep . . . Looks like the gang's all here!"

Inside the medium sized church they were packed in like a can of sardines. When Crystal saw Janay, she ran into her arms, sobbing uncontrollably. Janay's pain was visibly etched on her face, but she carried herself with regal composure.

"He's gone, Nay, he's gone!" Crystal cried out, feeling so much better in her sister's embrace.

"I know, baby. Let it out," Janay urged her.

"What're we gonna do?" Crystal sniffed. "I—I just don't know what to do."

Janay looked into her sister's eyes and saw it all. The pain, the sadness, the confusion, but the clearest emotion front and center was the guilt, and Janay understood why. Choppa didn't want her to get married. He had probably threatened to cut her off, and Crystal, being her spoiled self, threw a tantrum, a tantrum Dark used to his advantage. Janay's eyes turned to Dark and regarded him coolly.

"Hello . . . Dark, is it?" She allowed her sarcasm to drip.

"How're you, Janay? I'm sorry about your loss," he offered with a straight face, ignoring her sarcasm.

Bullshit. She replayed the last conversation with Choppa. He needed her, and she turned her back on him. Now all she could do was pray that God saw her sacrifice and that something good would come out of her decision.

The old Janay would've spit in his face because deep down, she knew Dark had some hand in her father's death. Her street instincts screamed it, and they had never been wrong. But the saved Janay accepted the fact that Choppa lived by the sword. It was simply his turn to die by it. Janay didn't answer Dark. She simply nodded and turned back to Crystal.

"Janay, what are we going to do?" Crystal cried, knowing she had been the cause. The guilt of sleeping with the man who had a hand in taking her daddy's life was killing her soul.

"Nothing," Janay replied.

"Nothing? But they killed—"

"It is God's wrath upon this family, Crystal, and the wrath of the Lord will not be turned away until this family comes to him. Until then, God will turn us against one another and allow the devil to be the cause of our demise," Janay preached calmly, looking Crystal squarely in her eyes.

Crystal couldn't take her sister's penetrating gaze that saw right through her. *Oh my God, she knows!* "Janay, I-I," Crystal stuttered, paranoid that her sister knew that she had a hand in their father's death.

"Shhhh, what's done is done. I'm not the one you or him have to worry about. You should fear no man. Only God." Janay's tone was more of a threat instead of a warning. She then turned to greet more of the guests that came out to offer their condolences.

After Boomer hugged Crystal she sat down next to Janay, wishing she could be more like her sister, and at the same time, feeling inferior because she wasn't.

Boomer brushed past Dark without speaking. He simply glared at him and sat next to Crystal, making Dark sit beside him like the outsider he was.

Don't worry, your day is coming too, old ass nigga, Dark seethed.

Their attention then went to Victor. Janay gave a slight smile as Victor came over to embrace her. "Janay." He said a few sentences in Italian and gave her another hug. "If you need anything at all, please don't hesitate to call me. You know I'd do anything for your father. I know you hear this all of the time, but they don't make them like him and Boomer anymore."

"I know, Mr. Conti. All the more reason why I'm out. But there is one thing you can do for me."

"Anything. What is it?"

She turned away from Crystal. "As of this moment do not deal with my sister or anyone she brings to you without checking with Boomer first."

"Your father said that you—and we just arranged—"

"We will talk another time, Mr. Conti."

Crystal had never met Victor, but did speak to his people. Victor shook her hand, and he stood in front of Boomer. They exchanged a few words.

"Crystal, baby. Who is that? That's him, isn't it?" Dark was on the edge of his seat. The man's whole demeanor screamed 'the connect'. Dark could hardly contain himself. "Crystal!"

"Jerome, my daddy is dead. How can you talk about business? We are at his funeral, for God's sake." She sobbed louder and harder.

Shan spotted Keeta in the middle of the church and made her way over to where she was. "Keeta, girl, how are you?" With the big, black hat and veil over her face, Keeta didn't know who Shan was until she heard her voice.

Keeta let out a sarcastic laugh. "How am I? You got balls. Bitch, you left my cousin high and dry and off with his kids with his boy. Ho, I ain't got nothing for you. You need to watch your back!" Keeta spat and left Shan standing there embarrassed and wanting to crawl under a rock.

Minutes later the preacher gave a beautiful eulogy filled with the standard lies on top of lies and soliloquies that turned gangstas into saints. Everyone then made a grand exit as they all headed to the cemetery. The funeral procession made its way up Woodward Avenue to the Woodlawn Cemetery for the burial.

The funeral procession was almost a mile long, so it gave Shan ample time to get comfortable in Nick's Range Rover and to get her thoughts together and get reacquainted with the who's who of Detroit. She did miss the city. In New York she felt too much like a loner. But now her run-in with Keeta really had her feeling alone.

"I see Keeta has a new man," she remarked. "I was wondering if that was the baby's daddy."

Nick shrugged. "I've never seen the nigga, so I don't know his story. Why didn't you ask her?"

Shan sucked her teeth. "Please. I tried to speak to her, but the bitch got all stank on me. I'ma call her and cuss her ass out."

Nick glanced over at her while he drove but kept his eyes out for any signs of a setup. He knew he shouldn't have come. They both were supposed to be lying low, but attending the funeral was a way to get a good pulse beat on the streets.

"Shan, what are you gonna do about Briggen?" he asked, nixing Keeta.

"What do you mean?"

"I mean, he is the father of your two kids. Do you plan on letting him be a part of their lives?"

"Truthfully, Nick, I don't know. But one thing I do know is he won't be a part of mine," she lied, knowing she had talked to Briggen the night before.

Nick nodded, taking it all in. He wasn't stupid. He knew feelings didn't just go away overnight, especially for women. But he would simply have to trust her, because he had bigger things to worry about.

"I see that nigga Dark fuckin' Big Choppa's daughter now. I'll give it to him. The nigga smart. Yo, he knows how to make moves," Kay-Gee complimented as he and Born rode in the back of the stretch Phantom with JoJo and Teraney right behind them. This was the crew that Born moved from Memphis. Detroit was now their new home and territory.

"That only makes him predictable. Never mistake movement for action. He gonna try to push Crystal back and run the show. That's why I went and hollered at Janay, to see what's really good," Born remarked.

"And?"

Born shook his head. "She always been hard to read. She talking that Jesus shit, but that gangsta shit still in her. I could feel it. I don't know. But for now, she's a wild card."

Kay-Gee nodded as he looked out on the dismal Detroit streets.

"Any word on who tried to set y'all up at Benny Thrillz?"

"Naw, but to be honest, I ain't been on that shit like that. It'll come to light. More important, we need a stable connect. With Mr. G in Italy and Nick cased up, shit been really flaky. Not to mention, what we *can* get has been pure bullshit. We need to get right. I want you to go to New York, get at Wise. Pick his brain," Born told him.

"Wise? How we gonna fuck wit' that nigga after—"

Born waved him off. "Ancient history. That was his cousin, not him. Besides, Doc was a weak link. Can't knock the nigga for exposin' it."

Kay-Gee chuckled. "True. I ain't look at it like that. Still, I don't trust them Brooklyn niggas. They grimy as fuck."

"That's good you don't trust him, then he can never catch you slippin'. Only those you trust can do that," Born jeweled him, looking him in the eyes.

Nyla didn't make it in time for the eulogy, but she did join the procession to the cemetery. She had decided to come out, see and be seen, because she was tired of the drabness of her life. It was time to get back in the mix. But she didn't want to go the club route, so Choppa's funeral was right on time. She knew she would always love Forever, but it was time to move on with her life. But it couldn't be with a nine to five. Forever had her spoiled. So if she couldn't settle down, she at least knew she could find a sponsor and she did. *Nick.* Janay had come to her because she needed someone to work him, get into his head and get the info she needed. And who was the person to do that? Tiny. Nyla's alter ego. When she and Forever would play bedroom games, it always drove him crazy when Tiny paid him a visit.

Upon her arrival at the burial site, she sat back and watched all the hustlers getting out and making their presence known. She spotted Nick exiting a Silver Range Rover. Nyla smiled to herself because she knew he would definitely remember Tiny. Just as she started to make a beeline toward Nick, she stopped dead in her tracks when he helped a much thicker looking Shan out of the truck. "That bitch." She gritted her teeth, balling up her fists. She knew this was not the place or time to make a scene so she had to control herself. "Damn that ho. First, Forever, and now Nick. What the fuck do this bitch got between her legs?" she whispered as if somebody would answer her question.

It had been months since Forever's death, and Shan just up and disappeared. Nyla had even gone so far as attending Briggen's court appearances, but it was to no avail. She couldn't catch up with Shan for nothing. She had all but given up on ever seeing her again. She knew she had moved away, but she didn't know where. But now, here she was, in her face, and had the nerve to be looking fly. Had the nerve to show up with the nigga who she played Briggen with and the man she was connected with. *Was she crazy?*

"It must be meant for me to kill this bitch," she mumbled angrily. Seeing her again only renewed her desire to taste some payback. Nyla left abruptly, having seen all she needed to lay her trap.

Everyone gathered in a semicircle around the casket, covered with flowers, and the preacher was getting ready for a final word and prayer. But their attention got diverted as everyone turned and watched the lone woman strut toward them. Her presence alone made the men stare and the women feel unworthy of the expensive shoes they stood in. The bitch was so bad, women gave their man a pass for looking, because they were looking too. Even the preacher stopped in mid prayer and looked. People close to him heard him mutter, "God . . . damn."

She approached the casket without looking left or right and tossed two roses on the casket. One black and one yellow. No one understood what it meant, but they knew it meant something. When she turned and walked away, she looked directly at Dark with a smirk playing at the corners of her mouth.

"Jerome, who is that?" Crystal asked with a hint of worry in her tone as the woman walked away.

"Joy. Cisco's wife," he replied, remembering her face from the night he had gone to murder her. She had arrived with some dude, but Dark couldn't see his face. He was all over Joy and her security was all over her and the mystery man. Dark was forced to fall back, realizing he couldn't pull off the hit.

After the funeral, Born stepped to Crystal and Dark. He gave Dark a pound and Crystal a hug. "I'm sorry for all this," Born told her. "Big

Choppa will always live on as a legend. If you don't mind, I wanted to speak with you for a moment," Born requested of Crystal.

Dark started to speak up and assert his authority, but then he felt confident enough in his game not to be pressed. Born and Crystal stepped a few feet away.

"Like I said, Big Choppa will be missed."

"I miss him already," Crystal remarked, holding back all but the trickle of a single tear.

"Shit about to get crazy, for real. Muhfuckas breaking bread with you and smilin' in your face, but ain't got your best interest at heart," Born said.

Crystal looked at him, tearless, and on the offensive. "Meaning?"

Born was a little thrown by the sudden flip in her attitude. "Meaning, the people around you."

"Like Dark?"

"I'm not speakin' specifics. I—"

"Oh no, but I think you are, Born," Crystal cut him off with a huff. "I am so tired of people tryin' to tell me about my man. I think I should know my man better than y'all, because I'm the one fucking him!" she snapped.

"Sometimes the best way to see someone is not look at 'em," Born schooled her.

"Look, Born," Crystal began, getting loud, "Dark is my man, and we're gettin' married! Period. End of story! If my own goddamn Daddy couldn't tell me nothin', what makes you think I'm listening to you? Like you said, Choppa is gone. But guess what? I'm here, and I'm in charge, got that?"

Born smirked, and inside he recognized that she was dumber than he thought. "Loud and clear," he replied sarcastically, then walking off.

Cisco's original Oak Ridge Team, his cousins, Dana and Wes, along with Big Darnell, and Reggie, all sat in Dana's basement while Mook and Mac broke down the situation.

"Look, the nigga's on the fast track to take over Big Choppa's family. That's major paper right there!" Mac said, trying to convince the crew.

Mook had already put Mac up on game. "They had to go, yo!" Mac added. He didn't really give a fuck, but he was the type that wanted to avoid a problem if he could. If they decided to ride with Dark, so what? Cisco was gone, and none of these other niggas had a plan.

"Man, I don't trust that nigga," Darnell spat. "You seen what he did to Dread. What the fuck gonna stop him from doin' us like that?"

There was general agreement all around. Mook checked his watch. These niggas were the living dead.

"Man, where the fuck is Rob?" Mook asked Mac, suspiciously.

"I called that nigga five times and sent him three texts," Mac replied.

"Hit him again," Mook told him and then turned to the crew. "So, what's it gonna be by a show of hands? We rollin' wit' Dark, or we gonna do our own thing?"

The vote was unanimous for doing their own thing.

"Fuck Dark!" Wes spat. "The nigga killed my cousin, so you best believe he gonna get his! Besides, we can fuck with my nigga Ray Ray. He doin' big things."

Mook shrugged, looking at Mac who had just hung up after trying to call Rob.

"Then that's what it is," he remarked. Then without hesitation, he and Mac pulled out their guns and took aim.

"Man, what the fuck—" Reggie stated, but his voice and life were drowned out under the barrage of bullets.

They were all caught totally off guard. Wes and Darnell weren't even strapped. Dana and Reggie at least tried to go for their guns, but the attempt was futile. Mook blew the top of Reggie's head all over the old picture of dogs playing poker hanging on the wall, while Mac fired four shots into Dana's chest from almost point-blank range, exploding her heart instantly. He then put the gun in her mouth and blew out the back of her head.

Wes tried to make a break but got stopped dead in his tracks with two shots to the back of the dome. At the same time, Mac put his gun to Darnell's forehead and hissed, "Pussy-ass nigga, I been wantin' to do this." He blew his brains out.

When the gunshots ended, their ears rang, and the room smelled of gunpowder, blood, and shit. Mac's phone rang. It was Rob.

"Yo, Rob, where you? You just missed the meetin'," Mac said and winked at Mook.

"I got caught up with this bitch. Mook wit' chu?"

"Nah, man, Mook already bounced. I'll bring you up to speed when I see you," Mac said, and then hung up.

"What up, doe?" Mook asked.

"Nigga say he was fuckin' a bitch. I don't know. He sounded mad paranoid. He don't trust that nigga Dark."

Mook laughed. "Smart man!"

Mac laughed with him. "He at the crib now."

"I'm 'posed to be gone, right?" Mook assumed.

"Yeah, I'll handle it," Mac told him.

One look around the room and it was clear it was time to get out of Oak Ridge.

"A'iight, maine, but yo—" Mook began, but Mac waved him off.

"I got you, maine. I ain't never give a fuck about none of these pussies runnin' with Cisco. I'll take care of it."

"Say no more."

Chapter Six

It was true that Rob had been fucking Demetria damn near nonstop for the past twenty-four hours. But he also had a bad feeling about Mac coming to town. Why hadn't Dark come? If it was supposed to be a major sit-down, and the boss ain't there, it's either a setup or the boss didn't trust them. Well, Rob didn't trust the boss. Now that Mac said Mook was gone, Rob called Darnell to get the heads-up.

No answer.

He called Reggie.

No answer.

Dana.

No answer.

By the time he got to Wes, he knew.

No answer.

He didn't believe in coincidences. Rob was a true street nigga, so he left nothing to chance. He told Mac to come over. He would hear him out, but he'd be on point. Rob and Mac were cool, but he knew if it came down to it, Mac wouldn't hesitate to throw him under the bus. And Rob couldn't blame him, because the feeling was mutual.

His buzzer rang, which meant Mac was at the door. Rob lived on the fifth floor of an apartment building. He walked out on the balcony and looked out. The infinity shaped pool was directly underneath the balcony, and beyond that, the parking lot. Nothing looked strange. No exhaust of a waiting car, no shadows lurking.

Still, he tucked his .40 caliber in the small of his back and waited for Mac's arrival.

Minutes later, Mac knocked and Rob peeped out of the peephole. Mac was alone.

"Yo," Rob called out, before opening the door.

"Nigga, you know who it is," Mac answered, being his usual impatient self.

Rob detected nothing in his voice. He thought, maybe he was being too paranoid. He relaxed a little and opened the door.

"Fuck you doin' in here? Smokin' that shit?" Mac cracked as he walked in.

"Naw, givin' your girl time to get dressed and hide in the closet," Rob shot back.

They laughed and dapped each other up.

"What up, though? Why you ain't come through? The nigga Mook wanted to holla at the whole team," Mac reported.

"What's good?"

"The team is expandin'. We 'bout to hop the border into Carolina. But since you ain't show, bitch-ass Darnell and, Reggie got, the nod," Mac lied, but got a little laugh to himself over his got-the-nod comment.

Rob shrugged it off. "Fuck it, more for us here. I don't know shit about Carolina no how."

Goddamn, this nigga watchin' my every move, Mac thought. He continued to make small talk as he tried to find an opening to pull his gun out and get shit over with. His adrenaline was on booster because he knew Rob was a street nigga, so he had to be on point to catch him slipping.

"Yo, maine, lemme get somethin' to drink," Mac requested.

"Nigga, you know where it is," Rob shot back. But all the while thinking, *This nigga been going to get it himself.*

Rob followed him into the kitchen. Mac took out the two-liter of Pepsi, and then grabbed a glass out of the dish rack. He had his back to Rob as he poured.

"Yo, I tried to call y'all niggas . . . all y'all, but ain't nobody answerin' their phone," Rob remarked.

"Yeah?" Mac said, sipping his soda and turning to face Rob. "I think they went out to the strip club or somethin'."

"Maybe."

The tension grew. Mac felt he had to make a move. *This nigga knows!*

he thought. Now Mac himself felt on the defense. He downed the soda, but before he brought his arm down, he threw the glass at Rob's head.

"Fuck!" Rob grunted as the glass barely missed him, and he reached around his back for his gun.

Mac saw him reach and knew he didn't have time to reach too. He lunged at Rob and rocked him with a left hook that would've dropped him any other time, but in a life-or-death struggle, pain is irrelevant. Mac grabbed Rob's hand that gripped the gun.

"Bitch-ass nigga!" Rob cursed as he used his free hand to pummel Mac's face with stinging blows.

Rob had the gun out, but Mac had his arm pinned back. He tried to angle the gun to shoot Mac in the foot.

Blam! Blam!

The bullets tore the floor up, but found no flesh. Both were reaching for their guns with one hand and stopping each other from pulling the trigger with the other.

But Mac was taller and stronger. "Nigga, you dead!" Mac barked.

He head butted Rob viciously. Rob stumbled back off balance. He let go of Mac's hand, pulled his gun, but sprinted around the corner into the living room to clear his dazed head. Mac let off a shot, splintering the doorsill but missing Rob. Rob let off two shots as he dived over the couch. Mac fired and missed. Rob then fired around the couch to keep Mac pinned down. That's when he discovered something ugly. His clip was empty.

"Shit!" he whispered. He knew if he didn't do something, it was over for him. Mac wouldn't wait; he'd come at him with guns blazing because he always kept an extra clip.

"Muhfucka, you might as well come out!" Mac taunted.

There was only one thing to do. He looked at the balcony. The pool was directly below. Rob had to jump. He knew if he landed wrong, he could break his neck, but it was a chance he had to take.

"Fuck it," he gruffed, throwing his gun aside and getting in a crouched position. He sprang off the balls of his feet and launched himself at the balcony. In two bounds he was out of the doorway and grabbing the rail.

Mac heard him, but all he saw when he turned the corner was Rob's body going over the rail, like he was hopping a fence. At first glance, Mac thought Rob was killing himself. But then, he remembered the pool, and he ran over just in time to see Rob, his arms flailing and legs bent, free-falling toward the pool.

Mac leaned over the rail and emptied his last few shots. Three of them split the water like miniature torpedoes, but one struck Rob in the thigh right before he hit the water.

"Aaaarrrgghh!"

Booosh!

Rob felt like he was breaking through a pane of glass and he was being smacked all over his body. On top of that, the chlorine seeped into his gun wound which only intensified the pain. But at least he was alive. He dragged himself out of the pool, staying under the extended lip of the balconies, limping his way to the parking lot. In the distance, he heard the sirens getting closer. If he could just make it to his car and lie low. He limped faster.

The Oak Ridge police skidded up the parking lot, three cars deep, responding to the 911 calls from several tenants. They spotted Rob half-limping, half-running, soaking wet, and his right pants leg covered in blood. They jumped out and trained their guns on him.

"Freeze! Freeze! Get down on the ground!"

"I'm shot!"

"Now! Get down now!" they bellowed as they surrounded Rob.

He quickly complied.

Mac saw the police skid up and arrest Rob. Several more cops entered the building. He knew they were on their way to find him. He looked down at the pool.

"Man, fuck that," he mumbled. Even if he could jump without the police knowing, he wasn't about to try. Still, he had to get out. The stairs were dead, and they'd be watching the elevators, so unless he grew wings, he knew he was trapped.

Unless . . .

Mac glanced over the balcony. The balcony below him was only a hang jump away. He didn't waste time. He tucked the gun securely in his waist and carefully climbed over the balcony railing. Mac slowly lowered himself until his body was about two feet from the balcony beneath him. To get a little momentum he swung his feet a few times. Then he finally released his grip landing solidly on the balcony. He glanced down to check, but no police had been looking up. Mac was good. He planned on hiding out right there until the police left, but then he looked up. A white girl dressed in only a long T-shirt stared at him with wide eyes looking as if she were about to scream.

Heather had been watching *Twilight* again for a second time until she thought she heard rumbling coming from the apartment overhead. Once she heard the shots she knew she wasn't just hearing things. She forgot all about the vampires and wolves and trained her ears on the sounds above her. Being this close to that gangsta shit made her pussy slick. Heather was a small-town girl in love with the idea of city life. That's why when she saw Mac on her balcony she wasn't about to scream. She was about to yell, *"That was you?"* She had seen him before. In fact, she had flirted with his boy Rob in passing a couple of times, but they simply hadn't gotten together yet.

Mac put his finger to his lips. "Shhh! Chill! I just need a place to lay low, li'l mama. I ain't gonna hurt you."

That was the last thing on her mind. She slid the patio door open. "Then come on, before they see you!" she told him.

Surprised but not hesitant, Mac came in. She shut the screen and the curtains behind him.

"I know you!" She smiled.

"Well, now, I know you. Thanks."

"I'm Heather."

"I'm . . . Mike," Mac lied, as they shook hands.

He could now breathe because he had gotten away. But that was the easy part. Now, he had to tell Mook he fucked up and Rob slipped from between his fingers.

"Yeah." Nick hit the speaker button on his cell that was lying on the table. He was sitting at his desk in his den counting money and placing them in neat stacks. He was in Detroit for only a few days.

"Hey sexy? Let me find out you forgot about me," Nyla teased as she stretched across her king-sized bed. "You just up and disappeared."

Pause.

"Who is this?" Nick muttered, half listening and not catching the voice.

"You must be kidding me, right?" Nyla purred, pouring it on thick. "I thought I had the sexiest voice you ever heard. If that was true, then how could you forget?"

"Now, li'l mama, I've been havin' a hectic day. My mind ain't right. Just tell me your name," Nick said, keeping it smooth but getting impatient.

"Tiny."

"Oh! What up, sexy? Goddamn, where you been?" Nick stopped counting and picked up his cell.

When she heard his voice brighten up, she knew he was still open.

"If you would've been checkin' for me, you'd already know," she flirted sassily.

"True, true," he admitted with a chuckle. "But you know the game. Tomorrow ain't promised—gotta make it happen today. But, yo, I'm checkin' for you now. What up?"

"Uh-huh, I bet," she replied.

"For real. Holla at your boy."

"Well, if it's like that, I'm trying to see you. A sista needs to get wit' you," she told him, cutting straight to the chase.

"Shit, you already know then. Let me take care of something, and I'ma get right back."

"Don't keep me waitin'."

Once they were in the hotel room, Nyla wasted no time going to work. She needed Nick totally open so he would lead her right to Shan.

Nyla took him in her mouth and began to give him pure head, no hands. He put his hand on the back of her head and began to fuck her face. Her tight jaw action and flexible neck had Nick ready to bust off. Sensing that, she pushed him back on the bed and climbed on top of him.

"I need you to fuck this pussy good, daddy," she moaned, gripping the base of his dick and sliding it deep inside her.

Nick grabbed her ass and let out a grunt from the back of his throat as Nyla began to work her pussy muscle on the head of his dick. He grabbed her hips and began bouncing her on his rod, hitting her spot.

"Yes, daddy, yes!" she squealed, loving the way he stroked her pussy.

"Turn over," Nick demanded. He wanted to watch that ass bounce while he beat it.

Nyla got on all fours and spread her legs wide, arching her back. Nick ran the full length of his dick up in her and began to long stroke her hard. She threw that pussy back like a champ. He grabbed a fistful of her hair and slapped her ass, urging her on.

"Fuck! Fuck this pussy, baby! Ow! Yes!" Nyla screamed, clamping her pussy muscles around his long and hard magic stick.

Nick fought to hold back, but he couldn't. He busted deep inside her, which sent Nyla over the edge, and she exploded right after him.

After they fucked again, Nyla lay with her head on his chest, playing with his nipple.

"A diva could get used to this," she remarked.

"I'm tryin' to spoil you for other niggas," Nick joked.

"You already did that the first time," she giggled.

"Then I'm doin' my job."

They laughed, and when it subsided, Nyla asked, "Now what? You pull another disappearing act on me? I missed you."

"Naw, yo," he assured her throwing his arm around her and squeezing her tit. "I ain't gonna let that happen no more. Even if I'm outta town, I may just send for you and we can hang out."

"Out of town, where?" she asked, her voice full of skepticism, but deep down, she was all ears.

"New York."

"New York?" *So that's where he had the little bitch stashed away?* Nyla's conniving mind played that revelation over and over. "I never been to New York City befo'," Nyla joked, sounding like a country girl.

Nick laughed.

"Stick wit' me, li'l mama. I'ma show you a lot of shit you ain't never seen before."

Later for all that other shit. Just show me Shan.

Shan had just gotten out of the shower and was drying off when her phone rang. She was waiting for Nick to call because he was supposed to tell her where to meet him. Nick had been gone for a week, and she was anticipating meeting his connect, so she had some serious butter-flies. The thought of being in a major position of power had her mind tripping. She was nervous and hoping she wouldn't mess up. Still in all, she fantasized about what she would do with all the money. Even though Nick would be only a phone call away, she feared not being on point. Thinking of him, she couldn't help but smile.

But when she answered the phone, it wasn't Nick.

"What up, baby?" Briggen whispered, staying one step ahead of the police.

A smile spread over her whole body in spite of herself. "Hello, Brig-gen. How are you?"

"Better now. I tried to call a few minutes ago, but I ain't get no answer."

"I was in the shower."

"Oh, really? Did you think about me?" he flirted.

She snickered. "No."

"Not even for a second?"

"Briggen, don't even go there."

"Go where?" He feigned ignorance. "I'm just sayin', but I got my answer. You thought about me. Thought about how when I used to slide in the shower with you and start at your neck and lick—"

"Briggen, stop!" she demanded, trying to sound firm. "Or I'ma hang up." Her pussy twitched, but she pulled away from the memory.

"Okay, okay, I'ma chill. I'm just sayin', you dressed?"

She sucked her teeth. "Bye, Briggen."

He laughed. "That means no."

She laughed.

"Damn, baby. You don't know how bad I wish I could see that pretty brown body. Nigga could be locked up a hundred years and still remem-ber your body head to toe," he sweet talked her.

"What about remembering my mind?" she challenged.

"Is that made of chocolate too?" he joked with a Latin accent.

She laughed harder. "Please, Briggen. Lose the accent. You so silly."

"Only for you, baby, only for you . . . I love you."

The words caught Shan off guard like he knew they would. Now that he had her laughing, he knew her defenses were down. He wanted to get his bid in before they went back up.

"You heard me?"

"I-I heard you," she stammered.

"Look at yourself in the mirror for me," he instructed her.

She did, gazing at her own reflection in the full-length mirror.

"You see that? That's what I go to sleep dreamin' about. Fuck the money, the game, and the grind. What you lookin' at right now, I'd give it all up for in an instant," he gamed.

The ice melted.

"Briggen, I . . . have to go," she protested weakly, her voice barely audible.

"I can see your nipples now . . . how they stand up when I run my tongue over them . . . pull them gently with my teeth. Remember how I used to do that?"

Her nipples must've had a memory of their own as they both hardened simultaneously. She let out a light, sweet grunt, hating how well Briggen knew her body and could command it with his voice.

"And how I used to wrap your legs around my head . . . damn . . . and tongue kiss that cherry until you came all over my lips."

Her breathing grew irregular, and her pussy grew moist. "Brig—"

"Touch it for me," he demanded.

She imagined her hand was his, and she did. She moaned that sexy song he loved. He gripped his dick in one hand and the cell in the other.

"My dick hard as a rock imaginin' you, ridin' me, bitin' your bottom lip every time I hit that spot."

"Oh, Brig, I missed you," she gasped, riding the fingers inside her pussy and massaging her clit with her thumb.

"You gonna make that pussy come for daddy, huh? Show daddy how much you missed him."

She lay back on the bed and cocked her legs up, getting wetter and hornier with every caress.

"Whose pussy is it?" he uttered huskily.

"Yours," she moaned. Even though it was a lie, but at that moment, it was true.

The emotions built up within her and consumed her mind and soul. She had never stopped loving Briggen. There was no use trying to hide it. As the climax broke to a crescendo, her phone beeped with another call.

Nick.

As she came all over her fingers, her thought was, *Fuck the connect.*

Finding Sharia's second phone was the jackpot. She only used it to call and text two numbers. One Mo'Betta knew was Demetria, the other he didn't know, but he knew one thing: whoever it was, was thirsty. He called at least four times a day and texted constantly.

Where U?

Answer the damn phone!

What the fuck are you doing?

Another gold mine was the fact that Sharia never erased her texts or e-mails to her Hotmail account. She had hundreds, and Mo'Betta went through every one. "Damn, this bitch scandalous," he said. He chuckled and added, "I mean, *was.*"

It was clear that not only was she planning on making Demetria turn on Briggen, but whoever she was working with wanted to take over his drug spots and customers as well. Her and this mystery man. But the best part was when he got to the text that came from the mystery man.

Tell Demetria 1197 Myrtle Lane. Keys r under the mat. Stay safe.

He had provided the safe house for her to lay low in, but ironically, he had now provided the information that would cause her death.

"Bitch was dumb as fuck!" Mo'Betta spat, thinking of how careless Sharia was for not deleting her texts and e-mails. But then again, a lot of people don't.

Mo'Betta arrived in Oak Ridge and used his GPS to find 1197 Myrtle Lane. He rode by the small yellow house once during the daytime. He parked up the block and watched the house for an hour. No movement. He went to the McDonald's three blocks over and ate a number four in the parking lot. Then he drove back by the house. All the lights were still off. He got restless and drove around until he found a mall. He flirted and got two numbers. One of them was a white girl. The moment he realized it was dark he left. Back on Mrytle Street he parked down the block and dug in. Mo'Betta wasn't moving until the sun came up. It didn't matter. The bitch was dead either way.

Three hours later, a black Benz E-Class pulled up in front of the house, and a dude got out. He limped to the door and knocked. Several moments later, the porch light popped on.

"Damn, she been home the whole time," Mo'Betta remarked. "She hidin' for real!"

But with the porch light on, he could see more than Demetria. He saw him. His eyes widened, and he laughed.

"Goddamn, cuz, you right on time!" Mo'Betta chuckled excitedly.

Rob went inside and the porch light went off. Mo'Betta frantically went through his contact list, looking for Rob's number. He didn't find one, but he found the next best thing. His baby mama, Renee. He hit her up.

"Yo, Renee, this Mo' . . . Yeah, what up, though? Naw, I need Rob's new number, 'cause I'm trying to get in contact wit' him."

She didn't hesitate because she knew they were cousins. He plugged it into his phone, and then sent him a text.

Yo, cuz, this Mo' . . . Shhh. I'm in Oak Ridge. I need to see you ASAP

A few moments later, his phone rang.

"Mo'?" Rob asked, obviously surprised.

"What up, big cuz? It's me."

"What the fuck—"

"Yo, don't say nothin'. Trust me. When we talk, you'll know why. Meet me at McDonald's up the street ASAP!"

"Yo, li'l cuz, I'm about to get into somethin'."

"Yeah, I know and that's the problem."

"Huh?"

"Just trust me. Meet me ASAP."

Short pause.

"A'iight, I'm on my way."

They hung up. Mo'Betta watched Rob come out, jump in the Benz, and pull off. He then did the same. He pulled up next to Rob's Benz, got out of his rental, and got in with Rob.

"Li'l cuz, fuck you doin' in Oak Ridge?" Rob said, happily giving him a pound.

"Handlin' some business. What up with the limp?"

Rob sucked his teeth and got animated. "Fuckin' bitch-ass niggas tried to take me out, cuz!"

"Who!" Mo'Betta questioned, ready to set it off right on the spot.

Rob explained the whole situation, then ended by saying, "Muhfucka tried to kill me, and I end up goin' to jail for fuckin' shootin' in an occupied dwellin—my own crib!"

Mo'Betta shook his head. "Jumped in the pool, cuz? Get the fuck outta here! But yo, I don't know Dark. I heard of him. Mac and Mook. I'll take care of them. They dead. But cuz, I'm on a lick right now that we can both come up on."

"Shit, put me down!"

"You know that nigga Briggen?"

"Yeah, muhfucka a heavy hitter."

"Exactly. But he cased up on the word of a bitch. We dead her, he walk, and he ready to break bread," Mo'Betta explained.

"Sheeit, say no mo'! Who the dead bitch?"

"The broad whose house you was just at." Mo'Betta smiled, loving the expression that spread across Rob's face.

"Get the fuck outta here!" Rob laughed, not believing what he just heard.

They dapped over how small the world was.

"Yeah, the bitch got popped and snitched my nigga out. So, without her, the Feds got nothin'. I'm tellin' you, cuz, the nigga eatin'," Mo'Betta emphasized.

"Then it's a done deal," Rob replied, thought for a minute, then pointed at Mo'Betta's car. "That's a rental?"

"Yeah."

"Get out and follow me."

Rob led him a few streets over where he parked his Benz in the parking lot of a closed dental office. He then got in the car with Mo'Betta, and they pulled off.

"Gimme the gun," Rob requested.

Mo'Betta reached under the seat and pulled out the taped up .38 snub. It looked like a well used murder weapon.

"You want me to come wit' you?" Mo'Betta offered.

Rob looked at him as if to say, *For what?* "Nigga, we family. I remember when you used to piss the bed and try to blame it on me! I know if you bring me a lick, it's legit. Let big cuz handle the rest. Remember, I'm the one who taught you everything you know!"

"Say no more." Mo'Betta laughed.

"Let me out here," Rob instructed when they got to the corner of Demetria's block.

Mo'Betta stopped.

"Go around the block. If I ain't waitin', go around again. Go slow. By then I'll be ready."

Mo'Betta nodded, and Rob went down the street. He drove off, keeping the radio down and his ears open. By the time he rounded the corner he heard a muffled. *Blap! Blap!* It wasn't loud, but the sound was unmistakable.

"Goddamn! Cuz ain't bullshittin'." Mo'Betta laughed, wishing he could've been the one to put in the work. He would've made the bitch suffer.

He came back around and saw no signs of Rob, so he kept going. By the time he came around the second time, Rob popped out of the bushes and half limped, half ran to the car. Mo'Betta glanced at the house as they pulled off.

"Why you turn the lights on?"

Rob laughed. "Them ain't lights."

Glancing in his rearview, Mo'Betta could see that it was actually a fire just getting started. He imagined it sizzling the skin of Demetria's corpse. Then he wondered if she was still alive. He started to say something to Rob, but he was interrupted by the ring of Sharia's second phone. He hadn't answered it before, but he had wanted to. Yet he didn't want to alert whoever it was that there was a problem. But now, it didn't matter. He answered.

As soon as he did, he heard, "Bitch, where the fuck have you been?"

The voice had a nasal quality to it and didn't sound like the average hood dude. Mo'Betta didn't say anything.

"Hello? Sh—" The caller hung up abruptly.

Mo'Betta thought about the voice but filed it away as he pulled out his own second phone and sent Briggen a text.

Welcome Home!

Chapter Seven

Yo, I fucked up! He got away."

Those were the last words Mook wanted to hear as he drove down Broad Street. But there they were, and all he could do is ask, "What the fuck you mean?"

Mac was pacing in the white girl's spot, using her phone so he could talk more freely.

"Yo, the muhfucka knew I was bringin' him a move, and the nigga jumped out of the goddamn window . . . literally!" Mac explained.

"What?"

"Twenty flights up and landed in the pool, yo!" He exaggerated. Fuck could I do? But he got arrested. I seen it wit' my own eyes. Now all I gotta do is find out his court date and his lawyer of record. My nigga, if I gotta hit him in the goddamn courtroom—"

Mook cut him off. "Whoa, maine! We on the phone!"

"My bad, but you know what I'm sayin'! I'ma handle it!"

You said that last time, Mook thought angrily, and Mac picked up on it.

"Yo, I know I said that before, but I slept on the nigga. He ain't no slow leak. But I promise you, shit gonna get handled," Mac vowed.

Mac paced the floor nervously. If he had been a smoker, he would've been chain-smoking because he knew he was in a bind. Quiet and as simple, he had killed all his friends, and now he was surrounded by enemies. Because Rob got away, Dark wouldn't trust him. And because he had tried to kill Rob, now he had to be on point. Rob was just as dangerous, and he had proven himself to be a worthy opponent. It wasn't that Mac was scared; far from it. He just knew the deck was stacked against him. He couldn't afford to lose Mook, too.

But Mook was in the small boat. He had vouched for Mac, so Mac's fuckup was on his head. He couldn't tell Dark, but he knew sooner or later, Dark would find out, and then . . .

"Look!" Mook sighed in frustration. "Do whateva you gotta do, ASAP! Shit ain't no game, yo!"

"I already know. I got it!"

"Yeah. Whatever." Mook hung up and tossed his phone onto the passenger seat. He made up his mind. If Mac couldn't catch Rob, Mook was damn sure going to catch Mac.

Dark was out on Belle Isle waiting for Mook. He liked to go out there to get away from the city and think. He had come a long way in a short time. It showed the power of initiative, focus, and determination. He had been on the offensive since the day he murdered Forever, and he hadn't looked back yet. Now, he had the daughter of the top spot eating out of his hand, and he was primed to be Detroit's next kingpin.

He sat on the bench looking out at the water. A few minutes later, a rumpled clothes wearing, fat white man came and sat on the bench on the opposite end.

He smelled like and looked like a cop. The man pulled out a bag of bread and began feeding the seagulls. He glanced over at Dark.

"How you doin'?"

Dark didn't respond.

"You know who I am?"

"No."

"You wanna know who I am?"

"No," Dark repeated.

"I know who you are. You's the man, homie." Sherman, mocked, using slang.

Dark peered at him coldly. "Man, get the fuck outta here. I'm sitting here minding my own business. Chillin'."

"Good. I just thought we could talk about Cisco and 'The List' before things get out of hand," Sherman suggested.

Cisco? 'The List?' Damn. What else does he know? Who is this cat? From his tone of voice, Dark felt it would be in his best interest to see what the cracker had to say.

When Sherman saw Dark refrain from getting up, he chuckled. "Smart man. Of course, you don't get to where you are and not be smart, huh, Dark? The guy on the verge of taking over the city? Because you see, I'm like . . . the pope of these streets. I bless 'em. But without my blessin', things become real hard for the unblessed. Especially ones with murder charges hangin' over their heads," Sherman insinuated.

Dark looked at him. "How much you want? Just get to the point."

Sherman chuckled as he tossed out a handful of bread crumbs. "No, Dark. You may tell your goons what to do, but I tell you what and how you're going to do it. You know why? Because you don't want to be on my bad side. Because when you're on my bad side, I use everything in my power to make your life a living hell. I'll go so far as settin' you up for Cisco's murder. Oh, I know the body's never been found, but you see, that works both ways. 'Cause without a body I get to make stuff up!" Sherman fell out in a fit of laughter.

Dark wanted to shoot him in the face. "So how does somebody go about gettin' your blessing?"

Sherman tossed more bread in the air, and birds swarmed as soon as the crumbs hit the ground.

"You're not only smart, you don't waste time. That makes you a genius in my book. Your name is on that *List*, but, of course, you know that. A lot of nasty stuff is on that *List*. Enough to put a man away for a long, *long* time. But we don't need to worry about that, do we, Dark? Because we're going to cooperate. Isn't that right?"

"How much?" Dark gritted.

"Noooo my friend. It's a little more complicated than that. You see, I recently had a problem with a guy. You know a guy named Fat Rich? Fat Rich from Zone 8? I-I'm . . . Fat Rich and I no longer see eye to eye, so I don't wanna see Fat Rich no more. You catch my drift?" Sherman explained.

Dark laughed. How ironic. He was being asked by a cop to kill somebody. "Naw, really I don't," Dark replied, standing up to leave.

Sherman stood up and got right in his face. "Dark . . . This ain't a request. I thought you wanted to run this city? Well, this is the price. You walk away, and I'll see you on murder one before the week is over," Sherman promised him.

Dark knew Sherman had the power to put him away. Inside, Dark was boiling.

Since Dark didn't walk away, Sherman knew he would handle it, so he turned back to the birds. "Will you look at that? That son of a bitch almost shit on me. That's the thanks you get when you feed the bastards?" Sherman ranted and then shook his head. "That's why I carry this."

He pulled out a box of Alka-Seltzer, crushed up a few of the tablets, and then mashed them up into a chunk of bread. As he did, he said, "You see, when you feed 'em you got to teach 'em not to shit on you. So you make an example."

He tossed the toxic ball of bread out on the ground, and a seagull greedily gobbled it up.

"Remember, Dark . . . I'll be watching you." Sherman leered.

Dark started to walk away until he saw the seagull that ate the chunk of tainted bread start to shake, and then squawk strangely. Suddenly, he tried to fly off, but the bird's stomach exploded and the carcass slumped to the ground. The other birds scattered.

"That'll teach 'em." Sherman chuckled.

Dark couldn't believe his eyes. The old childhood myth was true.

While they had been talking, Mook pulled up. He just missed the exploding bird trick, but he passed Sherman as he approached Dark.

"Hi ya, Mook," Sherman greeted but didn't stop.

Mook looked at him strangely. When he got to Dark, he asked, "Who the fuck was that?"

"The tax man," Dark replied sarcastically. "What up wit' Oak Ridge?" Dark held his gaze.

Mook couldn't have looked away if he wanted to. It was a split second, a split second, and he decided he had to ride it out. "I told you, maine, I'd take care of it. It's a done deal."

"Yeah?" Dark checked, still eyeing him hard, not letting on if he believed him or not.

"No doubt."

Dark nodded. "A'iight," he replied, then fixed his mind on how to handle Fat Rich.

Dark pulled up to the S&C's on Six Mile, a popular greasy spoon spot. He chirped the alarm, and got out. Just as always, a group of niggas took advantage of the beautiful night and were posted on the block like crows. He kept his eye peeled for Baby Boy. Not only because he had pistol-whipped and shot him, but he also had business with him. He kept his hand close to his waist casually, just to let niggas know he was chilling, but shit could get ugly fast.

Dark entered S&C's, and the first person he saw was Jamilla propped up on her stool behind the register. He couldn't front. For a hood rat, she wasn't bad. She had that Eve-type sassy attitude, short haircut, body and all. If a nigga cleaned her up, the bitch could be top choice. He just wasn't that nigga.

When he got to the counter, her face lit up with a sexy smile.

"What up, doe, Dark? You lookin' good tonight," she flirted.

"Better chill, li'l mama, or I'ma get your husband on you," he teased.

Jamilla sucked her teeth. "Please! You see a ring on this finger? Shit, he can't hardly handle this no way."

"Okay, li'l mama. I hear you."

She giggled. "So what you want, besides me?" She gazed into his eyes. "For real, what you want?"

Dark chuckled. Jamilla was putting her bid in hard. "I'd love to see you on my plate real soon, but right now, I need to holla at Quita," he told her.

"Quita?" Jamilla snapped, rolling her neck and narrowing her eyes. "Nigga, I know you ain't 'bout to ask me 'bout the next bitch!"

"Chill, li'l mama. I need to holla at her on some business shit."

"Okay, business shit," she huffed.

"On the real, ma, handle that for me," Dark said firmly.

Sensing his impatience, Jamilla didn't push the envelope. She sucked her teeth and yelled, "Quita! Somebody wanna see you!"

"Good look, Jamilla," Dark told her.

"Mmm hmmm." She rolled her eyes.

Dark tossed a couple of hundreds onto the counter. "Here. That's for you. Get an outfit. And the next time I come through, I wanna see you in it." Dark wore a grin that said, "You can suck my dick later."

"Nigga, you ain't slick." She licked her lips seductively, snatched up the two bills and buried the money in her bra. "Call me later."

Quita came out. When she saw Dark, her frown turned into a smile. "Long time no see."

"I know. Come on. We 'bout to take a ride."

"It's ten of ten. Time for me to punch the clock anyways. Let me get my jacket."

As they drove away from the restaurant, Dark pulled out his dick and looked at Quita, "Bitch, fuck you waitin' for? You know what it is."

"Where the money?" she shot back.

"Money? Bitch, I ain't get right last time. This on you!" Dark demanded.

"You lucky I like you." She sneered as she bent down and wrapped her sexy, thick, hot lips around Dark's dick.

For a young bitch barely twenty-one, she definitely had skills, teasing the head with her tongue, then devouring it and relaxing her throat and working her neck just right. Dark couldn't wait. He was ready to go up in that ass. He found a quiet back block and pulled over.

"Get out," he urged her, opening the door of his Ferrari Spider 458.

She was right behind him. He came around to her, bent her over, and pulled her skirt up. "You remember how I like it, superman?" She looked back at him.

He answered her by sliding his dick straight up in her ass, causing her to let out a shrilling squeal. She reached back and spread her ass cheeks. "Fuck, Dark, y-y-your . . . dick . . . is . . . so . . . fat," she grunted, but taking every inch.

"Shut the fuck up and take this dick," he demanded, grabbing her around the waist and banging her asshole like it was a grudge fuck. He knew, with a bitch like Quita, he couldn't just fuck her. He had to thug her too.

"Oh, daddy, this dick is so good! You gonna make me come," she moaned, throwing that ass at him.

"Then make it come for big daddy," he instructed.

"Yes . . . yes . . . yes!" she urged him until her pussy exploded, and the juices ran down her thighs.

She quickly turned and took Dark's whole dick in her mouth. Quita was definitely a hood rat, but being so nasty turned Dark on even more and he came deep in her throat.

"Swallow it," he told her. She did, licking her lips like she wanted some more.

"Damn, that was good. You been to jail before, ain't you⸮" She smirked.

"Fuck you tryna' say⸮" Dark snapped, ready to smack the shit out of her.

"I'm just playin' wit' you, dang."

"Don't fuckin' play like that."

"I'm feelin' you, Dark. You gonna be my new sponsor⸮" she pouted, playing with his half-erect dick right outside in the open.

"I don't do the sponsor shit. What happened to your man, Baby Boy⸮"

"He in the county. Plus I don't be fuckin' wit' him like that no more," she quickly added.

"Li'l mama, you ain't gotta lie to kick it. Real talk, he is who I really need to see."

"For real⸮ Why⸮" She sat up.

"Don't ask so many goddamn questions. Just tell me his government name."

"Jevon Monroe."

Dark pulled out his cell and called a bondsman.

"What you doin'⸮" she wanted to know.

"Bailin' him out."

"Why⸮"

"Don't talk wit' your mouth full," Dark spat, grabbing her head and filling her mouth with his dick.

"Fuck it then! Six!" Baby Boy shouted, bidding his hand.

He was dressed in a thermal shirt, with the top half of his county orange jumper tied around his waist and a doo-rag tied around his head as he bid his hand.

"Do you," the dealer told him, pushing the kitty to him.

"Downtown," Baby Boy said, as he picked up the kitty.

Before he could play, a big, black, buffed CO barked, "Monroe! Jevon Monroe! Roll yo' shit! You outta here!"

Everybody at the table froze and looked at him.

"Out?" He frowned up. *Who the fuck posted my bond?* He had three assaults with intent to kill, and his bond was fifteen percent on one hundred grand. He didn't have that kind of money. No one he knew had that kind of money. Damn sure not his dope-fiend-ass mother, and definitely not that trifling-ass Quita. She had even put a block on her phone so he couldn't call. It was him against the world, just like he wanted it because it meant he didn't owe anybody shit. He thought maybe one of his victims had got him out, but quickly dismissed it. They were all as broke as him.

"Monroe, you stayin' or what?"

"Fuck no!" He slapped the cards down on the metal table.

"Then bring yo' punk ass on!"

"Yo mama!" Baby Boy yelled right back at him.

An hour and a half later he stepped out of the county jail and looked around. When he saw Dark, he remembered him instantly. That was the nigga that had been fucking Quita. He also pistol-whipped him and shot him in the ass. He wished he had his pistol because he would've killed Dark right where he stood.

Dark read his expression and laughed. "Goddamn, li'l nigga. Right in front of the county jail?"

"I'll see you again," Baby Boy vowed.

Dark approached. "Hopefully, you'll be seein' me a lot, especially if you workin' for me."

"Work for you?" Baby Boy laughed. "Nigga, suck my dick."

Dark bit his anger off. Looking at Baby Boy's skinny ass, he knew he could break him in two.

"Li'l nigga . . . I'ma let that go 'cause I ain't here to beef wit' you. I'm the one that bailed you out."

"You?" Baby Boy spat in disbelief. It made no sense.

"Real talk, li'l nigga, you a soldier. Fuck wit' me, and I'ma make you a goddamn general. When we met, we was both out of order. But real niggas see past the bullshit. We'll make better friends than enemies," Dark offered.

Baby Boy couldn't front. The vibe Dark was giving off was official. Besides, he was right. Quita had him fucked up. He had no reason to kick his car, damn near putting a dent in it.

"I guess you the man," Baby Boy acknowledged, but with less hostility in his voice.

"I'm that nigga Dark," he replied arrogantly, knowing Baby Boy had heard the name. And he had.

His name rang all over the county as the man who had taken over Cisco's whole crew on some get-down-lay-down-type shit. Word on the street was he had also murdered Cisco and niggas were confirming that shit as if they witnessed it first hand.

"So what up? You gonna take this ride wit' me or what? Straight-up, I'm tryin' to fuck wit' you. That is, if you tryna to take shit to the next level," Dark proposed.

Baby Boy thought about it. He knew if Dark wanted to kill him he could've gotten him touched in the county. He had nothing to lose and everything to gain.

"Fuck it," he replied, grabbing his nuts and bebopped up to Dark's Ferrari and got in. The two of them drove off.

Because of Nyla, Nick missed his flight, so he instructed Shan to go ahead with the meeting. "It's not even a meeting. He simply wants to feel you out. No talk of business. That's my job, after you pass this test," he said.

"*After?* Are you sure I'm gonna pass the test?"

"Shan!"

"But, Nick, I'll be nervous," she protested like a spoiled little girl. "I don't even know what he looks like."

"He'll find you. Trust me, it'll be fine."

They were to meet at Manhattan's South Side Seaport at an exclusive restaurant called MarkJoseph Steakhouse. Shan approached the maître d' and said, "Powell party, please."

The maître d' checked the list. "Will you be dining alone, Madame?"

"I hope not," Shan answered cheerfully.

She was shown to her table and given a menu with no prices. Before she could order or call the nanny and check on the kids, she heard, "Oh, there you are!" The words were drawn out.

Shan looked up and saw a heavyset white man smiling hard, but sweating even harder, and headed right for her. *This* was the connect? As he approached, his eyes were right on her, or rather seemed to be right on her. When he got close enough and she was about to extend her hand, she realized he had obviously been looking at someone directly behind her. The man passed her, and she breathed a sigh of relief. She looked back just to see who the man had greeted. Some older white woman with the air of someone that probably owned half of Manhattan.

"Shannon?"

No one had ever said her name like that. No one called her by her first name. Period. But hearing it said like that with an accent she couldn't place, made Shan want everybody to start saying her whole name. She looked up, and her eyes were rewarded with a tall, dark-skinned brother with a short fade and eyes as green as emeralds that seemed to take in her entire being. Something in her made her want to stand up and greet this man, but he protested.

"Non, non, non—! Don't get up. I am so sorry that I am late. I hate Manhattan tra-feeq." He chuckled, extending his hand. "I am Edgard."

"Shannon," she replied, as close to hypnotized as she had ever been.

He kissed her hand. "I am, as you saaaay . . . pleased to meet you," he stated as he sat down.

"The pleasure is all mine," she replied, taking a sip of water but really wanting to fan herself.

"Neeak speaks very highly of you."

"I'm . . . sorry . . . who?" Shan inquired.

"Neeak . . . Neeak."

It took a moment, but she finally understood. "Oh, Nick." She giggled. "I'm sorry."

"Yes, Neeak."

"If you don't mind, what is your accent? It's beautiful," she remarked, not to be flirtatious, but he made everything sound like a song. So she needed to know exactly where they sang like that.

Edgard smiled graciously. "Thank you. My first language is French. My father is Moroccan and my Ma-Ma is Sudanese."

The waiter appeared, and Edgard ordered first. Butternut squash, apple soup, lamb chops, yellow rice, and roasted asparagus tips. Shan followed his lead and ordered the same, except in place of the soup she requested a caesar salad. After the waiter left, Edgard said, "But I came to meet you. Don't be nervees. There are no right or wrong answers. I simplee want to know about you, Shannon."

"Like what?" she probed.

"Like . . . why a beautiful woman like you would want to go into such a dirtee business, eh? I mean . . . besides the monee."

She shrugged. "Nick is family. And we are all we got."

"Ahh Shannon, I know its more than that. What's in it for you?"

"Freedom. Not having to depend on anyone for anything. Playing a losing game and winning. Beating the house," she mused. "All I'm really trying to do is win for me and my kids."

He chuckled. "So you are a gambaler?"

"Not really. I feel that I have nothing to lose, but everything to gain," she stated.

"If so, then who makes the odds? Who is thee house?"

She contemplated his point. "Fate," she answered.

Edgard shook his head. "Soreee, I cannot agree. Because fate means it was already written, no? So if it is already known, it can't be a gamble," he concluded.

"I guess I never looked at it like that."

Their meals arrived. They ate and talked for hours. After the restaurant, they sat down on the deck on the USS *Intrepid,* the retired battleship right near the seaport. It was chilly but Edgard had her all warmed up. Talking to him was like a breath of fresh air for Shan. His conversation was intellectually stimulating, which she found that she hadn't had in a while. Shan felt like she could listen to Edgard talk for days. Even if she didn't always agree.

"So are you saying that black people shouldn't believe in God?" Shan questioned incredulously, as they watched the sun set from the stern of the old battleship.

Edgard shrugged and replied, "Where has it gotten us? In my country of Sudan, the European give us Bibles, the Arab gives us Koran, but they get our resources, and we get famine, war, and genocide. So, if we are to judge a tree by its fruit, what kind of seed are we planting?"

"I mean, I see your point, but . . ." Shan shook her head, "I know there's a God. There has to be after all I've been through."

"There is, Shannon." Edgard smiled, then lightly touched her on the arm. "You. Don't be afraid of your own human potential, because, after all, a person must stand on their own two feet before they can fall to their knees. But when you are born on your knees, you are only a slave," he jeweled her.

He allowed his words to sink in as he studied her silhouette by the light of the dying sun. Edgard was a man who never mixed business with pleasure. But never say never . . .

"Shannon, you are a very intelligent woman. I will tell Neeak that if your loyalty matches your intelligence, then I will welcome the opportunity to work with you. And then, he will, of course, fill you in on all of the details."

Shan turned and smiled at him. Coming from him, the compliment really meant something because most men only wanted what was between her thighs. Edgard appreciated her mind.

"Thank you, Edgard. I do too . . . welcome the opportunity, I mean."

"An old man once told me the English word for *opportunity* breaks down into two syllables. Open ports of unity. He said the *port* is, how you say, for life's journey, but the *unity* is because we all have a single goal: happiness . . . I look forward to being a port in your journey, Shannon." Those last words dripped from his lips. He then kissed her hand and departed, leaving Shan to fantasize about . . . *what-if.*

Chapter Eight

N ew York!" Nick echoed as he made his way through the Dumbo section of Brooklyn.

"Yeah, baby. Surprised?" Nyla asked, holding in her conniving cackle.

She was standing in LaGuardia Airport, having just gotten off the 6:20 p.m. flight from Detroit. As soon as Nick left, not more than two hours later she had booked her own flight to New York. She had Shan's scent, and like a bloodhound in relentless pursuit, she wasn't about to lose it.

This nigga gonna think I'm a stalker, Nyla giggled.

Goddamn, I hope this bitch ain't no fatal attraction, Nick thought. The pussy was good, but he didn't want it in New York. Not that close to Shan. Tiny was his Detroit jump-off, so what the fuck was she doing in New York?

"Yeah, as a matter of fact, I am. When you get here?" he asked.

"Just now. Are you upset with me, daddy?" she pouted, playing to his ego.

"Naw, I'm just sayin' . . ." Nick stammered, not wanting to hurt her feelings.

"I just couldn't stand the idea of not seein' you," she cooed. "I know you got somebody else in New York, and I promise I'll play my position. Shit, if she cute, I'll stick my tongue all up in her gushy while you watch." She giggled.

Nick's dick jumped at the thought of seeing Tiny licking Shan's pussy. The seed was planted just like Nyla knew it would be. He had been fucking Nyla on a regular since her call. Her freakiness had him wide open, and the last time he was with her, he promised her that he would send for her, and obviously, she couldn't wait. He was getting real comfortable, and it made him feel even cockier to have two bitches in the same city. That gave him the idea of both of them fucking. Nick already pictured the two of them fighting over his dick. He knew he would have to spend a couple of thousand and do a lot of scheming to warm Shan up to the idea. She would enjoy the stroll of heaven as she affectionately referred to Fifth Avenue in New York City.

"Damn, baby, once again, you just made my dick hard."

"I'm for real. Anything for you, daddy."

Nick smiled, feeling like a true swordsman. "Yeah, well, hold that thought."

"I will. Anyway, I came to do some shopping too, so just call me when you're free. I'll only be in town a few days. What's more convenient for you, Harlem or Brooklyn?"

"Harlem."

Oh, so he got the bitch in Harlem, huh? she assumed, knowing he'd want to have her close by so he could have easy access. Nyla laughed at how easy it was to get information from a man. But she was even happier than she had been in a long time. Revenge was finally within her grasp. She would have her chance to make the woman suffer who destroyed her marriage, broke up her happy home, put her husband into a wheelchair, and then caused his death. She wanted revenge so bad she breathed it. She kissed into the air.

"Then Harlem it is. I'll be staying at the Aloft."

"Big spender, huh?" Nick teased.

It's your money. "Only the best, daddy. That's why I fuck with you. Mmmwah! Talk to you later." She blew him a kiss and hung up.

Briggen sat across from Rudy in the visitation booth, holding the phone and not being able to believe his ears. He was under the impression that Rudy had already filed his motion to get released.

"What the fuck do you mean why are you gettin' me out? Rudy, that's your goddamn job! And if you don't do it, you better put my muhfuckin' money back in my account and someone else damn sure will!"

Briggen threatened him. He was so mad spit sprinkled the plexiglas that separated the two men.

Rudy sighed. "You haven't heard me out, Calvin. I just don't want you to get out and end up dead or right back in here."

"What the fuck? I'm not payin' you to concern yourself with whether I come back to jail or not. You're my lawyer not my social worker! I'm—"

"Calvin, how long have I been your lawyer? Haven't I always found the loopholes? Haven't I always worked the angles? I've been with you almost from the beginning, and all I'm trying to say is, when is enough enough? I can't concern myself with your well-being? You are not going to be able to always worm your way out of these situations. Those streets ain't the same. It's damn near drying up, and you now have two kids to think about! Have you considered that? All I'm saying is, Calvin, you're a smart man. But this thing is bigger than you. Think about the kids, and when I do get you out, go legit," Rudy said encouragingly.

"Are you finished?" The two men glared at each other as if in a stand-off. Briggen had to admit. What Rudy was saying made perfect sense. He just wasn't ready to let the game go. He needed one more run. *One.* Then he could go totally legit. He knew it was cliché. The theme of so many sad hustler stories that ended with one more run, but he would be different. He had a plan.

"Look, Rudy, I'm just sayin', the path has been cleared. We can move now. File the goddamned paperwork and let's move," Briggen ordered.

"You're the boss," Rudy said with sarcasm.

Briggen caught the tone but let it go. He was too happy to let that bring him down. He had awakened a few days ago to Mo'Betta's *Welcome Home* text, and he knew he was home free. It was time to put his team back together, only better this time. Mo'Betta would be his right hand, but he wasn't about to make the same mistake he made with Woo.

Welcome Home. That text made his heart sing. *Yeah. Ol' Brig still got it.*

When he got back to his cell, he took out his phone. He couldn't wait to talk to Shan. She was a part of his come up, but after that, he definitely had plans for her. Payback was a muthafucka, and he felt that she couldn't get hers fast enough. He never betrayed her. But she would wish on their kids that she hadn't betrayed him.

"What up, sexy? How you?"

"Oh, hey, baby, I'm good. Early today, ain't you?" Shan inquired as she drove, heading to Midtown.

"Just thinkin' about you. You sound like you're drivin'. Where you takin' me?" he joked.

"Just goin' to meet some friends."

"Oh, do I know *him*?" Briggen asked.

"No, you don't know her. Actually two hers," Shan answered, hating herself for feeling the need to explain herself, even casually.

"Sounds kinky, can I listen?"

She laughed. "You so stupid."

"On the real, though, when you gonna come see me so I can see my new li'l girl and my man?" Briggen asked.

"I told you, baby, I know you want to see Brianna, but I'm not ready for that. I know I'm being selfish, but I just need some time, Briggen," she explained.

"I understand, but tomorrow ain't promised. I just don't want to take any day above ground for granted anymore. Besides, it's behind the glass. It ain't like I can stick my tongue in the pussy." Briggen chuckled, adding in his mind, *or choke the shit out of you.*

"Although I'm sure you'd try. Nasty ass!" She snickered.

"Please, baby, I don't know what these crackas gonna do. I need to see my family." He played on her heartstrings, purposely not telling her that as soon as the ink dried on the paperwork he would be out and about.

When she sighed, he knew he had her. "Let me . . . check on some flights, okay? And, Briggen, don't make this complicated for me. Things are complicated enough as it is."

"I won't, sweetness. I won't. I'm still in love with you."

The clerk of the court's wife was a fat slob. He wished he had never married the nagging bitch, but after three kids and seventeen years of marriage, it was definitely cheaper to keep her. Besides, he himself was no prize. He looked like Elmer Fudd and not the cartoonish character but a flesh and blood version. That's why when the curvaceous, sunflower blonde girl smiled so sweetly and cocked her head just so, he couldn't help but fantasize about smelling her panties.

"Excuse me sir. What's your name?" she asked with the sweetest country lilt he'd ever heard.

"Harold, li'l lady, Harold Kent," he replied, tipping his imaginary hat.

"Well, Mr. Kent, can I call you Harold?"

"Li'l lady, pretty little thang like you can call me cow manure, long's you don't spread it around," he replied, making a vain attempt at being witty.

She giggled like a schoolgirl. "You're funny."

"What can I do for you, Miss Lady?"

"A friend of mine had to go to court today, and I was supposed to meet him, but I was too late. I really need to catch him, but I don't have his number. I was hoping I could leave a message with his lawyer," she explained.

Harold nodded.

"What's his name?"

"Robert Lincoln."

Harold looked down in his computer and pulled it up. "Your friend's a little bit of a hothead, ain't he? Shootin' in an occupied dwelling and all."

"It was a break-in."

"Mmm-hmmm," Harold replied, not believing her. "It doesn't say he had a court date today."

"Maybe it's tomorrow," she said.

He shook his head, and then looked at her with a mischievous smile. "And anyway, how'd you know he had a court date if you haven't talked to him?"

She dropped her eyes. "Okay, you got me. He's not really a friend."

"Glad to hear it."

"I'm really a reporter for the *Tennessee Star,* trying to get the exclusive interview, and I need his lawyer's address to catch him," she lied.

Harold laughed. "I figured as much. You look like the reporter type, tryin' to get the big scoop," he joked, wiggling his eyebrows.

She giggled again. "The bigger the better," she flirted.

His dick twitched. "Got 'em . . . I'm not supposed to do this, li'l lady, but for that smile, I'll make an exception. His lawyer is Stanley Reed. Need the address, too?"

"No, thank you."

"Need mine?" He winked. "Maybe you could do a big scoop on me."

They both laughed. "I would love to, but I don't think your wife would like that," she pointed out, touching his wedding ring.

"Well, then, we'll be even, because I don't like her either," he replied truthfully.

"No comment. Bye, Harold. Maybe some other time," she remarked, wiggling her fingers good-bye.

He watched her walk out the door, and for the millionth time, cursed his life.

Outside, Mac waited behind the wheel of a rented Chrysler 300, smoking a blunt. When Heather got in, he passed it to her.

"Stanley Reed," she told him, inhaling the weed.

"Good girl," Mac replied, pulling off and merging into traffic.

"Mr. Reed, please."

"Do you have an appointment?"

"No, but I have this," Mac said, pulling out a stack of one hundred dollar bills. "Will this get me an appointment?"

The secretary looked up at him. Her boss had all types of characters stopping by and trying to get him to represent them. But this one here looked crazy, and she wanted to get his marijuana-smelling behind as far away as possible. She would tell the police later that he was tall, wearing those awful dreadlock things in his hair and donning a scraggly beard and smelled of marijuana. But that knot spoke volumes. She got on the phone, and then several seconds later, said, "Mr. Reed will see you now."

I'm sure he will, Mac thought.

He adjusted the wig and fake beard as he walked down the hall. Moments later, he opened the door to Mr. Reed's office. Mr. Reed, an

older man that fit the description of the consummate country gentleman, sat behind the desk.

"Hello, Misterrrr. . . .¿" Reed greeted, getting up to shake hands.

Mac ignored his outstretched hand. Instead, he turned and locked the
door.

"What the hell—" Reed started to protest.

Mac turned back holding a .44 revolver. Reed froze.

"Sit down, Mr. Reed."

Reed sat down.

"Close your mouth, Mr. Reed."

Reed shut his gaping mouth with a snap.

"This ain't about you, so don't make it be. You have a client, Robert
Lincoln," Mac told him.

Reed nodded.

"You can speak, Mr. Reed."

"Y-y-yes, I do."

"Then you're about to get on the phone right now and call him.
You're going to tell him exactly what I tell you. If you do, you'll live.
Are we clear¿"

Reed nodded, and then remembered he could speak. "Crystal."

"Very good. Now pay attention. You fuck up, you get fucked up,"
Mac warned him.

Reed gulped.

Rob's phone rang. He rolled over. It rang again. He woke up. It rang a
third time, and he answered.

"Yeah."

"Mr. Lincoln, this is your attorney, Stanley Reed."

Rob yawned. Scratched his nuts. "Yeah¿"

"Mr. Lincoln, you told me I would be defending you against a charge
of shooting in an occupied dwelling."

"You are."

"Not anymore. The police have informed me that, that gun was used
in several homicides."

"Homicides¿" Rob echoed. He sat up, now fully awake.

"Homicides, Mr. Lincoln. That changes my fee drastically. The police want to question you right away. Now, I suggest you get to my office immediately and bring another ten grand if you want me to represent you in this matter."

"Fuck!" Rob cursed.

He got up and began pacing the floor, trying to remember who he got the gun from. It was quite possible the gun had bodies on it. He thought about going on the run, but he quickly dismissed it. If the police had something they would've already arrested him. They just wanted to question him, which meant try to get him to tell where he got the gun from. They could eat a dick, because he wasn't telling them shit. But he had to go because running would only make him look guilty, and then an arrest would be inevitable.

"Mr. Lincoln, are you there?"

"Yeah, man. I'm here."

"Well, you need to be here within the hour and bring my additional retainer. I feel confident that we can get this matter cleared up quickly," Reed said, which made Rob feel better, just like Mac knew it would.

"I'm on my way," Rob assured him.

"He just pulled up," Heather told him.

"Yep. Remember, two blocks."

"Okay."

They hung up.

Rob got out of the car and crossed the street to Reed's office, carrying a McDonald's bag. When he entered, he said to the secretary, "I'm here to see Mr. Reed. He's expecting me."

"I know. Go right in," the secretary told him.

Rob walked down the short hallway and knocked on the door.

"Come in," Reed called out.

Rob entered, seeing Reed behind the desk looking almost . . . chalky. As if he was deathly ill.

"Mr. Reed, are you—" were Rob's last words as Mac stepped from behind the door and put the gun to the back of his head.

Rob froze.

"Game over," Mac hissed, blowing the back of Rob's head through his face.

Reed threw up, and then passed out. Mac stood over Rob and hit him three more times. He contemplated killing Reed and the secretary, but decided against it.

They couldn't identify him so they weren't a threat. Besides, they were white. One dead nigga was one thing, but two dead white people changed the game.

Mac grabbed the McDonald's bag and peeped in it.

"I should've said twenty grand, muhfucka," he laughed.

Mac dipped into the hall and out the emergency exit. It led to a back alley. He quickly took off the dreadlocked wig and fake beard, and pulled his hood on and kept his head down. As he reached the street, he took off the hood and walked naturally. On the second block, Heather sat waiting in his tricked-out 300. He got in.

"What now, baby?" she asked, feeling this gangsta shit.

He smiled. "You ever been to the D?"

"No. And I'm tired of Oak Ridge. How many bags do I need to pack?"

Crystal definitely knew how to play the boss diva. Everywhere she went, she was always accompanied by two big, black, buffed bodyguards and rode around in a bulletproof burgundy Hummer. Dark let her play the role because it kept her out of the way, even surprising her with a dachshund. He paid almost seven grand for it. And she took it everywhere with her. She treated it as if it was her baby. Dark figured it would give her something to do.

Every Tuesday and Friday she had her hair and nails 'done at her favorite salon, Majestic Beauty, on Grand River. She would arrive, her bodyguards would exit first, and then she would get out. The salon owner had offered to shut down the shop while she was there, but Crystal refused. What good was having money and power if you couldn't flaunt it in people's faces sometimes? She wanted those hood bitches to recognize a boss bitch when they saw one. How many of them had to place their thousand dollar weave on lay-a-way? Or better yet, wanted to live her life? Only in their dreams.

She entered the salon, and, as usual, Cherry, her hairstylist's, chair was empty and waiting on her.

"What's up, Miss Lady? And how are you today?" Cherry greeted, exchanging air kisses with Crystal.

"Girl, you already know. I'm fabulous!" Crystal cackled.

"Yes, you are."

The bodyguards posted up in the waiting area and one near her chair. Several females were waiting for their turn, but three females in the middle of the salon stood out because they looked like men in drag on their way to a costume party. Before the bodyguards could react, all three reached under their skirts and pulled out 9 millimeter guns and opened fire. The three shooters aimed straight for their targets. Ladies screamed and ducked as the bullets ripped. Both of the bodyguards dropped back to back with half of their heads blown off, leaking blood. Their bodies lay twitching on the floor. Cherry got hit in the exchange, and her brains squirted across Crystal's face, her dead body slumped over Crystal who couldn't stop screaming, all the while realizing that the streets weren't for her. She loved all the perks, but this shit wasn't worth all the stress and danger.

"Grab that bitch and let's go!" one of the shooters ordered in a deep baritone, confirming what everyone who remained alive already knew; that they were men dressed up as women.

The last thing Crystal saw was the butt of the gun smashing into her head, and then everything faded to black.

Choppa was true to his word. "I will take my connect to the grave before I let you have it."

Dark played those words back as he cruised around the city. What could he have done differently? He was caught between a rock and a hard place. If he hadn't gotten rid of Choppa, Choppa would have definitely gotten rid of him. Crystal had the connect, but then Janay stepped in and put a stop to the flow. Now he needed to handle Janay and get another connect. The Consortium had a connect for its members, but the prices went up, and Dark had plans on becoming their supplier. Shit, he felt that was his right.

When Crystal woke up, she was tied to a chair in some old garage with rusty, old car parts everywhere. She smelled oil, gas, and transmission fluid. Three dudes she had never seen before stood in front of her.

"I'm gonna ask you one time, bitch. Do you want to live?" Wise snarled.

Crystal nodded, her head still clearing. *Who are these niggas and what do they want? Are these the same people that tried to kill me in Benny Thrillz?* her instincts screamed.

Wise held up her phone.

"We already know Janay is 704. That's Charlotte, North Carolina. What we don't know is where. Start singin'," he demanded.

The first thing that popped into her mind was an image of Marquis's face. *Sweet Marquis.* Her nephew. She knew if she told them where Janay lived, chances were, Marquis would die. She couldn't stomach that.

"I-I can't . . . no," Crystal stammered.

Wise laughed. "Oh, bitch, you can, and you *will,*" he promised, then pulled out his gun and shot her in the knee.

"Aarrrr!" She screamed out in excruciating pain. "Somebody help me!" The pain was still less than the emotional torment of signing Marquis's death warrant like she did her father.

"I told you I wasn't gonna ask again, so stop me when you got something to say," Wise snapped at her, then shot her in the other knee.

It hurt so bad, she pissed on herself, but nothing came out of her mouth but cries.

"Still ain't talkin'?" Wise fumed.

He nodded to one of his two goons who snatched Crystal's shoes off and poured gasoline all over her feet, then set them on fire. The pain seemed to shoot straight through to the top of her brain, searing even her thoughts of survival. The pain was worth her life. She even willed it, but it wasn't worth Marquis's life.

Wise put the fire out. Her feet were charred and gnarled. She let out gut-wrenching screams. He ground his boot into her charred feet mercilessly. Crystal cried out, "Fuck you, nigga! Kill me, kill me, 'cause I ain't tellin' you shit!"

It took every ounce of her strength, but in her mind she was fighting for Marquis's life with the force of a mother's love, and no mother worth the name would give their child up.

"Oh, you finally got some heart, huh, bitch? You gonna wait 'til the day you die to finally live?"

Wise gripped his gun and pistol-whipped Crystal unconscious, but when he looked into her swollen and bloodshot eyes, he saw a wall he knew he would never get through. He shot her in the shoulder once just out of frustration, then put the gun to her forehead and ended it all with two shots, point-blank.

"Bitch was a soldier. I'll give her that," Wise remarked bitterly.

He flipped through her phone until he got to Janay's number.

J 704-571-2391

He stared at it, then, by mistake he hit the button, sending a call through. By the time he pushed end, it had rung once.

"Fuck it, if I can't go to the bitch, maybe the bitch'll come to me," Wise concluded. Turning to his goon, he ordered, "Make sure they find the body. We wanna make sure she gets a proper burial," he chuckled, and his goon caught on. Before the goon walked out, Wise added, "And bring the ugly-ass mutt with her!"

Janay was on her computer when her phone rang. Then it stopped. She looked and saw it was Crystal's number. She frowned. *One ring?* She called back, and it went straight to voice mail. Her instincts told her something was wrong and a cold chill shot up her spine.

"Lord, please protect my family."

Chapter Nine

Fat Rich from Zone 8 was a fat, Biggie-looking nigga that loved to gamble. He had it so bad that he'd gambled on a two-cockroach race. His favorite game though was five card. He was a pro and seldom lost. Unfortunately, his last night playing five card, he lost more than he gained.

"Come on, maine. Let a nigga get some get back, Rich," one of the gamblers he broke complained.

"You can get some get back, nigga. Get back at me tomorrow!" Fat Rich joked, and the other three gamblers laughed.

"That's that bullshit, Rich!"

Fat Rich and his man walked out of the gambling spot.

"Yo, you holla at the twins?" Fat Rich asked his man, as they walked toward Rich's cocaine white Porsche SUV.

"Yeah, them niggas said next week."

"Next week? It's always next week wit' them niggas," Fat Rich grumbled. "We need to call a sit-down before shit get out of hand."

"Hold up, I gotta piss," his man said, standing at the tree the Porsche was parked under.

Fat Rich started to get in, but he saw a fresh Nike print on the hood of his shit.

"Who the fuck been standin' on my white shit?" Fat Rich spazzed.

A rain of bullets was the reply. His man got hit first. Two in the top of his head came out of his neck, and his body flopped against the tree trunk—and slumped at the root.

At first Rich didn't know where the shots were coming from. He thought it was somebody in a window. He crouched behind his door for cover. But suddenly he heard something land on the roof of the Porsche. He tried to swing his gun into position, but Baby Boy took aim and blew the top of Rich's head off. He jumped down and hit Fat Rich two more times, point blank for good measure. He reached down and took Rich's money and jewelry.

An old Buick hooptie skidded up, and Baby Boy jumped in. They skidded off.

"Goddamn, young buck. You ain't no goddamn joke! Up in a tree for a muhfucka! You on some Vietnam shit!" the toothless crackhead cackled as he drove.

Baby Boy smiled to himself. He had to admit, it was a good idea. Even though he had to wait for four hours, the ten grand Dark paid him was worth it. Not to mention the bag of money Fat Rich had just won. Not bad for four hour's work.

The crackhead pulled into a vacant parking lot next to where Baby Boy had left his Suzuki 900.

"Yeah, young buck, you a beast. But let me get me so I can go," he requested.

"Yep," Baby Boy replied, putting the gun to his temple and painting the window with his brains.

"Dumb muhfucka." Baby Boy laughed, got out, jumped on his bike and disappeared into the night.

Baby Boy headed straight for Quita's apartment. He really had nowhere else to go.

Between her place, motel rooms, and various jump-offs, Baby Boy was basically homeless. But after hooking up with Dark, he knew all of that was about to change.

When he got to Quita's house, Ty-Ty, her little nine-year-old brother, answered the door. Baby Boy clenched his nose.

"Damn, Ty-Ty, I see you still pissin' in the bed." Baby Boy snickered, because he smelled just like piss.

"Fuck you, Baby Boy. Gimme some money," Ty-Ty spat back.

"Go wash yo' ass, and I'll give you twenty dollars."

"Ain't no water," Ty-Ty informed him.

Baby Boy sucked his teeth. Quita's sorry-ass mama probably smoked up the water money. Quita's seventeen-year-old sister was sitting on the couch watching TV.

"What's up, Quandra? Where Quita?"

"Sleep," she replied, without taking her thumb out her mouth.

Baby Boy went down the hall to Quita's room and opened the door. She was sprawled out on her stomach, wearing nothing but her panties, phat ass tooted up in the air. The room smelled like sex. His first instinct was to wake her up and beat her ass back to sleep, but he knew he was partly to blame for leaving her out there. He had been with Quita since she was nine and he was eleven. Now they were nineteen and twenty-one. They had been through everything together. Homelessness, no lights, rockin' the same clothes for days, no school, no food, everything bad you can think of, they experienced together.

He slapped her hard on the ass, and she jumped like she had been shot.

"Owww! I'ma fuck you up!" she shouted, not seeing in the dark who had done it.

Baby Boy plopped on the mattress lying on the floor and pulled her to him.

"Fuck me up, huh? Who you gonna fuck?" He laughed.

"Hey, baby!" she sang, and wrapped her arms around his neck, kissing him excitedly.

"Oh, now it's, 'Hey, baby.' But when I'm in the county, you block the phone!"

"Ain't nobody tell you to get locked up," she replied sassily between kisses. "Ain't nobody got no money to hold yo' hand."

"Yeah, we do now." He smiled and dumped Fat Rich's bag of money on the bed.

Quita's eyes got as big as two moons. She gasped.

"Bey! Who you kill?" Quita wrapped her tiny hands around a big pile of money.

"Stop askin' so many questions, nosy ass. Just get yo' ass up and get us a spot. We gettin' the fuck outta here," Baby Boy spat, looking around at the dismal surroundings.

"For real, baby? Ewww, I love you!" she squealed, knocking him on his back with her embrace.

He laughed. "I love you, too."

Quita stopped and looked him in the eyes soberly. "Why, Baby Boy? Why you love me?" she questioned intently, tears welling in her eyes.

Baby Boy just shrugged and replied, "Because I promised you I always would."

He was her rock. Despite everything, he was always right there.

"And now you ain't gotta do that dumb shit no more, Quita. I'm dead ass. And you quittin' that fuckin' Subway shit," he demanded.

"See how much you know about me? I been quit Subway. I work at S&C's."

"Whateva the fuck it is, I said you quittin'."

"*Whateva* you say, baby," she cooed as she unbuttoned his jeans and pulled his long dick out.

Quita was already soaking wet when she slid her panties to the side. Baby Boy was the only one she let fuck her pussy, so it stayed hot, tight, and wet. Just another quirk in their strange relationship that fit them like a glove. And he fit her like a glove as she began to ride his dick, squatting on it and bracing herself on his chest.

"Oh yes, this your pussy, daddy. I been a good girl, see? Nobody been in your pussy," Quita swore to him. It was the truth.

But she didn't have to tell him, because he could feel it. He gripped her thick hips and ground his dick deep up in her. It didn't take him long to get off his first jail nut, but when he laid her on her back, he dug out the pussy until morning light and they both fell asleep satisfied.

"**Drug Kingpin's Daughter** *Found Slain*" That was the headline of the newspaper, but the word had already been all over the city ever since Crystal got snatched up.

The reporter from Channel 2 Fox News started her segment: *A gruesome murdered body found belonging to a woman today on the East Side. She was the daughter of a drug kingpin whose organization stretched as far as Memphis, Tennessee.*"

But once the word got out that her body was found buck naked with a dog's dick in her mouth on Nine Mile Road, the streets were abuzz with assumptions and rumors of war. The Consortium members were all abuzz as well.

"I bet you that muhfuckin' Dark did it," Tareek from the East Side told his man.

While across town, Tommy from the Number Streets was vexed. "We need to call a meeting ASAP! This nigga Dark got questions to answer!"

Everybody blamed Dark simply because nobody trusted him. But Dark had his own problems. He was now out of a connect. As for Crystal, his mourning period lasted long enough for him to say, "Man, goddamn, that bitch had a helluva head game."

Mook chuckled as he and Dark rode along Woodward Street.

"You a cold nigga. I thought you was marryin' the broad."

"Marryin' her connect," Dark corrected him. "Now I'm gettin' a divorce before the goddamn weddin'. We gotta make somethin' happen ASAP. I need a connect."

"Fo' sho'," Mook agreed. He could hear the desperation in Dark's voice.

Several minutes later Dark's phone registered a text.

Belle Isle where we first kissed @ 8:30

There was no name, but Dark knew exactly who it was. He glanced at Mook.

"What you 'bout to do?"

"Why, what up?"

"I need to handle somethin'."

"Take me to the crib. I'm waitin' on Mac anyway."

"Yeah, tell that nigga we all need to powwow."

"Yep."

Dark dropped Mook off, and Mook breathed a sigh of relief. He was glad Mac handled his business. Now, they could concentrate on getting that gwap.

Dark arrived on Belle Isle and parked, pissed off that Sherman wanted to meet so early in the morning. He spotted Sherman on the bench, feeding the seagulls. He walked down and took a seat.

"I hope you left the Alka-Seltzer at home," Dark snapped.

Sherman chuckled. "And I'm glad you brought your sense of humor. Last time you were a tough guy, and tough guys are a pain in the ass to work with."

"I handled that."

"Yeah, I see. Only you clipped the wrong guy."

Dark scowled. "Fuck you mean wrong guy? You said Fat Rich from The Zone. Ain't but one Fat Rich muthafucka from Zone 8!"

"Did I? Are you sure? I'm gettin' too old for this shit. I meant Tommy . . . Tommy from the Number Streets," Sherman informed him.

"What! Ain't no fuckin' way! What kind of game you tryna play?" Dark ranted.

"Hey!" Sherman ranted right back. "Whateva game I fuckin' wanna play! You know why? Because it's *my* ball! If I say jump, you don't say how high, you ask how long should I stay up there! This ain't a one-night stand, it's a marriage, and I'm the man in this relationship. Are we clear?"

Dark was really less upset than he put on. Even though he was under Sherman's thumb, it wasn't him putting in the actual work. Besides, he was just clearing the way for his own expansion.

"So you sure this time? Tommy?"

"For now, I'm sure."

"Yeah, well, I need somethin' from you."

"Let me guess. A connect," Sherman gathered, having been assigned to Crystal's case.

"Yeah, a connect."

Sherman smiled. "See, this is what a marriage is about. Give and take . . . Gimme a couple of days and I'll have you straightened out."

"Yeah," Dark grunted, then turned and walked away. Sherman pulled out his phone and sent a text to Nick.

Nick got Sherman's text.

Need to see you ASAP

He replied back:

Not in the city. Gimme 2 days

He received a text right back:

24 hrs

Nick sighed hard, but he knew he had to comply. He had already sold his soul to the devil, and her name was Joy. Sherman was just her tool. But at the moment, his mind wasn't on business, it was on pleasure.

Ever since Tiny had mentioned it, he was obsessed with getting her and Shan in a ménage à trois. It wasn't like he'd never had one, but getting Shan to agree would be a challenge, which he was up to. He felt like he could convince her, because, at heart, he knew she was a freak. And with Tiny in his ear, he was totally open.

As soon as he left Tiny's suite, he headed straight for Shan's brownstone, just like Nyla knew he would. He just didn't realize when he left that Nyla was right behind him in a rented Honda Civic. But what neither one of them knew was, Courtney and Michelle were right behind both of them.

"There he goes, Chelle," Courtney pointed out as soon as Nick jumped in the Range and pulled off. "Don't lose him."

Michelle sucked her teeth cockily. "I'm from Newark. Can't nobody lose me." She snickered, because her driving skills were on 1,000.

But as soon as she started to pull off, a pea green Honda Civic cut her off.

"Dumb bitch!" Michelle spat, falling back speed-wise, but keeping pace with Nick.

She didn't sweat the Honda at first. In fact, she used it for cover, but when the Honda made the same three turns as Nick, Michelle said, "Yo . . . I don't think we the only ones trackin' this mark."

"I see that," Courtney agreed.

When the Civic did it a fourth time, they knew it wasn't a coincidence.

"Damn, yo, who is this bitch? She tryin' to fuck us out of our lick?" Courtney chuckled.

"Whoever it is, the bitch is an amateur. If the nigga don't see her, he *needs* to be robbed!"

Nick didn't see her because he was thinking with the other head. He led Nyla right to Shan's brownstone and got out. Michelle and Courtney kept going. At the end of the block, Nyla pulled over and parked while Michelle made a right.

"Circle the block," Courtney told her.

"That's what I'm doin'."

Nick got out and rang the bell. He never called before he came. Even though he had a key he didn't use it, but nevertheless he still felt as if this was his spot. He waited. No answer. He rang again. Still no answer. He got impatient. So he called Shan.

"Hello?"

"What up, ma? I'm on the porch. Open the door."

A hiccup of a pause. "I'm not home."

"Where you at?"

"Detroit."

"Detroit? What for? Why you ain't tell me?"

"Because."

"Because? What do you mean *because?*"

"Because I brought . . . I brought the kids to see their father," she replied haughtily.

Nick felt his temper rise. Not because she went, but because she didn't tell him. "Without tellin' me?" he questioned. "It's not safe for you to be roaming around with the children. You should have checked with me first. I would have sent somebody with you."

"Lupita is with me. Plus, I didn't have to tell you or check with you," she shot back. "So don't start trippin', Nick. This baby has been crying all day, and Li'l Peanut is acting up," she said, trying to pile up motherly reasons to distract him.

Nick sighed hard. "Yo, whateva," he replied, attitude apparent. He hung up, turned and went back to his car and drove away.

Nyla got low as she watched Nick drive right past her. Once he turned the corner, she got out and walked down to Shan's brownstone. She climbed the stairs and peeked through the octagon-shaped front window. The place was laced, which only made her madder. Here was another man she had her hooks in, taking care of this home-wrecking hoochie.

"Oh yeah, you gonna get yours real soon, you bitch," Nyla hissed as she headed back to the car. She had gotten what she came for; now she could go home.

By the time Michelle and Courtney came full circle, Nick was just getting back into his car and leaving. They parked up the block and watched Nyla get out, climb the stairs, and start peeking in the window as if she was staking the house out.

"What the fuck is she doin'?" Courtney questioned.

"I don't think she tryin' to rob that nigga," Michelle suspected. "She checkin' for Shan. That nigga creepin'."

"Shit, what nigga ain't? Besides, she might be the wifey and Shan is the jump-off," Courtney suggested.

"Naw, I doubt that."

"Why?"

"'Cause the bitch drivin' a Civic and Shan drivin' an Infiniti," Michelle pointed out.

Courtney nodded. "Yeah, you right."

Both of them got quiet. They were in deep thought as they watched Nyla pull off.

"So what we gonna do?" Michelle questioned.

"Stick to the plan. This nigga could be that lick we waitin' for, yo," Courtney replied.

"Yeah, but we fuck wit' Shan. She cool peeps. She a little green, but goddamn, if a bitch schemin' on her, I'm just sayin'."

Again, they got quiet. They both were go-getters, and they liked Shan, and the fact that she was a go-getter as well.

"So how we tell her we know? 'Yo, Shan, we was followin' ya man 'cause we were about to hit him, when some bitch came through schemin' on you,'" Courtney suggested sarcastically.

"Naw, we tell her, her man creepin'. Try to get in her head, and maybe she'll be wit' it and help us hit him. As long as we don't kill him," Michelle reasoned.

"Which we can't guarantee," Courtney shot back.

"True. But do we fuck wit' sis or not?" Michelle asked.

Courtney sighed hard. "Man, fuck it. Money ain't always everything. Us bad bitches gotta stick together. We will make her a part of our team."

"That's what it is then," Michelle said and nodded in agreement.

They pulled off with the sounds of Kendrick Lamar's "Bitch, Don't Kill My Vibe" bumping from the speakers.

After Nick hung up on her, Shan felt bad. She didn't feel obligated to him, but he didn't deserve the disappearing act. She had thought about telling him before she left but she kept telling herself she was only taking the kids to see their father.

Until she laid eyes on Briggen.

He came through the door, and she couldn't stop her heart from leaping loud, just like a dog pawing at the gate when it sees its owner. He may've been dressed in them ugly-ass khakis, but he looked good in it. Not being on the move all the time made him gain weight, but to her, he had simply filled out. He had a fresh haircut and razor-sharp shape up. His skin tone was still flawless, and his lips were what she focused on. She remembered how he used to . . .

"No!" she had to tell herself. *I just brought the kids to see their father.* But when Li'l Peanut cried out, "Daddy!" she couldn't stop her heart or her lips from breaking into a smile.

"Hey, beautiful," he greeted Shan, but his eyes were glued to Brianna, sleeping peacefully in her mother's arms.

"You talkin' to me or her?" Shan flirted.

"Both, because one is just the reflection of the other. But, damn, I wish I could hold her."

"You will . . . soon," she said encouragingly, but not believing it herself.

You just don't know how soon, he thought. Instead, he acted dejected. "I hope so."

"What is Rudy saying?" Shan wanted to know.

Briggen shrugged. "What he always says. That he's on it. Hopefully, I'll know something soon."

He spent the first part of the visit speaking to Li'l Peanut and talking to Shan about the baby. The more he did, the more he thought about what Rudy said. Looking from the other side of the glass at his very first baby girl being so tiny and vulnerable was getting to him. *Stay focused,* he told himself. *This is the same bitch that stabbed you in the heart and twisted the knife.*

"Real talk, Shan, when I'm through with this, it's going to be all about spending more time with my seeds. Being away, I can see what's most important, and that's my family," he told her, looking her in the eyes. "Do you have a problem with that?"

"You sure that's not the bars talking, Briggen? Seem like every nigga in jail say they gonna be the perfect husband, the perfect father, the perfect man, but get out and act just like the perfect nigga!" Shan got philosophical.

"You right. But for me, I don't want to lose my family. I don't want to lose you," he said.

Her voice subtly caught in her throat, but she hid the hitch. "We can't ignore how we split up. What makes you think you haven't lost us already?"

"Because you're here."

"I only came to bring the kids—"

He shook his head with a knowing smile. "That's what you told yourself in order to justify coming. But I can see it in your eyes; you . . . are here, too."

Shan hated the fact that he knew her so well.

"Why did you fuck me over, Shan?"

She looked up at him speechless. The hurt visible in his eyes and in the expression on his face.

"Time's up, Thompson!" the guard told Briggen.

"Say good-bye to your daddy, Peanut." Shan was glad to be getting out from under his microscope. She wanted to talk about *them*, but not at this time. No. The time wasn't right.

"I'm comin' home, baby, and I'm comin' home to you. You know I'm still in love with you, right?"

She couldn't help but feed into the moment, because deep down inside, that's what she wanted.

"I love you, too," she replied as she hugged both of their children. Shan then watched them lead her husband away in chains.

When Nick arrived in Detroit, he arranged a meeting with Sherman on the fly, but he headed straight for their hideaway apartment. He didn't want Shan to think he had come to Detroit just for her. But he had to see her. His ego couldn't take losing her to Briggen.

When he knocked on the door, Shan and the nanny had been in the bedroom putting the kids down for their afternoon nap. She gave their nanny the pet name "The Rock" because she was the same nanny that Briggen found for her. She sent for her the minute she set foot in New York, and Lupita asked no questions.

Shan came out, gently closed the door behind her, and then went to the front door. As soon as she opened the door, he was all over her.

"Nick!" she gasped. He smothered any protest there may've been with a breathtaking kiss. "Why are you knocking? Where is your key?"

Shan slammed the door shut behind him by pinning her body against it. She had on a Victoria Secret one-piece shorts jumper that zipped up in the middle, so it was easy for him to get the sweetness underneath. Before she knew it, he had her jumper wide open and her bra off her breasts while he feasted on her nipples and pushed her panties aside to play with her clit.

"Nick, wait—" she pleaded weakly, already caught up in the energy he had brought. "Lupita might come up front."

She had never seen him like this before. He was always passionate, but now he ravished her. Her first thought was to stop him. But the truth was, she didn't want to. Her mind was still reeling from her visit with Briggen, the first man in her life. And now this surprising behavior from the second man in her life had her feeling herself.

"Take this shit off!" Nick yanked down her jumper, dropping to his knees and replacing his finger with his tongue to play with her clit. Shan grabbed the doorknob trying to crush it in her palm as her whole body convulsed in an orgasm that crept up on her. Nick licked and sucked that pussy until Shan begged, "Fuck me, baby! Please put that dick in me!"

He hoisted her off her feet and positioned her on his rock hard dick as she wrapped her legs around his waist and her arms around his neck. Nick gripped her ass, spreading her cheeks and pushing himself in and out, deeper with every stroke.

"This my pussy, *my* pussy," he grunted, using each stroke to spell his name in it.

"Make it yours," she squealed, bouncing on his dick. The sound of wet pussy being fucked filled the room.

He finger fucked her asshole while grinding into her pussy, causing her to claw his back and cream all over his dick. It took him a while to nut, but when he did, his dick still remained rock hard. He was blowing her mind with a stamina that she had never seen before. By the time he had her on the thick carpet and put the curve in his dick to work, she was moaning, "It's your pussy, baby, your pussy. It's yours!"

A couple hours later, they were awakened by the ring of Nick's phone.

"Yeah," he answered groggily.

"Benny Thrillz at ten o'clock," Sherman told him, and hung up.

Nick rubbed his eyes, and then shook Shan. "Come on. Get up and get dressed."

"Nooo," she whined, wanting to snuggle.

Nick popped her on the ass playfully. "Come on, let's get this money."

Even though she wanted to sleep, hearing the word *money* was her motivation. And the combination of some good dick and a man that helps you get your own money could be undeniably addictive.

Exactly an hour and a half later, they arrived at Benny Thrillz. Nick turned to Shan and asked, "Okay, QueenPin, you ready?"

"You sure you don't want to go in with me?" she asked nervously.

Nick chuckled. "That'll kinda defeat the purpose, won't it? Don't worry. You'll do fine. We've been over this a hundred times. You got this. Go get that gwap, hustla."

Shan laughed, and it released some of her anxiety. She took a deep breath and got out. As she walked, she gained more confidence with every step. It reminded her of the feeling she got promoting her own shows and she found her rhythm.

Dark checked his watch. He hated waiting. Shan breezed in and his eyes were instantly drawn as they would be to any bad bitch's entrance, but his mind was on getting money. That is, until he saw her headed to his table. He watched her approach, and he tried to remember where he knew her from.

Shan slid into the booth and said, "Sorry I'm late."

Dark smiled and licked his lips. "You got me mixed up wit' somebody else, li'l mama, but I wish I was that someone else."

Business-like, Shan replied, "You're Dark, right?"

His smile turned upside down and his antenna went up.

"Dark?" Shan smirked because she knew it was him. "Look, you wanna do business or you wanna play games? I'm Nick's people. I'm the one you'll be dealin' with."

Where all these hos come off thinking they can play a man's game? Dark thought, thinking of Crystal dead with a dog's dick in her mouth.

"I wanna talk to Nick."

"You are. I'm Nick as far as this is concerned. Now, yes or no, do we do business?" Shan asked directly, her demeanor solid but feminine.

Dark needed product like yesterday, so he decided to go with the setup until he could find an angle to play.

"Okay, li'l mama, I—"

"Redbone. The name is Redbone. Not li'l mama, shorty, or sweetie. Respect me and I'll respect you," she broke it down to him.

Dark had to admit he liked Redbone's swag. Then it hit him. "Redbone, yeah . . . you used to promote parties not too long ago," he remarked.

Proud of being remembered but not wanting to let Dark in, she replied, "Something like that. So what's the number?"

"What's yours?" he shot back.

"Same thing The Commission was getting it for, a little less if you play fair," she told him, trying to remember everything Nick went over with her.

"The *Consortium*," he corrected her with a knowing smile.

"Excuse me?"

"You said The Commission. It's The Consortium."

"Oh, well, you know what I meant."

"True, but always mean what you say. In this business, words count," he gamed her.

"I'll try to remember that," Shan replied with a hint of sarcasm.

She took out a small TracFone and slid it across the table to him.

"Hit me when you're ready. Remember, I'm in charge now," she told him with just a hint of sass, enough to be sexy.

Dark pocketed the phone. "Expect my call within the hour, fo' sho'."

Shan nodded and stood up. "I'll be waiting."

"I like the sound of that." He winked.

Shan's reply was a confident strut toward the exit that read, *untouchable*.

Dark's phone registered a text.

Who's next?

"Goddamn! Broad daylight? My young boy is a beast!"

Chapter Ten

Tommy took his grandmother to church every Sunday. He rarely missed a day. She had raised him when his mother died, and since he didn't know his father, she was all he had. She always tried to instill in him the love of the Lord. So even though he was heavy in the streets, he felt like giving one day to the Lord was a hustler's tithe. He shut down all operations and could be found in the front pew of Ebenezer Baptist Church right next to his grandmother.

Ebenezer was known for having one of the best choirs in Detroit, so the church was always rocking with loud, raucous praise and a lively youth ministry drawn by the music. That was how Baby Boy blended in. The pastor always emphasized, 'come as you are', so Baby Boy came as he was, a cold-blooded killer dressed in Dickie cargo pants, sagging, exposing his underwear, a hoodie, and work boots. He even put sixty-six dollars and six cents in the offering, an inside joke with himself.

"Brothers and sisters . . . before we go, I ask you . . . no! I implore you . . . to look deep inside and say, 'Self . . .'"

The congregation repeated, "Self!"

"Let go!"

"Let go!"

"And let God!"

"And let God!"

"Because, he is our only salvation," the preacher concluded, dabbing his precious face with a silk handkerchief with his diamond-studded hand. "Now if there's anyone who wants to dedicate their lives to me—I mean—Jeee-suss . . . come up now and proclaim!"

Several people around the church got up and headed to the front and Baby Boy was the third one. People would only remember he was young looking, no more than sixteen, and thin. But since he kept his head down and things happened so fast, no two people could give the same description.

As soon as the train of people reached the front, Baby Boy pulled his chrome .44 Bulldog and aimed it dead in Tommy's face.

In all his years of coming to church to praise the Lord, Tommy never knew he'd actually meet the Lord face-to-face, but there he was in the form of a cold, steel barrel. And when the shots exploded in his brain, they exploded with the finality of Baby Boy yelling, "Let the church say Amen!"

Three shots to the dome and Baby Boy blew bits of Tommy's head back over the next three pews. The church broke out in a screaming panic. Tommy's grandmother fainted. Baby Boy fired off two more shots in the air to make people scatter and get low as he made his escape through the back door.

Once outside, another faceless crackhead awaited him in another nondescript hooptie, and his rotting body would soon be found in the forgotten ghetto.

"Yo, pull off! Fuck you waitin' for?" Baby Boy shouted.

"I-I got you, man," the crackhead said, as he lurched away from the scene, licking his ashy lips. "Come on, li'l nigga. When I'ma get mine?" He scratched his arm.

"I got you," Baby Boy smirked, as he sent Dark a text.

Who's next?

Mo'Betta sat back on the couch, stunned. Keeta took one look at his expression and asked, "What's wrong, baby?"

Mo'Betta shook his head. "My cousin, yo . . . the nigga killed my cousin."

Hearing the words come out of his own mouth made the anger start to boil deep down in his gut. It bubbled up into rage and began to leak like lava in the form of tears out of his eyes.

"Oh my God, baby! I'm sorry—" Keeta tried to comfort him. She had never seen him cry, and her love made her want to comfort him.

But Mo'Betta moved her away hard and stood up. "Don't fuckin' touch me!" he shouted. His whole body went rigid with rage.

He knew exactly who did it. Mac . . . Mook . . . Dark. He may not have known who pulled the trigger, but these would be the three he would hold responsible and would get his payback from!

He had just called Rob because he hadn't heard from him. With Briggen set to get out in a few days, he was supposed to come to Detroit and meet him. So he called to see what was up.

"Hello?" the male voice answered, but it was clear that it wasn't Rob. The voice wasn't even black.

Mo'Betta hung up. He hit speed dial again, and the same voice answered.

"Please, don't hang up. Who is this?"

"Who is this?" Mo'Betta spat back. His instincts were screaming, "It's the goddamn police!"

"Did you know Robert Lincoln well?"

Not knowing what was up Mo'Betta answered, "What about him?"

"He's dead. He was shot to death."

Mo' couldn't believe his ears.

"Who is this? Do you know anybody who would—"

Mo'Betta hung up. His mind was reeling. *Rob can't be dead.* He had to know if it was true. He pulled out his cell going for his Internet browser. He googled Robert Lincoln. An article popped up from the *Tennessee Star*:

Man Gunned Down in Lawyer's Office.

He read the article. Read the setup . . . Dreadlocked gunman . . . forced Reed to make the call . . . "I've never been so scared in my life!" the secretary quoted. He read it all. There was no doubt who it was, and he pictured their headline:

Three Dead-Ass Niggas

Janay stared down into her only sister's frozen face. One last time. She looked so peaceful.

Before the mortician worked his magic, she looked hideous. But it was important to Janay that her sister have an open casket funeral, therefore, she spared no expense. She wanted to remember Crystal how she looked in life and not how she was found in death. Besides, if the killer had the audacity to show up at the wake, she wanted to catch the expression. Any hint that registered surprise because that would mean that person had seen how fucked up she looked before the fact and would give themselves away. That was the only reason she didn't have a private funeral back home in Memphis. Detroit sheltered the killer. She had Born make sure he let the streets know how she was killed and when and where the funeral would be held.

Janay didn't know what she would do if she did recognize the killer. She had wrestled with that all night, like Jacob had wrestled with the angel, going back and forth. Jacob refused to turn the angel loose. The old her had stirred, but she refused to allow it to reign.

"Get behind me, Satan," she had gritted. Janay tensed up as if she were in a physical battle and not a spiritual one.

She assured herself, *It was God's plan.*

But even God has tools to carry out his plans, her dark side countered.

Vengeance is mine saith the Lord.

Why should God have all the fun while you suffer all the pain?

Crystal lived by the sword so she died by the sword. Janay clenched her teeth.

That goes for the killer too! Her dark side spat.

Let go and let God. She decided as she breathed a sigh of relief.

"But a dog's dick?" the devil questioned.

She stood torn before the body of her sister, one hand clenched in a fist, the other open and caressing Crystal's cheek one last time.

"I-I love you, Crystal," she said, totally poised. She had cried herself out in private; now she wouldn't give the satisfaction to anyone seeing her cry in public. Plus, she could feel all of the stares watching her every move. She knew all eyes were on her. The heir to the throne. Choppa's daughter burying her baby sister.

Dark was the first to approach. He started to embrace her, but her gaze dared him to do it. It was an awkward moment. He diverted his gaze and looked down at Crystal's eternally sleeping face.

"Despite what you think, I loved Crystal. And I promise you, I *will* find who did it," Dark vowed.

Watching him look at Crystal's face, she felt like Dark hadn't done it himself.

"Will that bring my sister back?" she asked. Then Janay walked away to sit with Boomer and Marquis.

Born watched his aunt and Dark from the corner. He scanned the small funeral home, taking in who had come to show respect, mourn, or just be seen. Tareek from the East Side came up to Born and gave him a gangsta's hug.

"Peace, Lord," Born greeted.

"Peace, Lord, how you?" Tareek returned.

"The God just doin' the knowledge, yo. Shit is crazy, huh?"

"Crazy ain't the word," Tareek responded, shaking his head. "Shit is gettin' straight the fuck outta hand! I know you heard about Fat Rich from Zone 8?"

"Indeed."

"What about Tommy? You heard about him?"

"Tommy?" Born echoed.

Tareek nodded ready to give the full report. "They got the nigga in church! His grandma was so fucked up, she had a heart attack and died on the spot," Tareek explained.

"Goddamn!" Born shook his head. "Niggas gettin' it in."

"God, I'm tellin' you, somebody tryin' to take over the city, and they tryin' to take out the whole Consortium. One by one!"

Born nodded. "Yeah, yo, I was thinkin' the same thing."

Tareek looked around to make sure no one was close enough to over-hear him and said, "And real talk, I think it's Dark."

Born looked at him. "Dark? Come on, God. He was the first nigga they tried to kill, remember? I was fuckin' there when they killed Six-Nine. God bless the dead. And they almost got the God as well," Born countered.

"But they didn't. Think about it, God. What better way to camouflage the shit than to make it seem like you a target, too?" Tareek concluded.

Born nodded in deep contemplation. "Yeah, yo, that shit do make sense. Nigga obviously on some mastermind shit."

"Exactly, God. That nigga a thinker. But we need to call a meeting, yo. ASAP. Because the God won't be next, I promise you!" Tareek said with conviction.

"No doubt. And, God, I see your point. We gonna get that done ASAP. Let The Consortium know we meetin' and attendance is mandatory," Born instructed.

"Say no mo', God, say no mo'," Tareek answered and gave Born another hug and bounced.

Born moved around the funeral home like a politician. He spoke with the twins from the North End, who came so deep you'd think they were going to war. Born told them about the meeting.

"Yeah, maine, definitely," they agreed.

Before he left, he went over to console Janay. He gave Boomer a hug, then Marquis, and finally Janay. It was the first hug she had all night, because she wouldn't allow anybody to embrace her since she was so in fear of embracing a snake.

"How you, Auntie?" Born greeted, calling her his name for her when he wanted to convey family ties.

She mustered a smile. "You know me. I'm maintaining."

"Shit is crazy in the city," he told her.

"I heard."

Born nodded. "I know you feeling a way about how they did Crystal."

Janay looked at him, because she knew where he was going. "Born, I told you before. It's the Lord's plan. We may . . . not understand it, but we have . . . we have to accept it."

He could see the struggle in her soul and hear the hesitancy in her reply. He kissed her on the cheek. "I'm here . . . never forget that."

"I know," she replied, finding strength in his presence.

As he started to walk away, she grabbed his hand. He looked back at her. "It's not Dark," she told him. "It's not him. Somebody just wants it to look like it's him."

Born nodded, then walked away.

Janay and Boomer were preparing to leave with Boomer carrying Marquis, who was sleeping.

"Yo, Janay!" Dark called out. He approached her. "I understood what you said, but that ain't how I roll. We might not have been married yet, but Crystal died as my wife," Dark told her.

She turned to answer him but something caught her attention out of the corner of her eye. Mo'Betta and two of his shooters were laying on Dark. Mo' had thought about setting it off right then and there, but he knew if he disrespected Crystal's wake there would be consequences. Consequences he didn't fear but wanted to avoid. So he waited. But as soon as he saw the nigga he couldn't hold back.

"There he go!" Mo hissed, and he went into action mode.

Wise and his team were prepared, ready to move on sight as well.

What caught Janay's attention were the movements of Mo'Betta's shooters. Once she saw the glint of the steel, she cried out, "Marquis!"

Gunshots erupted from two different directions and all hell broke loose.

"Get down!" People were yelling and screaming.

"This is a funeral! What is the matter with these fools?" Someone hollered.

Janay ran to catch up with Boomer and Marquis. Even though she was less than ten feet away, the time elapsing made it seem like everything was moving in slow motion. She would have taken one to the head had she been closer . . . Boomer saw what she saw a split second after she saw it. He eyed the sparks from the barrels aimed at them, or he thought were aimed at them. Ironically, he bear-hugged Marquis with as much of his body as he could, turning his body and putting Marquis directly in the line of fire from the opposite direction as his team went into action at the same time.

The first shots hit young Marquis in the throat, and then his chest, exploding his heart and mercifully killing him instantly, making it impossible to feel the next barrage of bullets that riddled his little body and Boomer's simultaneously.

"Noooooo!" Janay bellowed, as she watched her son and uncle die in one big embrace.

The only thing that saved her life is that she lunged for them when the barrage of bullets meant for her went over her head.

"The Lord is my shepherd . . ." Mrs. Millie began to pray as he lay face down on the carpet.

"Allah is the Greatest . . . Allah is the Greatest . . ." A Muslim chanted clutching his prayer beads as he crawled along the floor seeking cover.

"These niggas have lost their minds!" Someone in the distance yelled out.

Mo'Betta couldn't believe Dark would be on point like that. *How did he know? How could he be so prepared?* Mo'Betta thought. Wise's team was Dark's, and they were shooting back at Mo' and his team.

They took their attention off Dark long enough to give him time to take cover and return fire. Dark took aim and squeezed off five shots, busting the window of the parked car of one of Mo's shooters. Pissed off, the shooter ran toward Dark, but Dark got a shot off, exploding the shooter's chest and taking him off his feet.

"What the fuck?" Wise uttered, finding there was a team in place and already taking aim at him. He was going to use the opportunity to hit Janay. But taking aim at Mo'Betta and his people, he missed her. Two of his shooters got hit because of the surprise attack.

Dark took aim at Wise's people, thinking they were two arms of the same hit team. Mo'Betta's people shot it out with Wise, neither knowing who the other was, thinking they were with the people the other was shooting at. Even the Twins from the North End's people got involved, thinking they got set up for an ambush.

Instead of the ultimate payback, it was the ultimate confusion.

When the smoke cleared and all of the teams made their getaway, several people had been shot or killed, including three girls, one of the Twins' people, several shooters, and Dark.

And then there was Janay. Everything in her world had gone black the moment she saw those bullets enter her son, seeing his eyes grow big as blood splashed from his chest. Seeing him fight for another breath, only to fail, his chest deflate, head drop, and body slump.

"Nooooo!" she would hear herself scream that for the rest of her life. She snatched Marquis from Boomer's lifeless arms and cradled him to her chest. She didn't hide from the bullets; she didn't see or hear anything but the intensity of her own heartbeat and the absence of her son's.

When the police and ambulances arrived, that's how they found her. Head thrown back, screaming her soul out for her dead son.

Part II

The Beginning

Chapter Eleven

Briggen stepped into the light of the April sun to feel the free shine. The sun never felt so good on his face. Not only was he free, but he was free on his own terms, having put together the plan and having it executed to perfection. That thought made him feel that he could take over the world.

"What up, big bruh?" Mo'Betta greeted, climbing out of his Cadillac XTS. Since Briggen was out, the first thing on his agenda was to upgrade to a newer model.

He gave Briggen a gangsta hug. "What up, though, Mo'? It's good to meet you in the flesh," Briggen returned.

"Fo 'sho'."

Briggen looked at the young boy, mentally assessing him. He reminded Briggen of Forever in a lot of ways.

"Ay, yo, you did good. Real talk. And now that I'm home, I'ma show you how to get real money," Briggen promised.

"I'm wit' you, big bruh. I'm wit' you."

"Let's get outta here. I need to go see my lawyer."

They drove across town to Rudy's office. As they drove, Mo' broke down the situation with Dark and the shootout with him and who he thought was Dark's people.

Briggen listened in silence. He definitely wanted to fuck with Mo'Betta. He needed a strong right hand. But he wasn't trying to inherit any beef, even though he already had his own beef with Dark and Nick. Briggen knew he wasn't in any position to go to war, but once he got his ones and guns right, he would serve Dark and Nick with some much needed and deserved payback!

"Check it, though, dawg. I know losin' your cousin Rob fucked you up, but we play this game with our heads, not with our hearts, feel me?" Briggen gemmed him.

"No doubt, but—"

"Everything after *but* is bullshit. This same nigga killed my brother, so if anybody wanna eat him, it's me. But you can't underestimate this nigga, 'cause you see what happens when you do," Briggen remarked, reminding him of how the shootout caught him by surprise.

Mo'Betta didn't respond, so Briggen knew he was listening.

"Be clear, maine. This nigga gonna die. That, I promise you. But we gotta be ready, get our gwap up, and we move. We move hard, you wit' me?"

Mo'Betta reluctantly nodded. He was the type to want to shoot on sight, hit innocents, raise the murder rate, and make shit hot whether or not he got his man. In other words, he was an emotional nigga, the game's worst enemy.

"No doubt, big bruh, no doubt."

Briggen nodded and sat back.

When they got to Rudy's office, the secretary let them right in. Rudy was on the phone when they came in, but once he saw them he said, "Listen, I need to handle something. I'll talk to you later." Then he hung up.

He rose, came around the desk, and embraced Briggen like a brother. "Welcome home, Calvin. Welcome home."

"Thank you, it definitely feels good," Briggen answered, then added, "Rudy, this is my man, Mo'Betta. Mo', this is Rudy Harrington. Best lawyer in the city."

"Excuse me, Calvin? Best lawyer in the *city*? I'm the best in the *state!*"

They all laughed. Mo'Betta and Briggen sat down. Rudy perched on the corner of his desk.

"So, let me bring you up to speed. Because of Miss Demetria Atkins's unfortunate demise, the prosecutor has nothing. I don't see them going anywhere with this issue," Rudy explained.

"That's what's up," Briggen nodded happily.

"But—" Rudy added, holding up a finger. "Know that this isn't over."

"What you mean?" Briggen frowned. "You just said—"

"I don't mean this case. I'm talking about the future. The Feds don't like to be beat. We won this round. Rest assured they're already preparing for round two," Rudy warned him.

Briggen smirked cockily. "Maine, listen, let them niggas do their job and I'ma do mine. Besides, that's why you get paid the big bucks, right?"

Rudy shook his head. "Same ol' Briggen, huh? I guess you didn't think about what I said."

"Naw, I did . . . believe me. I just need one more run, yo, and I'm done."

"Whatever you say, Calvin," Rudy replied, thinking, *You and every other hustler.*

Briggen stood up, but Mo'Betta was slow to follow. He was trying to wrap his head around where he had seen Rudy before. And then it hit him like a radio station coming crystal clear after mad static. He stood up, shook Rudy's hand, and asked, "Can I get your card? Shit, if you the best, I'm definitely trying to keep you on retainer."

"Some of my favorite words." Rudy chuckled as he handed Mo'Betta the card. They headed for the door, but before Mo'Betta closed the door he gave Rudy a wink that made Rudy frown because he didn't understand the implications . . . not yet.

"Look! For the thousandth time, I don't know shit! And if I did, I wouldn't tell you cocksuckas!" Dark spat as he lay in the hospital, recovering from surgery.

The two detectives turned red in the face.

"We'll see who's the cocksucka when those guys come back and finish the job!" one of them spat.

They turned and walked out the door just as Mook walked in. "Police, huh?"

"Who else? Comin' around askin' stupid-ass questions," Dark gruffed. "But shit, I was dead ass. I don't know who the fuck it was!"

"Maine, mad niggas from The Consortium gettin' hit. Whoever it was probably tried to punch yo' clock," Mook surmised.

Dark shook his head.

"Naw," he replied, because up until then, it had been him killing The Consortium members for Sherman. Then he realized, maybe it was Sherman. Maybe Sherman wanted to cover his tracks, and now he wanted to get rid of Dark. But Dark was having none of that. It was time to show that cracker he could be touched too.

"Maybe it was that nigga Briggen," Mook suggested.

"That pussy in jail. Besides, his whole team got ate. So I doubt it. I got an idea, though, and when I get out, we'll see about it," Dark said.

"Say no mo'. You know Mac came through. He ready to get it in. Oak Ridge is wide open for you."

Dark nodded. "I wanna meet him first."

"Cool. Say the word, and I'll make it happen."

While they were talking, the nurse walked in. Their eyes met at the same time. "Lisha?"

"Hello, Jerome," she said, not at all happy to see him, but still in all, glad he wasn't dead.

She had just started her shift, and when she saw his name and why he was there, all she could do was shake her head. *Will the black man ever wake up?*

"I ain't know you a nurse," he remarked, watching those hips looking right in her outfit.

"It's a lot you don't know," she mumbled.

"Huh?"

"Nothing."

Mook felt the vibe. He checked his watch. "Yo, I'm gone. You sure you don't want me to have a coupla niggas lay 'round?"

"Naw, I should be gone soon anyway."

"Holla if you need me."

"Yep."

Mook walked out, and Dark turned his attention to Lisha. "So what is it I don't know?"

"I thought you ain't hear me," she answered.

Dark eyed her down and licked his lips. "Come here, Lisha."

"No, Dark. Now, do you need anything? I have to make my rounds."

Dark scowled. "So, it's like that?"

Lisha sighed and came closer to the bed. "Look, Dark. I'm trying to get my life together, okay?"

"Does that mean you are no longer fuckin' and suckin' on that bitch?"

Their voices were getting louder. "Dark, I can't keep going backwards and it's obvious that you are stuck in the past."

"How you figure that?"

"Look at you! You ain't gonna ever learn, but I have, so—" she said, letting her voice trail off into the obvious.

She tried to step away, but Dark grabbed her arm. "I still want to see my son, Lisha."

"Why? So you can teach him how to be like you? Raise you a little gangsta? What can you possibly offer a child, Dark? Tell me!" she asked, peppering him with questions that deep down, felt like slaps in the face.

"How to be a man!" he raised his voice.

Lisha laughed and pulled away. "Like I said, I gotta make my rounds."

She walked out, leaving Dark to reflect upon the absurdity of his own statement.

She lay on her back staring at the ceiling listening to the tick of the clock on the wall. The room was completely white. The halogen light overhead bright and hypnotic. She felt like she was up from a dream. As if she had spent her life in blissful ignorance, but only to be awakened to the cold reality once the sedatives had worn off. Her willpower to stay conscious had overpowered their ability to lull her to sleep. She was more awake than she had ever been.

In the beginning she had tried to pray.

"Dear Lord . . ."

But her voice felt heavy. Her prayer, wingless, dropped like a stone into a bottomless abyss, the cold echo mocking her with an anguished sense of emptiness.

The doctor walked in. "So, you're awake."

She didn't respond. He looked at her lying flat on her back, strapped to the bed across the chest, legs, and ankles. She was in the psychiatric ward of the hospital. He felt for her. He heard the heartbreaking story.

Her father had recently been killed in prison. She was at her sister's wake when her child and uncle were gunned down right before her eyes. The paramedics couldn't describe the scream, the primal cry she had yelled until her body had no choice but to succumb to the powerful sedative they injected in her. Since she had awakened, she hadn't said a word.

The doctor pulled up a seat. "Ms. Carter, I will not release you until you answer some questions and assure me you're no threat to yourself or others," he explained.

"What do you want to know?" she asked, her voice hoarse from disuse.

He was taken by surprise. He didn't expect her to cooperate right away.

"Do you know where you are?"

"In the hospital."

"Do you know why?"

"Yes."

There was a short, and obviously painful pause.

"Why, Ms. Carter?"

"My son . . ." was all she could get out.

The doctor didn't push it. "Ms. Carter, are you going to hurt yourself?"

"No."

"Do you wish to hurt others?"

"No."

Satisfied, the doctor nodded. "Now, Ms. Carter, we'd like to keep you for a couple of days, just for observation. But I'm going to unstrap you. Do you think you can behave yourself?"

"Yes."

By hospital protocol, he was supposed to have at least one nurse with him. But he was 6-feet 3-inches, 220 pounds, and Janay was, at best, 5-feet 6-inches, 120 pounds. He didn't worry about any potential problems.

He started with her ankles, then her legs. She didn't budge. Before he undid the chest buckle, he looked her in the eyes and said, "Now, Ms. Carter, I'm going to trust you, okay?"

She nodded. Her gaze glazed.

He undid the chest buckle. In one smooth motion, Janay grabbed the metal bedpan off the table and hit the doctor dead in the face with it, breaking his nose. He winced in pain as blood ran down to his mouth.

"Fuck!"

He went down and Janay didn't let up. She hit him three more times, until he slumped to the ground unconscious. There was no way she was staying in the hospital three more days. Not while her son's killer was breathing. She didn't know if they could legally keep her, but she wasn't taking any chances. So she took matters into her own hands, in the form of a bedpan.

Janay grabbed her clothes and got dressed. As she finished, the doctor moaned and began to come to. She picked up the bedpan and beat him until he slumped again. She didn't give a fuck if she had killed him. She didn't give a fuck about anything anymore, not even herself. She had lost everything, and now those responsible and anyone who stood in her way would lose everything too. She dropped the bloody bedpan on the bed and walked out.

Mac and Mook kicked back, smoking a blunt, while Heather took a shower.

Mook's 70-inch HD was on TV One's, *Celebrity Crime Files* as they discussed the situation.

"Muhfuckin' Dark said a few more inches and the bullet would've hit his heart," Mook told him, handing him the blunt.

"He a lucky muhfucka. Who you think behind this shit?" Mac questioned.

"Ain't no tellin'. The nigga brought a move to so many niggas, maine. It could be anybody, yo."

Mac nodded in agreement. "That's why I don't trust the nigga!"

"And you think I do? But right now, it's just betta to get along than to get it on. But once we get our weight up, shit, its whateva," Mook shrugged.

Mac gave him dap and the blunt. "Say no mo', my nigga, say no mo'."

Heather came out of the bathroom with the towel wrapped around her and headed for the back bedroom. The exotic weed had Mook ready to fuck something.

"Goddamn, maine, your li'l snow bunny thicka than shit."

"Yeah, yo, she a rider. Bitch do whateva I say."

"Word?"

"Word. Why? You wanna hit that?" Mac grinned.

"Nigga, you already know I go in on them bunnies!"

Mac laughed. "Ay, Heather! Heather . . . Come 'ere, yo."

She came out, still wrapped in the towel. "What's up, baby?"

"Ay, do that dance you be doin' for my nigga Mook," Mac instructed.

"Now?" she asked, smirking, because she knew what it was.

"Yeah."

"But I need some music."

"I got that." Mook grabbed the remote and turned on his Pac CD and went to "How Do U Want It."

Heather didn't hesitate. "I love Tupac!" she gushed with that country twang that sounded so good to Mook's ears.

She began to gyrate her hips in a grinding motion, spreading her thick thighs for balance.

"Naw, wit' out the towel. And slow," Mac told her, licking his lips.

She began to do a slow striptease, pulling the towel up to reveal her wide hips, and then slowly opened it. She wasn't black thick, but she was definitely country thick, with size D cup breasts that were full and firm. She reminded Mook of Lindsey Lohan, and he wanted to fuck the shit out of Lindsey Lohan.

When she dropped the towel, Heather began to rub and caress her whole body, loving the attention and getting wetter in anticipation of what was to come. She put her nipple in her mouth while she played with her clit, turning her dance into a call for action.

Mac had seen enough. "Bitch, come 'ere," he commanded. She didn't hesitate to obey.

Mac pulled out his dick. Heather bent over at the waist and took it all in her mouth with one big slurp and an experienced throat. The way she had Mac grunting and groaning, it didn't take Mook long before he wanted to join the party. He got up, dropping his pants around his ankles and slid his long, hard dick in her creamy, wet pussy. Mook loved white girls, so sliding up in Heather's pussy curled his toes in his Timbs. She let out a gasp and began throwing that juicy pussy back at Mook, encouraging him to fuck her harder. She even began sucking Mac's dick with no hands, reaching around to spread her pussy lips, urging Mook deeper. Mac wasn't as big as Mook, so as soon as she got a taste of Mook's dick, Mac became a third party.

"Hmmm, fuck me, oh, fuck, big daddy . . . oh daddy, oh . . . he's fuckin' this pussy!" she squealed, going wild on Mac's dick only because Mook was beating it so good.

When Mac turned her around and she began sucking Mook off, she made sure to keep steady eye contact. Her gaze told him, *I choose you*.

Mook had to have her.

Shan, Courtney, and Michelle were downtown in Manhattan trying on shoes. Since Spring was only a couple of weeks away they had to get ready. They each had a distinct style to match their distinct swag. Courtney went for the aggressive diva styles, while Michelle was more edgy and chic. Shan's choices were quiet, sensitive, with a splash of sassiness. When it was all said and done, they had twelve thousand dollars' worth of shoes between them. But when they got to the counter Shan whipped out her Black American Express card and said, "It's on me, ladies."

She didn't mind being so generous because she had made more in the last couple of days than she had ever seen in her life. All for basically taking calls, collecting money, and doing what Nick called, "Directing traffic." The game had been good to her, so she didn't mind giving back to the game.

Courtney and Michelle looked at each other. If they hadn't decided to fuck with Shan already, they did right then. She had proven to be a bitch down by law.

Shan read their expressions. "Oh, believe me, next time is on y'all!"

They all laughed.

When they got back to Shan's crib, Shan checked with the nanny and the kids, and then she sat down for a drink with Courtney and Michelle in the living room.

"Damn, sis, you must got that nigga wrapped around your finger to be ballin' like this," Courtney insinuated.

Shan smiled, knowing Courtney was fishing. "Let's just say . . . It's fair exchange."

"I ain't tryin' to be all up in yours. I was just sayin'—" Courtney replied, trying to find the words to come at Shan with.

"What she tryin' to say, sis, is, do you love this nigga, or is he just a meal ticket?" Michelle questioned.

"Why do you ask?" Shan was hesitant in responding.

"Because that nigga creepin' on you and his bitch might become a problem," Michelle informed her.

Shan wasn't really surprised that Nick had a chick on the side. She didn't really consider him her man per se . . . her thing was, *a problem? How might she become a problem?*

Michelle nodded. "Like she might be on some stalkin' shit."

"How would you know?"

"Because we were followin' him, and so was she. But when he got here, she stopped followin' him and started stalkin' your shit out," Courtney explained.

"You were following Nick?" Shan scowled, completely taken aback. *What kind of shit these bitches on?*

"Yeah." Michelle nodded. "Because we was gonna rob him."

Shan looked at Michelle. "Him and me too?"

"If we were, you think we'd be tellin you? Look, sis, this is our hustle, just like you got yours. You stick niggas up wit' the pussy, we stick 'em wit' steel. At the end of the day, we all eat, feel me? But we fuck wit' you. Bad bitches gotta stick together instead of knockin' one another. So when we saw somebody tryin' to bring you a move, we switched gears." Michelle explained, being totally honest.

At first Shan was heated, but by the time Michelle finished, she was actually flattered and appreciative. They had abandoned their own interest in order to hold her down. That was real to her, and it gave her an idea.

"They say everything happens for a reason, and I believe this is that reason," Shan said. "Y'all have proven to me to be real. It might have been a funny way to find out, but it is what it is. Bottom line, since y'all kept it real, I'ma do the same."

"Speak on it, sis," Courtney remarked.

"Nick ain't really what you would call my man. It's complicated. But he is my supplier. I make moves here and in Detroit, but I don't have anybody to hold me down and watch my back. But y'all already proved that you got my back, so you might as well get paid for watching it."

Michelle and Courtney sat back, sipping their drinks as they thought.

"Shit," Courtney said, looking at Michelle, "I ain't never been to Detroit."

"Greener pastures." Michelle snickered.

"Exactly!" Courtney agreed.

Michelle turned to Shan. "Okay, sis, we wit' it!"

"But . . ." Shan interrupted, "if y'all gonna be fucking with me, no more stickups. I gets real paper."

"As long as we can get the real paper too, then it's on," Michelle told her.

The three of them shook on it.

"Now, tell me about this stalkin' bitch," Shan said in frustration.

By the time they finished describing her and how she moved, Shan's instinct knew exactly who it was. But how did she track her? From Nick? Was she at Choppa's funeral? She didn't see her. Shan didn't know how or why, but she knew that their paths had crossed again.

Nyla.

Chapter Twelve

Janay stood in the moonlight streaming through the window of
the abandoned apartment. She was using it to see the .38 Bulldog in
her hand. She had bought it off the street. The guy even threw in a
box of bullets and a cellphone. But for what she had in mind, she only
needed one.

With a cold, steady hand she slid one bullet into the chamber, gave
the cylinder a spin, and jerked the cylinder shut. She looked down at the
steel winking at her as it glinted in the moonlight. The moon was full.
She took it as a sign. Her life was over. For whatever reason, God had
taken everything and everyone from her. She felt like Job of the Bible,
and Marquis had been the final straw. Now she had nothing else to lose
and joining Choppa, Boomer, Crystal, and her son is all she wanted.
So she had decided to send up one last prayer. One last request in the
form of chance. She would play Russian roulette with herself. If she
won, well, she'd never know it. It would just all be over and God would
have had mercy on her, accepted her prayer, and welcomed her into his
bosom.

But if she lived, she took it as a sign of God's rejection. To her, he'd
be saying, "Fuck you, bitch! Suffer. Live with the shit that you are. Your
prayer is denied."

Janay took the gun and looked at the moon. Then in one motion she
put the gun to her head, closed her eyes, and pulled the trigger.

Click!

For a split second all of eternity stopped and she didn't know if she
was dead or alive. But when she heard the click as the gun hit on the

empty chamber, she knew she had lost. God had rejected her. She had been sentenced to suffer.

But I won't suffer alone.

Janay loaded the gun and stuck the rest of the bullets in her pocket. As she walked, believing she no longer warranted or wanted God's grace, she felt free. There would no longer be any right or wrong. She would simply do what she must. Whenever it ended, it wouldn't matter, because in her heart, she was already the walking dead.

She pulled out her phone and googled an article on Fat Rich's death, since it was the most recent. She read it twice. It told her nothing. It wasn't until she read an accompanying article that she knew where she needed to start.

Man Found Slain in Car

Police found Lorenzo "Pookie" Tate dead in a late model vehicle believed to have been used in an earlier gangland-style murder. It appears Tate may've been the driver for the earlier homicide. It is believed that he was only a patsy, and the real killer is still on the loose."

She then googled the church slaying. This time she was looking for the patsy and again she found him. His name was James "JJ" Wright, a fact she found out by googling his obituary. She now knew where both men were from, and now she knew where to start.

Janay headed for the ho stroll on Woodward and Eight Mile. The strip was peppered with stiletto-wearing whores, mostly addicts, and not always a sure thing that they were even women. So Janay shined like a diamond amongst glass trinkets. Women gave her murderous glances, but the glance they received in return sent them scurrying until she had an entire corner to herself.

It didn't take long for a trick to choose her. He was white. An accountant. He drove a Mercedes. He was a regular on the strip. He had never seen Janay before. She was a jet-black stallion he couldn't wait to ride.

He boned up instantly. "How much?" he questioned.

Janay didn't answer. She got in the car. "Pull off," she ordered.

She was forceful. He liked that. Maybe she would spank him.

"I-I-I can . . . pay whatever," he replied nervously.

She stuck the gun to his nut shack. He damn near passed out.

"Then pay attention to what I say," she seethed. "If you do, you'll live. If not, you die. Do you understand?"

He nodded vigorously.

"Take me to the West Side," Janay demanded.

"I don't know where—"

"I do. Drive."

Two stoplights later, a cop cruiser pulled up beside them in the outside lane. Janay pushed the gun a little more into his nut sack. He winced.

"I'm not going to jail, but you will definitely die," Janay warned him.

The cops glanced over casually. He mustered up a smile and nodded. They returned the nod but not the smile. The light turned green. The cops turned into the intersection.

"You did good."

"Please don't kill me. I-I have money."

"So do I."

For the next few hours, he drove Janay all around the West Side. Her only question to its inhabitants was, "Y'all seen Pookie?"

The answers ranged from no to nothing. Most people didn't even know he was dead. After two hours, another crackhead named Evelyn took one look at the Mercedes and the white driver and her instincts screamed, "Jackpot!" She came up to the car and leaned on the passenger window. Janay concealed the gun.

"You seen Pookie!" Janay questioned.

"Why? You lookin' fo' him too?"

"He a friend of Pookie's. He ready to spend, but only if Pookie cop," Janay explained.

Evelyn sucked her teeth. "Shit, daddy, Pookie dead. But I promise you I can take you there," Evelyn flirted, flashing her rotten toothed smile.

"When he die?" Janay questioned.

"'Bout a week or two ago. Last time I seen him he was wit' that crazy-ass Baby Boy," Evelyn replied.

"Who is Baby Boy?"

Evelyn looked her up and down. "Bitch, who is you, po-leece? Fuck you askin' so many—"

That's all she got out before Janay stuck the gun under her chin. "Who . . . is . . . Baby . . . Boy?" Janay gritted.

"You got it."

"Answer the question."

"He Thelma son. Crazy as shit. He prolly kilt Pookie! I don't want no trouble, Miss Lady!" Evelyn pled.

Janay released her with a push. Evelyn tripped on the curb, then fell on her ass.

"Then watch your goddamn mouth," Janay warned her as they pulled off.

She then went to the North Side, where JJ was from, and asked about him. This time she also asked, "Was he with Baby Boy when he came through?"

Finally after two hours a block hugger said, "Baby Boy from the West Side? Yeah, Baby Boy scooped him up. I ain't seen him since."

Baby Boy! Janay's mind repeated. That's who she was looking for.

She told the white man to stop in a secluded spot. It was four in the morning and Detroit was quiet. The streets were dark. She put the gun to the white man's forehead.

He melted into a mountain of sobs and quivering flesh. "Oh, God. No! You . . . you said—"

"Fuck what I said," she hissed. "I lied. You ever lie before?"

He was afraid to answer.

"That's what I thought. You probably lied to your wife tonight, didn't you?"

"Oh, God. Oh, God—"

"Didn't you?"

"Yes, yes, I did!"

"So why should a liar expect the truth?"

"My God—"

"Don't call on him. He's a liar too," she spat evilly.

He shut his mouth and moaned.

"You got kids?"

He nodded.

"You love 'em?"

"Yes!"

Janay's finger trembled on the trigger. She had power over life and death. From now on, the only power she would believe in was her own.

"Go home. Appreciate every day you have with them. If I ever see you out here again I'll know you don't appreciate them. I'll go to your house and kill them all. Do you understand?"

"I do. I do. I do."

"Give me your wallet."

He handed it over without hesitation. She took his license and put it in her pocket.

"Now I know where to find them."

She got out of the car and walked off. The man watched her disappear in the shadows until he unthawed enough to drive away.

"Oh my God, Briggen!" Nyla squealed, getting on her tiptoes to give him a hug.

He stepped inside her house as she closed the door behind him.

"When did you get out?"

"A coupla days ago," he answered, sitting down on the couch, and pulling out an envelope full of money.

"Briggen, no. I can't."

"That's for you and Tameerah, yo. Where she at?"

"At school. And Briggen, we are fine," Nyla replied, curling up on the other end of the couch. "We don't need your money," she assured him.

"Why? You still mad at me?"

"No. Briggen. I forgave you. It wasn't you. It was her. I told you that in my letters."

"Nyla, it wasn't her working solo. Forever played his part in it too. So don't blame it all on her."

"Briggen, you are only saying that because you in love with her. The bitch is a snake. Just like she destroyed my marriage she tried to destroy you as well."

"Nyla, I see that I can't change your mind about Shan, so I'ma let it go. Here. Take this money." He forced the envelope into her hand.

"Briggen, Forever left us money. We are fine. Use this to get back on your feet. Since you are still in love with that bitch, trust me, you're gonna need it."

"Nyla, I'm not accepting no. Just take it and say thank you. Damn, girl!"

"Okay. If it makes you feel better, thank you," she snapped, obviously still into her feelings.

"Don't thank me. That's my niece. Y'all family. You know, regardless, I'ma make sure you good," he vowed.

Nyla smiled warmly. "I have to admit, you a good man, Briggen." Just saying the words reminded her of Forever, which led to thoughts of his death, which connected a full circle to the person she blamed for it all. *Shan.*

Briggen caught her expression. "What?"

"Nothin'," she lied.

"Come on, Nyla. You know I know you. And you bein' you, I know you thinking about Shan. Let it go. You can't bring him back."

"I hate that bitch!" she seethed.

"Stop sweatin' her, Nyla."

"And you're not? Shit, you should be! I told you that bitch was cold, Briggen. I ain't tryin' to rub it in your face. But while you was locked up, this bitch ran off with your kids, your money, left you for dead, and was shackin' up with yo man Nick! He got this ho livin' good in New York while Forever in the cold ground," she spat with anger, tears pouring from her eyes.

Briggen slid over to comfort her. He put his arm around her, and she put her head on his chest.

"Chill, Nyla, let that shit go. Every dog has its day."

"I can't, Briggen, I can't. I tried. I swear I did. But she deserves it, and you know she do!" Nyla was in a full boohoo mode.

"Don't worry about it," Briggen told her again.

She hugged him tight and kissed him on the cheek. "You're a good man, Briggen. She didn't deserve you." Nyla continued to sob.

She kissed him again, this time on the corner of the mouth, and then on the mouth.

Briggen was surprised at first, but he reacted like any other nigga would with a sexy bitch all over him and returned the kiss. When their tongues met, it electrified them both. Nyla slid over on his lap, but the energy that hit him made Briggen pull back.

"Yo, Nyla, this is all wrong," he tried to protest.

"I missed you so much," she purred, pulling at his belt and zipper and releasing his half hard dick.

Missed me? Briggen was confused.

Nyla pulled her sweatpants off to reveal that she was pantiless. She straddled him, gripped his dick, and slid it in her wet and waiting pussy. She sucked in her breath and threw her head back.

"Yesss, daddy, oww fuck!" she screamed, coming almost instantly. "Oh, yes, Forever! I missed you sooo much!"

Briggen heard the name, but he was too much in the zone to feel any kind of way. In fact, it turned him on to be his dead brother in Nyla's sexual fantasy. He only wished that Forever could walk in and see this. He admired his dick going in and out.

"Fuck your pussy some more, make me come hard, baby, I need it!" she moaned, bouncing on his dick while she gripped the back of the couch.

Nyla was definitely in a zone, but not the zone Briggen thought she was in. She definitely fantasized that Briggen was Forever, but she knew he wasn't. She just wanted to sink her claws in him. She wanted to fuck Shan's man like Shan had fucked Forever. Besides, she wanted to try and get in Briggen's head and get him to help her get Shan. She was obsessed with Shan. Nyla had to have her, and there wasn't anything she wouldn't do to get her.

Sherman entered his Detroit city dwelling two minutes before Conan, his favorite late night host came on. He headed straight for his refrigerator. He grabbed a beer, popped it, and then headed for the stairs. When he got to his bedroom, he clicked on his light—and immediately froze.

Dark was sitting on the bed, with a gun pointed straight at him.

"Bang, bang, you're dead." Dark's voice was chilling but calm.

Sherman tried to play it off, but he couldn't mask his fear to a man who could smell it a mile away. He didn't know if Dark was serious or not.

"Am I supposed to be scared, Dark?"

"You are."

"Kiss my ass."

Dark laughed, stood up, and held the gun loosely at his side. "You slippin', Sherm. You could've been your own next homicide case," Dark remarked.

"You don't think I'm prepared for that? You don't think I keep my bases covered? You fuckin' prick! I was playin' this game since before you were shittin' green!" Sherman taunted.

Dark slammed Sherman against the wall, kept his forearm against his throat, and put the gun to his cheek.

"Who are you workin' for, Sherman?"

"Fuck you!" Sherman spat.

Dark cut off his windpipe. "You think I give a fuck about killin' you, cracka? One shot and I solve my problem! You got me takin' out The Consortium. I want to know why right now, or I'll fuckin' murder yo' bitch ass and take my chances!" Dark raged.

Sherman took one look in Dark's eyes and realized he was through being a pawn. He knew Dark would make good on his promise so he relented. "Okay . . . Okay! It's *The List!*" Sherman admitted.

Dark eyed him intently, then released him from the death grip. "What about it?"

Sherman rubbed at his throat.

"Cisco knew some . . . things. Don't ask me how, but he did. He had me over a barrel. The shit he knew could send me away for a long time . . . or worse. He agreed to sell me *The List*, but he said he wouldn't tell me exactly who the person he had told was until I paid him. It was a security measure. But before it could go down, you killed him," Sherman explained.

"Killed who?" Dark asked, playing dumb.

"Whatever, Dark. We both know the truth. Bottom line is, he's gone and I don't know who it is, so I'm taking drastic measures. Kill 'em all!"

"I'm on *The List*. You gonna kill me too?" Dark challenged.

"If I were, you'd be cashing in instead of being played like a pawn," Sherman chuckled.

Dark aimed the gun at him. "You're not in this alone. Who are you workin' for?"

Sherman glared at him without answering. Dark cocked the hammer. "Answer the fuckin' question," he demanded.

"Cisco's wife . . . Joy. She has Congressman Duffy in her pocket."

"Get her on the phone. You want me to be the cleanup man, I'm set-tin' the rules. If not, we'll burn this fuckin' city down so nobody will run it!" Dark threatened.

"You think you're pretty smart, huh, Dark? You don't know shit! You wanna play in the big leagues, do ya? You're not ready! Duffy will eat you alive." Sherman taunted as he pulled out the phone and hit speed dial. "Don't say I didn't warn you!"

Rudy sat behind his desk, talking on the phone when Mo'Betta walked in. He had been expecting Mo', but he didn't expect what he did next.

As soon as Mo'Betta closed the door and Rudy put up the wait-a-minute finger, Mo' walked over and hung up Rudy's call by pressing the dial tone button.

"Nigga, what the fuck are you—"

"I could ask you the same thing, muhfucka, but I don't have to because I already know!" Mo'Betta accused, cutting him off.

Rudy stood up. "Get out of my office!"

Mo' looked at him and smiled. He then pulled out Sharia's cell and pressed send. As soon as it started ringing, a phone somewhere in the office rang, corresponding to the rings.

Rudy knew he was busted.

"You a snake ass nigga, Rudy. Right up under the nigga nose, sche-min' on him the whole time. Tellin' him to get out of the game, talkin' that 'think of your kids' shit. The whole time you plottin' with that scandalous-ass bitch to take over his operation!" Mo'Betta laughed.

Rudy sat down. "I don't know what you're talking about."

"Oh, you know! See, the dizzy bitch ain't have the good sense to erase her texts or e-mails! Shit go as far back as some nigga named Woo and some bitch named Tami. I may not know who they are, but I'm sure Briggen will! It's clear you was the mastermind behind it all. It may not be all there, but it's enough for Briggen to connect the dots!" Mo'Betta warned.

Rudy knew there was no way he could deny it. He was in too deep. "What do you want?" he seethed.

Mo' stepped to the desk, leaned on his palms close to Rudy's face, and replied. "No, the question is, what *don't* you want to happen? You know if I take this to Briggen, you a dead man. So, my question is, do you want to die? And if not, what is your life worth to you?"

Rudy eyed him. "How much?"

"Everything you got wouldn't be enough. So I'ma make a deal with you . . . I want in," Mo' told him.

His and Rudy's eyes met, like two snakes slithering and intertwining. Rudy couldn't help but crack a smile.

"In?" he echoed.

"I want the whole operation, and you're going to give it to me, Rudy. You may be a snake nigga, but so am I. King goddamn cobra. Don't forget that, because if you do, I promise I'ma have fun makin' you pay." Mo'Betta made a threat that he was anxious to keep.

Rudy could see the young boy meant every word.

"Calvin's been on top for too long." Rudy grimaced at his own words. "I've been there every step of the way. You think he offered to bring me in? You think he said, 'Rudy, your loyalty is priceless?' Hell no! All he did was toss me the fucking crumb retainers and lawyer fees! Peanuts compared to what he was getting! Woo understood; he felt my pain. Sharia, she understood. Everybody that Briggen ever used and threw away, I turned them into my soldiers," Rudy boasted.

"So, what's the plan . . . partna?" Mo'Betta wanted to know. He was all too ready to roll over on Briggen. Excited that he thought Briggen was his big fish but he ended up catching a killer whale. In all actuality, he didn't give a fuck who had it, as long as he ended up with the prize money.

Mo'Betta was feeling himself, because he felt like he had figured out the riddle of the Sphinx. He had listened to Rudy when he first met him, listened to his style of speech. The way he talked proper, but mixed in slang with it when he needed to. The inflections in his speech, he realized, were from the same voice on Sharia's phone. At first he was going to put Briggen up on the game, but why? As long as Briggen didn't know, Mo'Betta would have the upper hand. So if Rudy's plan fell through, Mo' could always tell Briggen. He could effectively play both sides of the fence. The young boy had it all figured out.

The tension in the room seemed to him like the electricity of an ever present generator. The Consortium meetings were often used to air grievances and squash beefs, but when you didn't know who you are beefing with, and it could be anybody in the room, any little issue could spark an explosion. No one wanted to travel too far out of the city because niggas had their teams with them, ready to set it off. They were all seated at 7p.m. sharp in the conference room at the Inn in Plymouth. The twins brought an army, and Tareek wasn't far behind in numbers. Looking around, it was clear that shit was serious. The only members left at the table were Dark, Tareek, Keith and Kevin known as the twins, Kay-Gee, Briggen, and Born. But all eyes were on Dark, while he was all eyes on everyone else. Every man was strapped and ready to get it poppin'.

"First off, before we get started, welcome home my man Brig," Born greeted. The room erupted in cheers and barks. A few of the members got up, went over to him, and handed envelopes and gave hugs.

After Briggen acknowledged the welcome with subtle nods and smiles, and after everything settled down, out of the corner of his eye, he saw Dark staring at him, but he didn't comment.

Born turned to Tareek. "Tareek, you sponsored this meeting. It's only right that you begin," Born said.

"No doubt," Tareek replied, getting straight to the chase. "Bottom line is— what the fuck is goin' on? Shit is obvious somebody amongst us is goin' against all we stand for or somebody on the outside tryin' to take us out. So do we have to go to war with one another, or do we stand as one?"

"Yo, I'm feelin' you, maine—" one of the twins started to say, but was interrupted by Shan as she entered the room.

"Sorry, I'm late," she remarked as she blew into the room like a breeze. She was already nervous, so to have all eyes on her entrance had her even more flustered.

When Briggen saw Shan, his heart felt as if it no longer pumped blood. "Shan?"

Hearing the familiar voice, but not believing his presence, she turned and saw Briggen. "Briggen?"

Then both, almost at the same time, asked the other, "What the hell are you doin' here?"

For Briggen, her presence was totally out of place. She wasn't even supposed to know about The Consortium, let alone be in a meeting. But there she was, looking good, and at that moment, his heart began pumping blood again. As for Shan, she didn't even know Briggen was out. It was like a slap in the face that he didn't feel compelled to let her be the first to know.

He must be fuckin' somebody new, her thoughts fumed, *or else why didn't he tell me? I'm his wife! I bore his seeds. And seein' him here means he on the same ol' shit. That game about his family was all bullshit. But now, I can play the game too!*

"Yo, who is this?" Kay-Gee wanted to know.

"She's representin' Ni—" Born started to introduce her, but Shan cut him off.

"Excuse me, but *she* can speak for herself," Shan said, knowing she had to be assertive in a room full of men. "My name . . . is *Redbone,* and I'm working with Nick. I represent his interest. You want to talk to Nick, talk to me. Period."

"Nick?" Briggen blurted out. "Fuck you mean you represent his interest?" This made him that much more anxious to get at Nick. Not only was he fucking his wife, the mother of his seeds, but now he had her in the middle of some street shit. "Yo, Shan, let me holla at you right now!" Briggen stood up.

"There's a time and place for everything. A fact you've made crystal clear. Now is *not* the time," she shot back with nonchalant sass.

"Damn, li'l mama trying to go hard. We got a bitch at the table?" Tareek remarked, impressed with both her swag and her sexiness.

Briggen went for her. "Who the fuck is you talkin' to?" he fumed.

Kay-Gee restrained Briggen. "Yo, we don't handle personal matters in The Consortium meetings. You know that," Kay-Gee told him. "Handle that on your own time."

"Oh yeah, she definitely handle business," Dark chuckled, eyeing Briggen tauntingly.

Briggen glared at Dark. Reluctantly, Briggen sat down.

"Now," Shan said, removing an out-of-place lock of hair from her face with her pinkie, "you were saying?" A bunch of curls were piled high up on her head into a ponytail.

Tareek cleared his throat. "Yeah, so . . . I'm here for answers and I'd prefer to do it without bringin' the heat to niggas," he concluded, mentioning no names, but looking directly at Dark.

Dark chuckled. "First off, all that indirect shit, y'all niggas can pass me wit' that. I know most of y'all don't like me. I really don't give a fuck. Y'all look at me like I did somethin' to Cisco. Believe me, every nigga get what his hand calls for—"

"You got that right," the other twin blurted out.

Dark ignored it and kept talking. "But bottom line is, muhfucka just tried to kill me! Was it you, Twins?" He glared at them. He then turned to Born. "Was it you, Born? Was it you, Tareek?" He rested his gaze on Tareek.

No one responded until Tareek erupted with, "Nigga, if it was me, I wouldn't have missed!"

"Whateva. My point is, I'm a target just like the rest of you niggas. The question is, who aimin' for us?" Dark questioned.

He already knew half the plot. Hell, he was writing the script. But the other half, (who Sherman had used to hit him) itched to know so he could make it personal.

"Dark has a point," Kay-Gee agreed reluctantly. "Ain't no way a nigga gonna put a hit on himself. So let's look at this without all the emotions because shit will get out of hand, and we all goin' to war."

Heads nodded and murmurs of agreement flowed all around the table.

"I think we should all take an oath . . . to be our brothers' keeper. And if we find out anyone has broken this oath, then it's an immediate death sentence. No exceptions. We all strong, but no one of us can go to war with the combined five," Born proposed.

"I'm feelin' that," Tareek seconded the proposal, and the agreement was evident around the table.

"Yo, I just wanna say . . . to you," Briggen began, looking at Dark. "Oath or no oath, me and you ain't got no beef. I'm on some grown-man shit, so let bygones be bygones."

Briggen struggled through the whole speech, but he knew it had to be said. Dark didn't know that Briggen knew he had killed Forever. He wanted Dark to think he was just referring to shooting up his crib.

Dark may've not known that Briggen knew about Forever, but he still wasn't fooled one bit. He knew Briggen only wanted peace because he was weak at the moment. He knew once he got his weight up again, he was coming, and he would come hard. Dark didn't intend on letting him have that chance.

Everyone in the room vowed to be at peace with everyone else at the table. Under penalty of death a lot of the tension had eased up.

"Now that we are back on the same page, let's get down to real biz," Born said, turning to Shan. "The floor is yours."

"Thank you," Shan smiled at Born, before addressing everyone. "Nick is laying low. But he says he understands the situation. I don't know if you were aware or not, Mr. G is no longer our supplier. Nick says he can plug the holes, but we have to go up on the price Mr. G was charging."

"Go up?" Born protested. "Fuck kind of game is Nick tryin' to play?"

"No games," Shan replied, looking Born in the eyes. "Just business. He said, since the parties behind the attempt on his life haven't been found, transportation and security are costing us extra. Do you expect us to eat the cost alone? And where is the respect? You are trying to bite the hand that feeds you?"

Nick's message was clear. *Bring me those responsible, or pay for their mistake.* He was in control. Dark eyed the reaction around the room. It didn't make much difference to him because he was getting a much better deal due to his arrangement with Sherman and he couldn't wait to get Nick out of the way. Still, he wanted to cover his tracks so he spat, "This that bullshit, yo."

"So it's like that?" Briggen asked, eyeing his wife across the table.

"Take it or leave it," Shan replied, letting him know she was in control.

"We'll take it . . . for now," Born agreed. "But you tell Nick, should we decide to go elsewhere, we all go elsewhere, and he'll lose the city. Period."

Shan nodded.

"Any more business?" Born questioned.

The door flew open, and in walked Janay dressed in all black Cavalli. The black represented her grief as well as the fact that she was still in mourning.

Despite the murmurs spreading throughout the room, she went over to Born and kissed him on the cheek. She looked around the room and did a double take when she saw Shan.

"What brings you here, auntie? And I must say as always, your timing is perfect. But please tell me that you want to take your father's seat." Born could hardly contain himself.

"Awww, man. Come on, Born. What's up with all of the bitches coming up in here thinking they can run shit? Don't y'all hos know that this is a man's game?" One of Tareek's goons who stood behind his chair popped off.

"You must be new." Janay smiled and walked over to him. "Allow me to reintroduce myself."

"You hear this bitch?" The goon turned away to get a laugh with Tareek.

Before they could see it coming, Janay pulled out her pistol and shot him right on the side of the head.

Shan screamed. Born and Tareek's crew broke out in pandemonium while everyone else sat there caught by surprise. Dark was loving every minute of the action. This girl Janay never ceased to amaze him. He wished he had been fucking her instead of Crystal. Briggen was glad to be back in the mix, but unable to keep his eyes off Shan who looked as if she wanted to faint.

Born snatched Janay up and tossed her in his chair at the head of the table and was yelling for order to be restored in the meeting. He looked at the slumped body sprawled on the floor, and then back at Janay.

"Born, I didn't come here to be disrespected or insulted," Janay snapped, trying to stand up.

"Then what the fuck did you come here for? To shoot muhfuckas?" Tareek yelled out. "You know that is going to cost you, right? Rules are rules. I don't give a fuck whose daughter you are. No disrespect, and may Big Choppa rest in peace."

"None taken. I'm here to put a price on Wise's head. He killed my baby sister, and I can't let him get away with that. I'm offering one hundred bricks of uncut coke." Janay knew things were kind of dry, and with Nick raising prices and her cutting her connect off from Dark, this would get their attention.

The entire room became noisy again. Forgetting about the dead body lying on the floor, "One hundred bricks? Uncut?" was all she heard.

"One hundred bricks. Uncut," she repeated.

"How do we get in touch with you?" One of the Twins asked. "Ain't you on the run?"

"You take care of Wise, and you won't have to worry about finding me. I'll find you." She pushed Born off of her, got up, and walked out.

Shan sat there trembling. Witnessing another chick blow a nigga's head off and up close wasn't what she came here for. As far as she was concerned she was that bitch. All eyes were supposed to be on her! Not on the chick who came in and stole her spotlight. But now all she wanted to do was get the fuck away from the gangstas. But not before Briggen caught up with her at her car. He took her by the arm, but she snatched away.

"Bitch, have you lost ya' goddamn mind?" he spat.

"Mutha—"

Her words were cut off by his large hand mugging her entire face. "What the fuck has gotten into you? This nigga got you out here like this—acting like you can play a man's game! Where the fuck are my kids, Shan?"

He was so mad that she could see the whites of his eyes turning red. "Get off of me!" She reached up and scratched his face.

"Just remember. All bets are off the table. I'm coming after Nick, and then yo' ass. And just to think, I was gonna let bygones be bygones after you dogged me out."

Tears welled up in her eyes. She had so many mixed emotions. But she would have to put Nick on alert. For some reason she felt Briggen wouldn't cause her any harm.

"Who is she, Briggen?" she screamed.

"What are you talking about?"

Shan sucked her teeth. "Calvin, don't act stupid! I know you. You been locked up all this time. What bitch did you have waitin' for you? Who was it, Sharia? Or some bitch you met on the chat line in prison?" Shan accused. "You didn't even have the decency to tell me you were getting out?"

Briggen couldn't hold back his laughter. *Listen to this bitch.* Yeah, he had fucked Sharia, but in a totally different way. Then, he thought of Nyla. *If you only knew.* "I know you not feelin' some kind of way because I didn't tell you I was home? You left *me*, remember?"

"Yes, I am feeling some kind of way, Briggen. Fuck you!"

"Shan, I just got out. Literally. And they called this emergency meeting. I was going to surprise you and show up in the flesh. Like we talked about, remember? I wanted to surprise you, but do it right. But how the fuck you think I feel? I come home and my wife out here playin' gangsta? Where are my kids? I'm the one who should be pissed off!" Briggen told her.

Shan's heart wanted to believe him when he said he wanted to surprise her, but her head was much wiser. Still, being torn gave Briggen the upper hand. And she had to admit he made a valid point regarding the kids. Here she was out here playing gangsta. *What about their kids?* But still she was pissed that he didn't let her know he was home.

"You expect me to believe that? You stopped off to see how many bitches before checking on your children?"

"Ma, stop. I was comin' home to my wife and kids. But what difference does it make? You ain't home and I don't even know where my kids are!" He walked away to calm himself down. Seeing her at the meeting was fucking with him. He was used to being in control.

"Don't walk away, Briggen."

He turned back and came to where she stood. Reaching out to pull her close he asked, "Why would I be in the streets wit' all this waitin' for me?"

Shan pulled away. "Exactly! Why would you? And how you know it's waitin'?"

Just the thought of somebody else guttin' his wife had Briggen on fire, but he kept his composure. "You sayin' it ain't?"

"I'm sayin', I want to take it slow, okay? You did some foul shit to me, and I did some foul shit to you. I still love you, but just because you're home, we can't pretend that all the other shit in our lives didn't happen," Shan explained, making sense of the emotional mess between them.

Briggen nodded. "Okay, I feel that. Look. Both of our heads are fucked up. Can we at least discuss this over a drink? My treat."

Shan smiled. "No. My treat."

They ended up sipping VSOP at a table in the bar of the MGM Grand Hotel where Shan was staying.

"I want you to know I respect your hustle . . . Redbone," Briggen winked.

Shan giggled. "I figured I needed an alias. Plus, I used it before."

"Yeah, well, you need a lot more than an alias, baby. This ain't like promotin' shows. I can pretty much figure out what's goin' on, and real talk, Nick puttin' you on Front Street. You don't see that? Do you know how dangerous this game is for a nigga? Let alone a woman." Briggen wanted to talk some sense to Shan.

"Brigg—"

"Shan, this is a man's game, and I'm worried about you. I can't believe he got you out here like this. You have two small kids. That tells me that he ain't shit."

"I can handle myself," she declared with confidence. "Like it or not, I'm all grown up now. I made the decision to play and there is nothing you can do about it. There is no turning back."

"There is turning back, Shan. Come on now! You—"

"Briggen, face it. I'm all in. Plus, I've learned from the best. My brother Peanut. You. And now, Nick."

"That's bullshit." Briggen sat back, took a sip of his drink as he tried to digest Shan's words. But he couldn't believe how adamant she was. "Okay. It's on you. You got all the answers. Now let's talk about that price. Don't I get a husband discount?" he asked.

Shan snickered. "You know I'll look out for the fam', son!" she jokingly replied, using a New York accent.

Briggen laughed. "Yeah, a'iight."

"No, seriously, I got you."

"Yeah, but do I got you?" Briggen quizzed, gazing into her eyes.

The VSOP had her head right, and the way Briggen was looking at her let her know it was time to say good night.

"Oooohkay. I need to umm—"

"I know." He smirked, "Take it slow."

"Exactly. Plus, we need to have a serious conversation about us. Mainly, how we ended up like this."

"Let's talk now."

"No, not now. Now is not the time. We both need clear heads."

"Then when?"

"I'll let you know."

"When can I see my kids?"

"You have my number. Call me when you are ready to see them."

They stood. She told the waiter to put the bill on her room tab. Briggen walked her to the elevator. She turned and gave him a warm church hug and kiss on the cheek. "I'll call you tomorrow," she told him.

The elevator came. He got on with her.

"Where are you going?" she asked suspiciously.

"Chill out, girl. I just wanna see you to your room," he replied.

She looked at him skeptically.

"I'm not gonna go in," he assured her.

"I know you ain't," Shan snapped, pressing the fifteen button. *This nigga think he is slick. He is not coming nowhere near my room.*

"Yeah, ma, 'cause you never know. Muhfucka see yo' sexy ass all alone, and he might can't control himself," Briggen remarked casually. Then without warning, he hit the emergency stop button. The elevator stalled between the ninth and tenth floor.

"Briggen, what—" she tried to say, but he sucked the protest right out of her as he snatched her to him and tongued her down greedily.

There was no way she could ignore the passion and desire in his kiss, especially since it sparked the desire she had been fighting all night to suppress. She couldn't lie. Her husband still turned her completely on.

She tongued and clawed at his clothes as he snatched up her skirt and began pulling her panties down.

"Brig—" She breathed with a gasp. "The-the camera."

"So?" Briggen replied, too far gone to care. His dick was out, and he lifted her off her feet and brought her down on his hard rod.

Shan had never had sex in such a public place, and knowing someone was probably watching her get dicked down excited her. She wrapped her legs around Briggen's waist and used the leverage to bounce and meet his every thrust.

"Shan missed her big daddy!" she moaned.

"Daddy's home, baby. Take it for daddy!"

"I am. Ohhh, I am! It's still your pussy," she screamed, speaking from the heart and not from the moment.

The intercom came alive. "Hello? Is everything okay?"

Neither responded. All they could hear was the sound of a hard dick mashing a soaking, wet pussy as Shan's sweet sex song filled the elevator.

"Uhhh . . . just wanted you to know . . . that uhh, we can see you."

Briggen gripped her ass and dug up in her guts like he had been gone years instead of months, pounding his rhythm into her softest place. Shan couldn't stop coming. The elevator started moving and the sudden lurch only added to the intensity, making Shan cry out as she began to come along with Briggen.

By the time they got to the fifteenth floor, maintenance and the hotel manager were waiting, but Shan and Briggen's clothes were back in place as if nothing had happened.

Looking in their eyes and at their suppressed smirks, Briggen and Shan knew they were busted.

"Musta got stuck," Briggen remarked as they walked by.

"Yeah, I'm sure somethin' got stuck," the hotel manager replied.

Briggen and Shan burst out laughing as they disappeared into her room. But as soon as the door shut, he went to beating Shan's ass.

Shan struggled to crawl to the door, reach up, and unlock it. She didn't have anyone else to call since Courtney and Michelle were back in Jersey. She was grateful that Keeta took her call and said she would come see about her. But not before cussing her out some more. Keeta burst in, almost tripping over her body.

"What the fuck happened?" A pregnant Keeta looked down at a bruised up Shan in bewilderment. "I don't know if I need to call the police or an ambulance!" Keeta pulled out her cell phone.

"No! Keeta, no! I called you over here to pop my shoulder back in its socket. But first you gotta help me out. I don't need no damn ambulance."

"Shan, who did this?" She bent down and gently grabbed Shan's good shoulder.

"Ouch! Ouch! Ouch! Ouch!" Shan kept repeating as she gingerly stood up and they slowly walked over to the chair where she sat. "Oh my God! My whole body hurts. My shoulder. Be careful, Keeta. Go ahead. Pop it back in place. I remember you did Briggen's when he got in that fight and afterward, he was good as new. And yes, it *was* him."

"Briggen did this, Shan?"

"Go get me a washcloth and wet it. Hurry up!"

Keeta rushed to the bathroom and came back with the damp washcloth. "This is fucked up," she spat. "I understand that he's mad at you, but damn. Hell, I'm mad at you too. I started to hang up on your ass."

"Girl, thank you. I appreciate this."

Keeta watched as Shan put the damp cloth in her mouth, bit down on it, and squeezed her eyes shut. Keeta took a deep breath and felt her way around Shan's shoulder. Finally feeling the right spot, she popped it, and then snapped it into place. She stood back as Shan screamed, biting down on the cloth, tears streaming down her cheeks. She looked as if all the color drained from her face.

"You need to go to a hospital! Look at you. Two black eyes, your mouth is all busted up, and I ain't even a doctor. You need to get your shoulder looked at by a professional. I just gave you a temporary fix."

"Keeta, please." Shan slowly stood up. "Just let me lie down. The only thing I need you to do is get me some pain pills. *Believe me, I'ma get this nigga back.*" Shan lay down on the bed and let out a long moan. "Keeta, hand me my phone and go find me some pain killers."

"Girl, you in a hotel. The most you'll find is some Tylenol. I got some weed in my bag. You want that?"

"I need both. Go find me some pain pills first. Ask a white person if you have to. They always have prescription pain killers. And get me a lot of it. Grab the key card by the lamp. I don't think I can get back up."

"I got it."

As soon as Keeta left, Shan dialed Nick. He picked up on the first ring, frantic.

"Shan, I've been blowing your phone up! You were supposed to call me as soon as the meeting was over. All types of shit is running through my mind. What happened? Why you ain't call me as soon as it was over?"

"What happened? What *didn't* happen? I have a migraine, Nick. I had to lie down."

"Shan, migraine or bullet, you still could have answered the damn phone. Don't do this shit no more. If you can't do something as simple as call in after a meeting, then I'ma have to take you off of this."

"Damn, Nick, you going a little bit overboard, don't you think? I handled the business. So what I didn't call you immediately? Shit got a little crazy. Right after I gave them your message some chick comes in and she turned it all the way up."

"Some chick?"

"Yes. Born's cousin or aunt. That's all I know about her. But she got some beef with some dude named Wise. I'll have to tell you the rest when I see you. I know you don't want me talking over this phone. And then, Briggen was there. He said that he was going to get at you for having me out here like this on some street shit."

"Briggen?"

"Yes. Briggen, Nick. I didn't even know he was home. So, you see why my head is hurting. I just needed to lie down. I'll fill you in when I see you. I just took some more Tylenol. I'll call you later." She hung up before he could ask her anything else. Her mouth hurt even more from trying to talk as if her lips were not busted up. Now she had to figure out how she would duck him out so he wouldn't see the bruises and black eyes.

Chapter Thirteen

Baby Boy sat back in his La-Z-Boy recliner, big Willie Dick style, feeling his own come up. He knew he deserved it. Not only had he gotten him and Quita out of the projects, he had taken her brother and sister, Quandra and Ty-Ty, with them. The apartment was laced with all the toys a bunch of kids could want, because in reality, that's who they were. Ghetto kids that had never had a childhood but yet had never grown up. Stuck in a void unknowingly.

Ty-Ty was playing Madden on the 90-inch HD on the wall. The stereo system blared the sounds of Yo Gotti while Quita and Baby Boy blew fruit in multiple flavors.

Quandra walked into the living room. "I need some money to go shoppin'," she announced like a spoiled little sister.

"Fuck outta here. Y'all just went shoppin'," Baby Boy replied.

"I need some'm to wear to the *American Idol* tryouts. They comin' to Detroit," Quandra announced.

"Ohhh, for real?" Quita gasped. "Baby Boy, give her the money! Quandra can sing! She can!"

"So! If she that good, they ain't gonna give a fuck what she wearin'," he countered.

Quita sucked her teeth, grabbed the remote, and turned off Yo Gotti. "Show him, Quandra," Quita said like the proud big sister.

Baby Boy's first reaction was aggravation because Yo Gotti was his shit, but before he could open his mouth, Quandra opened hers.

His next reaction was almost . . . fear. Because something jumped out of Quandra that he didn't know existed. She seemed to transform from this awkward, bird legged young girl with a thumb sucker's overbite to a woman who had lived a thousand lives, and each one of them was filled with pain. She could project her voice like Beyoncé, but unlike Beyoncé, she had a soulfulness to her voice that would cause even the hardest thug to ball up and suck his thumb to sleep. Her voice made him believe there was a God.

When she finished, all he could say was, "How much you need?"

Satisfied, Quandra put her thumb back in her mouth and walked out of the room.

Baby Boy's phone registered a text. All it said was:

The Twins

He was happy for the work, because the way Quita spent money, he'd have to kill half of Detroit just to keep up.

TWO WEEKS LATER . . .

"Okay. Enough about me getting my ass whipped." Shan still had faint traces of her bruised and black eyes that Briggen gave her. "Trust me. The nigga is going to get his. I'ma hit him where it hurts. His ego, his pride, and his pockets. I even convinced Nick to fall back. So trust me, ladies, I got this. Know that every dog has its day. Now, what I want to ask y'all is, do you think if a woman has . . . multiple sex partners, that makes her a ho?" Shan asked the question as she, Courtney, and Michelle sat having a pedicure at the spa. They were clad only in thick, cloud like white bathrobes, hair wrapped in towels, and glasses of champagne in hand.

"Multiple as in the Knicks startin' five?" Courtney cracked.

Shan laughed and blushed. "No! Like two . . . or three."

"So let me see. I can only count one, Nick. Two, Briggen the ass whipper. And who is the third?" Michelle asked.

"My example is hypothetical," Shan told them, but in her mind, she was picturing Edgard. His sexy sophistication and that accent! And she couldn't lie, she was even feeling young ass Born—the way he ran The Consortium meeting. He seemed so . . . powerful.

Shan didn't know what was happening to her. It was like, making this new money was the first step in really taking control of her own life. It awakened things in her she didn't understand. So she brought it to Courtney and Michelle because their bond was growing stronger.

"Truthfully, I don't think fuckin' the Knicks makes you a ho, really," Courtney expressed, taking a sip of champagne.

"I do!" Michelle interjected.

"Shut up, Michelle! You only a ho if the man is in control. So if he makin' the booty call and you waitin' up, you could be fuckin' one nigga and be a ho! But if you makin' the call, layin' down law like—*nigga, lock the door on the way out* type shit. Nah, you just a boss bitch!"

They all laughed.

"I'm feelin' that. I'm feelin' that," Michelle agreed. "'Cause if you fuckin' this nigga because his game tight, then you just a ho to his reality."

"But, it just doesn't seem . . . right. I mean, y'all know my situation. Shit just got way complicated, especially with Briggen home. So it's like . . . I'm torn." Shan said, struggling to put her feelings into words.

Michelle sat up in her chair and did her best white girl impression. "Oh yeah, Oprah, I'm just such a good girl—but it's not me. I'm torn! And for the life of me I don't understand. He beat my ass and I'm still . . . torn."

Courtney jumped right in and took on Oprah's role. "Well, Mary Jane, that's because you're letting the men in your life do the pulling instead of you doing the pushing, bitch. Take control, ho! He beat your ass! You shouldn't be torn about shit. You're being dumb. You better get some payback on that ass!"

They all fell out laughing. Except for Shan.

"Y'all laughing too hard. And I don't sound nothin' like a white girl, y'all! Come on, now! And trust me. I have a plan."

"You know what you need? You need to swing wit' us tonight on one of our working nights," Courtney emphasized.

"I ain't tryin' to catch no bodies!" Shan cracked, only half-joking.

"Long as a nigga don't start nothin'," Michelle chuckled. "On the real, though, we goin' out tonight and show you how the brick do!"

Later that night, the three of them got dipped up, rented a stretch Phantom, and hit up Manhattan. They flirted from the Sky Lounge to the Copacabana, accepting no drinks but buying them for dudes, even dudes with females attached on their arms. They were on their boss diva shit, aggressive and taking the initiative. By the time midnight struck, they were toasted and feeling like the world was theirs.

They rode through the projects and saw a dude posted up, hugging the block.

"Oh, hol' up! Stop! Stop! Stop!" Michelle called out to the driver.

The Phantom lurched to a stop as she put the window down. "Oh, you a cutie. What's your name?" she called out.

Dude was on his thug shit. But he could easily be a model. He had the Tyson type pretty ruggedness with chinky eyes going on. He tried to play it smooth, though, squinting his eyes. "Yo, who that?"

"Yo' future baby mama if you play your cards right! Come 'ere, daddy!" Michelle giggled.

He diddy bopped up to the Phantom and peeped in. When he saw three bad broads inside, he was all smiles, revealing a platinum grill.

"Okay, I see you," he flirted. "What's good wit' y'all lovely ladies tonight?"

"You," Courtney chimed in. "What up wit' that fruit? We lookin' for some!"

"Well, then, you came to the right place," he remarked, pulling out and then holding up a half ounce of sour diesel.

"That's what I'm talkin' about. What up? You tryin' to party wit' us?" Courtney asked.

"No doubt," he responded as Michelle opened the door.

As he climbed in, Courtney slapped him playfully on the ass. "Mmm, firm."

Dude chuckled, but on the low, the way she did it made him uncomfortable. But he let it go. He sat between Courtney and Shan. The Phantom pulled off.

"What's your name, cutie?" Courtney questioned, licking her lips seductively.

"Man, yo."

"Man, huh? You sure you enough of one for three females?" Michelle teased.

He sat back, big dick style. "Like I said, Man," he repeated, grabbing his thick print.

Michelle eyed the print greedily, and then replied, "We'll see. But for now, roll that fruit!"

It took them a minute to convince Shan to hang out, but once they did, she was glad that they had. Man had rolled some fat ones and she inhaled deeply. She felt like she was floating and angels were singing in her ear. The sour had her head so relaxed she never wanted to come down.

They rented a room at a motel in Fort Lee, right off the George Washington Bridge in the cut. Shan sat in one of the little chairs by the window.

"Yo, you don't talk much, huh, ma?" Man asked, eyeing Shan's luscious thighs.

"She autistic," Michelle joked.

Shan giggled. "Bitch, fuck you. I'm not autistic."

"What's autistic?" Man asked, looking confused.

Courtney patted him on the cheek. "Don't worry, baby, at least you cute," she mocked. That one went over his head too.

"So what up wit' that thing, love? Let a sista see what you workin' with," Michelle urged him.

"Shit, you ain't said nothin'," he replied, standing up and starting to unbuckle his belt.

"Naw, naw, not like that . . . slow. Tease a bitch, yo. Dance," Courtney purred, coloring her tone with seduction.

"Dance? Yo,' I don't dance." He scowled as if she were questioning his gangsta.

"That shit is sooo sexy," Michelle remarked. "It turns me on to see a nigga dance. What about you, Nikki?" Courtney asked, calling Shan by her alias for the night.

All Shan could say was, "Yeah."

"I ain't no dancer," he said, but Michelle could see he was on the edge, so she pulled up her skirt, to reveal she was bald and pantiless.

"Mmmmm, dancin' makes this pussy purr."

Courtney added, "Mine too," and jacked up her skirt.

The nigga started two-stepping.

"Slow," Michelle ordered.

He began to do a slow striptease, taking off his clothes while the girls cheered him on. Courtney even threw ones at him. Shan was amazed at how quickly they had broken his gangsta down, turning him into a Chippendale wannabe.

Man even started getting into it, grinding his hips and making faces. He stood in front of them, buck naked, his rock-hard nine inches sticking straight out and bouncing to his gyrations.

"Now, take off *your* clothes," Man demanded lustfully, ready to take charge.

"Easy, chief. We got this," Michelle remarked, as she got up and gently pushed him on the bed.

She hiked up her skirt and straddled his face. His tongue went to work.

"Slow down, baby. This ain't fast food. It's gourmet," Michelle half giggled, half groaned.

He gripped her ass, sliding his tongue in and out of her pussy.

Courtney lit up another blunt. "Hurry up, sis, I'm next!" She remarked.

"We gonna run a train on him?" Shan gasped, her awe mixed with erotic anticipation.

Courtney giggled. "Not on him, on his tongue. We do this all the time—pick a nigga up and trick him out. See how easy it is to flip the script? Turn the tables? Imagine if bad bitches ruled the world." Courtney entertained the thought, blowing the sour smoke out and handing Shan the blunt.

Shan inhaled the words as well as the smoke while she watched Michelle ride Man's tongue to a body quaking orgasm.

"How was it?" Courtney asked as they exchanged places.

Michelle shrugged. "I came."

Courtney mounted his face and began working her hips to his tongue. Shan passed Michelle the blunt.

"That dick do look good though," Shan remarked, pussy getting wetter as the sour worked its way into her panties.

"Shit, do you. Remember, though, you only a ho if you ain't in control."

Shan got up and slid her panties off. She scrambled for a condom, ripped open the pack, grabbed his thick dick, wrapped it, and rushed to slide him into her pussy. She let out a belly shaking moan. "Fuck! I came already!" she spat.

"That's that sour." Michelle giggled, blowing the blunt.

Man tried to hold her by the hips, but Shan pushed his hands away, pinning them by his sides. She was in control. With Courtney sitting on his face, he was just a headless body. A fuck doll. A piece of dark meat. She bounced on his dick, being turned on even more by Courtney's aggressive talk.

"Yeah, nigga, eat this pussy! Fuck, yeah, right there. I'ma come all in your mouth, fuck!"

By the time Courtney got her first nut Shan had got her second. They both jumped off him almost at the same time.

"Goddamn, yo! Good look!" Courtney remarked, pulling down her skirt and sitting down.

Shan sat down as well.

"Oh, hell no!" Man barked, mouth slick from multiple cum shots. "What y'all bitches think I ain't gonna get mine?"

"Now you know how it feels, huh?" Shan cracked, and they all laughed.

The laughing made it worse. He jumped off the bed and drew back as if he was about to slap fire out of Shan. But before he could release, he felt the cold steel of a barrel against his jaw.

"Nigga, you was going to hit me?" Shan was flabbergasted.

"I wish the fuck you would!" Michelle gritted.

"Oh, now y'all gonna rob me?" He ignored Shan

"Rob you? Nigga we could *buy* your broke ass! But you fucked up. Now we gotta teach you some manners!" Michelle spat.

She pushed him down on the floor, keeping the gun aimed at his head.

"Yo, just chill, yo . . . before shit get ugly," he said, as if having total control of the situation.

"Yo, Nikki! This nigga was about to put his hand on you. What you wanna do?" Courtney questioned aggressively.

"Yo, shorty, my bad. I'm sorry," he groveled. Seeing how Michelle held the gun, he knew he was fucking with a vet.

Shan had never had a man grovel at her feet. The shit made her feel like a made bitch. The sour talking to her ego said, "Fuck it, shoot him."

"Naw," Michelle said, keeping her eyes on Man. "I asked, what *you* wanna do? We got your back, but tonight . . . you put in your own work."

Shan looked at Michelle. "I'm-I'm not a killer."

"Then don't kill him. But show him what happens when you try to play a bad bitch, yo."

Man was getting more nervous, not knowing that it was his own fear feeding Shan's resolve. "Come on, ma. Don't do this. I-I said I was sorry!"

Michelle handed her the gun. Shan took it and aimed it at Man.

"Ma, don't listen to her!"

Shan felt the trigger, and for some reason, she thought of her clit. The weed had her zoned. Running her finger over the trigger, she swore she felt it on her clit. That's how the first shot got fired. Her clit twitched, and her finger reacted. Lucky for Man, the gun was aimed at his shoulder.

"Aarrrghh, you shot me!" he cried out in agony.

Shan squeezed again just to feel the jolt, the kick back and the explosion of power.

Boom!

This time it hit his leg. Man fell out like he was dead, his mind screaming for him to play dead so this bitch would stop shooting.

Courtney kicked him in the ass. "Nigga, you ain't dead!"

Shan held the gun poised but didn't squeeze again. She looked down with new eyes on the bloody mass of flesh on the floor. Michelle and Courtney looked at each other with sly smiles across their lips and nodded subtly. Then Courtney said, "Party's over. So unless you gonna kill him . . ."

Shan stood up, eyes still transfixed on the blood. With the cold steel still in her hand a surge of power coursed through her veins. She felt like a true gangsta. But then she thought about the ass whipping Briggen gave her and her gangsta turned to rage.

"I'm ready," she replied meaning it in more ways than one.

If the ghetto is a concrete jungle then Janay had become a panther, stalking her prey. She hardly ate or slept, staying in seedy motel rooms and only moving in the shadows, even in broad daylight. Hell, she hadn't even buried Boomer or Marquis. Their bodies were still cold at the morgue. No one knew what had hit the West Side, but several people from crackheads to prostitutes to hustlers were dropping. The sun would rise on another corpse, and the streets would buzz. The hustlers were found with jewels and money. Robbery clearly wasn't the motive. No one knew, but the motive was silence. Dead men tell no tales. So no one could tell that there was a jet-black beauty looking for Baby Boy.

"Yo, I ain't seen 'im."

Boom!

"His mother live on Bull Terrace."

Boom!

"Oh my God, please don't kill me for what my son did! He live wit' Quita an' nem!"

Boom!

Step by step, death by death, she got closer until . . .

Click-clack!

That was the sound that brought Jamilla out of her revelry. Just getting off work at S & C's, Friday night, and she was on her way to hook up with what she hoped was a tricking ass baller. All she thought about was how she was gonna spend the nigga's money. That is, until she heard that sound that every ghetto head knew preceded a bullet in the head. The sound of a bullet entering the chamber.

"Please! Just take the car, I—"

"Shut the fuck up and get in!" Janay instructed her.

Jamilla got in on the driver's side door, but Janay made her climb over to the passenger side and she got in behind her. When Jamilla looked up, Janay hit her dead in the face with the pistol, breaking her nose. Blood poured freely. She was dazed, but her fear kept her from passing out. Janay stuck the gun in her face.

"Where did Quita move to?"

"I-I don't know! She quit! I ain't seen her!"

"Call her. Tell her you got that money you owe her," Janay instructed.

"But I don't owe her no money!"

Janay just stared at her. Jamilla got the hint. She hit speed dial.

"You better pray she answer."

On the fourth ring, her prayers were answered.

"What up, bitch?" Quita answered playfully, seeing Jamilla's name come up.

"H-hey, girl. I-um-um got that money I owe you," Jamilla said, as instructed.

"What? Oh, oh, yeah, okay," Quita replied, almost blowing free money. "Where you at?"

"'Bout to come through. Where you live?"

"One ninety seven Hunter Street, apartment 118. Why you sound like that?"

"Allergies. My nose is . . . stopped up," Jamilla replied, looking at Janay with pleading eyes.

"Don't be comin' over here wit' them nasty ass germs," Quita giggled.

"Hang up," Janay told her. "What's the address?"

Jamilla must have sensed, or seen it, in Janay's eyes, but she knew she was going to die. She blurted out the address, and then she tried to grab the door handle and dive out the car. Janay squeezed the trigger, hitting her in the temple and blowing her brains all over the car window. Since she had gotten as far as opening the door, the dead weight of her body fell out, and there it would be found, half in and half out.

Janay got out and headed for 197 Hunter Street, apartment 118.

Mr. Howard climbed out of his work truck with a relieved grunt. He had just gotten home completing another hard day as a brick mason. Tired but satisfied he had always prided himself on working hard, and his family had benefitted. He owned a nice brick home on the outskirts of Detroit. His wife of thirty-two years was happy, and his five kids had all made something of themselves. Well, all except for Keith and Kevin, his twins. They had taken hold of that street life and hadn't let go. They were a close family, and he loved his boys. He just worried about their safety.

He should've worried about his own.

Click-clack!

"Don't move, old man, or I'll blow your brains all over the yard,"

Baby Boy cautioned, holding Mr. Howard's collar tight with the gun to the back of his head.

"Easy, son. You don't want to do this," Mr. Howard warned him. He was a man used to being in control.

Baby Boy had timed his approach perfectly, catching Mr. Howard right after he unlocked the front door. He shoved him inside so hard that he fell onto the carpet. When he tried to get up, Baby Boy kicked him hard in the nuts, taking the fight right out of him.

"Stay down!" Baby Boy hissed.

"Baby, are you al—" came the question floating in from the kitchen.

Baby Boy heard her voice before he saw her. Mrs. Howard came in, typical black matronly type, graying hair and a ready smile. Only she didn't smile when she saw Baby Boy masked up and standing over her groaning husband holding a gun.

"Oh my God!" she gasped.

Baby Boy backhanded her, causing blood to squirt from her mouth. She crumbled to the carpet screaming.

"Bitch, shut the fuck up! Who else here, huh? Lie to me and whoever I find is dead!"

"M-my daughter and my niece," the old woman said. "Please don't hurt them!"

"Don't move and I won't!"

Baby Boy backed down the hallway watching the two old people. He found the niece, a seven-year-old in pigtails and their youngest daughter, an eighteen-year-old in tight cutoff sweatpants and a T-shirt. He snatched them into the hallway. The niece screamed. Baby Boy punched her in the mouth.

"Keep her quiet or I will!" he vowed to the daughter.

The daughter shot daggers from her eyes. He ordered them both into the living room next to the old people.

"My brothers gonna kill you for this!" the daughter spat with sass.

Baby Boy laughed. "You think so? Let's call 'em and find out. Call 'em!"

The twins were still not taking lightly the fact that someone was taking out The Consortium Members one by one. They moved with mad soldiers. To get to them, a man would need an army, or so they thought.

They forgot the one place no man can guard.

His heart.

When the phone rang, they were at their safe house, bagging up and counting money.

"Who that?" Keith gruffed.

Kevin checked the caller ID. "Li'l sis," he replied, then answered the phone. "Hel—" he started to say, but he was greeted with an ear piercing scream.

Baby Boy had shanked her in the eye with a pencil. He snatched the phone from her trembling hand and said, "If you try to send anybody or call the police, I will kill your whole goddamn family. Do what I say and they will live! You got three seconds to answer!"

"I hear you," Kevin replied, his insides aching for his little sister's pain.

"Put me on speaker," Baby Boy commanded.

Keith complied.

"My eye! My eye! He stabbed me in the eye!" She screamed. "Oh my eye!"

Keith dropped the money in his hand and looked at the phone.

"I hope I got y'alls attention because y'all got a big decision to make. Who lives? You or your family?" Baby Boy asked.

Both Keith and Kevin were riveted to the phone.

"You try to send anyone and I will kill them all. Are we clear?"

"Yeah," Kevin answered.

"What the fuck you want, nigga? Money?" Keith barked.

Baby Boy laughed. "I want your life, and you're going to give it to me, or you get to listen to your family die in your place."

The next thing they heard was their niece cry out in such a grotesque manner they didn't even want to imagine what he had done to her.

"You hear that? That's what it sounds like when you lose a thumb!" Baby Boy cackled, looking at the little girl's thumb in his hand and the bloody straight razor in the other.

Kevin and Keith were both enraged and heartbroken. Their helplessness dripped from their eyes into burning tears.

"A million dollars, yo! We'll give you a million dollars, man, just please let our people go!" Keith begged.

"I wish I could, but you already heard my price . . . or maybe you didn't."

The next thirty seconds were like an orgy of pain. It seemed like an eternity to the twins as they listened to the sounds of their family being tortured. The cries and screams of the girls. The deep moans and bellows of their father, and the soulful cries to God from their mother as Baby Boy took them through a hell none would forget. Having had enough, Keith was on the verge of pulling out his dreads. The sounds were unbearable. Truthfully, he would rather be dead than hear the family he loved so much suffer.

"What do you want us to do?" Keith was now frantic. "Just tell us!"

The intensity of the screams stopped, and only the pants and whimpers were now heard.

"Kill yourselves. Right now. Take out your guns and blow your own brains out. If it will make it any easier, pretend it's me doin' it," Baby Boy taunted them.

The twins looked at each other with questioning gazes.

What should we do? Was the unspoken question communicated. Family was sacred to them. They had vowed never to let this street shit bring them harm, but ironically, since they had made it so hard to hit them, it made it that much easier to get at their family. They could let their family die in order to save themselves. But that would be cowardly . . . or they could do as he said and end it all.

What would you do?

The ten seconds it took them to think was too long for Baby Boy, so he shot their niece in the thigh. She blurted out a wounded cry. The gunshot made Keith and Kevin jump. The second gunshot in their sister's foot made them cry out at the same time she did.

"We'll do it! Goddamn, we'll do it!"

"Then do it and don't try to play me! I'm takin' Ma Dukes wit' me, so if either one of you survive, she won't!" Baby Boy promised.

Keith and Kevin looked at each other. They knew their hand was totally forced.

"Man . . . I'ma do it," Keith said. "We can't let them die for us."

"We ain't gotta do it for real! We can just shoot—" Kevin whispered.

"Yo, you heard what he said. I'm not takin' chances wit' Mama's life,"

Keith vowed, pulling out his gun and putting it to Kevin's forehead. "You might as well kill me K, 'cause I'ma kill you."

Kevin knew his brother was right. This was the only way to save their mother. Reluctantly, he pulled out his pistol, clicked off the safety, and put it to Keith's forehead. Tears lined their twin cheeks. It was like looking in the mirror.

"I love you, bruh."

"I love you too! On three."

A split second before they pulled the trigger, their mother screamed out as Baby Boy stabbed her in the hand with a steak knife.

One . . . two . . . three . . .

Boom! Boom!

Two of the twins' soldiers snatched open the door, guns in hand, ready to set it off. They found the twins both on their backs, brains leaking and bodies twitching. They rushed to the window, but it was unbroken so no one had shot through the window. They looked down at them seeing them both with a gun in hand.

"Ain't no goddamn way . . ." one soldier remarked.

When Baby Boy heard the twins' shots, he knew they were dead. He hung up. "For your sake you better hope they ain't bullshittin'," he snapped, snatching their mother up by the hair. "Now, let's go."

He looked at the daughter. "Still think they gonna kill me?" He smirked.

She may've been in excruciating pain but her spirit was raging inside. She glared at him through her only eye and vowed that one day he would suffer . . . way more than she did.

Baby Boy read her expression and winked. "Anytime, baby. I'll be around."

With that, he snatched the mother out the door.

"Please don't," she begged.

"Bitch, shut up! Where's your keys?"

"In-in my purse! Where are you taking me?"

"Fuck!" He had to go back in and get the keys, but before he could, he heard his name called out in the still black night.

"Baby Boy."

He spun around to fire, but took two bullets in the upper chest and shoulder. The gun flew from his hand. The old woman didn't wait. She scrambled away and ran back in the house, locking the door behind her.

Baby Boy lay on his back struggling to get up. "Who the fuck—"

Janay stepped out the shadows and approached slowly, gun aimed for the game ending head shot if he even blinked wrong.

She had gone to his apartment building and waited until a figure emerged and mounted a red Yamaha TZ500J. One of her victims told her what he drove. Janay followed him and watched him as he parked it and then as he stole a car. She would've moved then, but it was too open. So she followed him here to the Howards' house, having no idea who they were. But when she heard the screams she knew he was up to no good. She waited. When he came out she was ready.

"Remember me?" she asked, her face a perfect mask of killer calmness.

He scowled and squinted. "Who the fuck are you?"

She got closer, her face fully illuminated by the light of the moon. "You tried to kill me."

"I never seen you before in my life." He grunted, shoulder and chest on fire.

She could tell he wasn't lying. Her instincts read his expression perfectly. She shot him in the knee. He howled.

"Fuck! I told you, bitch, I ain't never seen—"

"Who do you work for?"

"Eat a dick!"

"Wrong answer."

Boom! Blood gushed from the other thigh, then she ground the toe of her boot into the fresh wound.

"Aarrrghh!"

"Who . . . do . . . you . . . work . . . for?" she gritted.

"Dark, yo, Dark! I work for Dark!" he relented.

"Dark?" She scowled. But Dark had been hit in the same attack. Who was behind the hit?

In the distance, they heard sirens. She eyed him, feeling no remorse, only irony. Janay had hunted down the wrong man.

"My bad. I thought you were someone else," she remarked, turning on her heels and disappearing back into the shadows.

"I'ma kill you, bitch!" Baby Boy yelled as he tried to get up, but only fell back down.

Several seconds later, the street flooded with cherry high beams. Then the searchlight covered him.

"Put your fuckin' hands up!"

"Don't move!"

Baby Boy reluctantly complied.

Chapter Fourteen

Shan was on some real bullshit. He took her and her girls out, sent her flowers, cards and candy. How much apologizing could a nigga do for giving up an ass whipping that a bitch deserved? Plus, it'd been almost two months since he whipped her ass. Let bygones be bygones. It was time to make money. At least that's how Briggen saw it. It had been several days, and she still hadn't hit him with any dope. His money was too funny to be coppin' from somebody else, especially since she had the best prices along with the best dope. But he knew if she hit him off on consignment, he could get it all off. He was the hustler, but now she had the upper hand and had the audacity to be hand-feeding him. Then when she did hit him, it was some short shit.

"Briggen, you know how it get sometimes. Shit just tight right now," she had told him, giving him a couple stacks and a quick kiss. *Plus, you need to sit back and meditate on that ass whipping you gave me.*

Then she had dropped the kids off saying, "They need to spend time with their father." But the kicker was when she didn't come back to pick them up for almost two weeks.

Shan banged on his door like a mad woman, pissed because he told her to come get the kids or else. As soon as he snatched the door open, he said, "What the fuck is wrong with you? The kids are asleep, so don't come in here hollering and shit."

"You said to come and get them! You was acting as if it was a life or death situation. I told you I was working and traveling." She brushed past him with Courtney and Michelle on her heels. She wasn't getting caught with Briggen alone ever again.

"That was four o'clock this afternoon. Look what time it is."

"Whatever, Briggen. Pack my kids up so I can go. Or do you want me to come back later on today?"

His attention went to Courtney and Michelle. They wore smug looks on their faces. He grabbed Shan's hand. "Let me holla at you in the back for minute. Away from your bodyguards."

"Yeah, well make it short. I got people to see, places to go." Shan was feeling herself. Especially with her muscle in the living room.

"Okay, what's up?" she asked as soon as he shut the bedroom door.

"You on some real different shit lately."

"Different?" she echoed, acting like she didn't know what he was talking about.

"What you think? Just 'cause you gettin' a little paper and a nigga ain't got his weight all the way up, I'm 'posed to play Mr. Mom?" Briggen bitched, not feeling this role-reversal shit.

"Oh, that's what you call spendin' time with *your* kids?"

"I'm just sayin—"

"What are you saying, Briggen?"

"I got moves to make as well. But everytime I try to make one, you blockin'."

"Blockin'? What does it matter who gets the money in the family? We're a family, right?" she asked intently.

"Yeah, yo," he sighed. "But, goddamn, a nigga is used to goin' hard," he weakly protested, and Shan knew exactly what it was. Briggen wasn't used to looking at the world from flat on his back.

Shan walked up on him and wrapped her arms around his waist. She kissed him sweetly. "Baby, just give me a minute, okay? I'm just tryin' to stack for us, and then we can chill, okay?" she whispered in his ear.

"I can't chill no more. I need some bricks on consignment. Stop playing with me, Shan," he replied as the reality of the situation set in even more.

"Okay, I got you. I'll set something up for this afternoon." Shan kissed him passionately, and he returned the energy. She wrapped her arms around his neck, and his dick grew hard against her belly. Subtly but with pressure, she began to ease him to his knees. He kissed along her neck to her cleavage. She pulled her skirt up. When he got to his knees, she pulled her panties aside and cocked one leg over his shoulder. He ran his tongue along her pussy lips.

"Mmm, just like that, baby . . . Yeah, baby, suck that clit for mommy. Suck that clit," she purred, her hand on the back of his head.

Briggen had always had a killer tongue game, so it didn't take her long to come. When she did and the shudder subsided, she put her leg down and smoothed over her skirt.

He looked up at her dumbfounded. "What up? What you doin'?"

"Baabyyy," she whined, taking his hand and pulling him to his feet. "Don't be like that. I gotta go, but I promise I'll be back early, okay? I want to spend some time with you before I go back to New York."

With a quick smack she kissed his lips. Before he could protest, she stepped out of his embrace.

"Ay, yo, Shan, this that bullshit!" Briggen spat.

"I promise I'll take care of you later on," she said, adding, "You need anything?"

He started to say some slick shit but replied, "Naw."

"I'll call you. Muah!" she threw him a kiss. With that, she went to peek on the children and then was out the door. Excited that he was like putty in her hands. Just as she planned, she was fucking with his ego, his pride and his pockets.

Briggen was vexed. He grabbed the phone wanting to grudge fuck. He called Nyla.

The phone rang five times before switching to voice mail. She was already busy.

Nyla was riding Nick's dick reverse cowgirl style, giving him a view of her luscious ass as it jiggled and bounced while taking that dick like a pro. He admired his dick disappearing and reappearing in her tight, creamy pussy.

"Ohhh, yeah. Daddy likes that, don't he?" she moaned, licking her lips as she looked over her shoulder porno style.

Nyla couldn't lie. That curve could easily have a bitch fucked up. But she had an agenda, so it was only a means to an end. But she was damn sure enjoying the trip!

"Make it bounce for daddy, baby," Nick grunted, increasing the pressure of his stroke.

"Like this? Like this? Oh, fuck me, daddy! Just like that," she squealed, her wet pussy talking to him as the air was forced out with greater and greater pressure.

Nyla came all over his dick, coating it with her milk and making her pussy so hot and wet Nick couldn't help but come tumbling after her.

She leaned back and turned, laying her head on his chest.

"Dayummm, baby, I could sure get used to this every morning." She giggled.

Picture that, Nick thought, but said, "You and me both."

"Yeah, but yo' bitch ain't havin' that," Nyla expressed concern. "Shit, we can't even get a decent ménage à trois goin'."

"Naw, li'l mama. Shit just been crazy hectic for me. But trust me, it's gonna happen," he replied firmly. Ever since she had mentioned it, the more he wanted it. Especially now that Briggen was home. He had a point to prove.

"I mean, don't say it if you ain't got shit under control. I don't wanna create no waves," she remarked, purposely challenging his manhood.

He blew her off. "Shit is definitely under control. Like I said. It's gonna happen."

"Okay, daddy, I got you," she replied, thinking, *Yeah, I got you.*

Born and Tareek met in the parking lot of the Oakland Mall at noon. They pulled up driver's door to driver's door. Born, in his black Aston Martin Vanquish, and Tareek, in his blue BMW 750i. Each had one soldier with them who got out and mingled while the bosses talked.

"Peace, Lord. How you?" Born greeted. They both were members of the Five Percent Nation and from New York.

"Peace, peace," Tareek returned. "I'm good . . . but shit ain't."

"How so?"

"I guess you ain't heard about the twins."

"Naw, yo. The God was outta town. What up?"

"They killed themselves," Tareek replied, letting the words sink in, "or each other."

Born shook his head in disbelief.

"Yo, God, I don't get it. Niggas said his people heard two gunshots. They rush in and them niggas dead, gun in hand. Shit is crazy 'cause don't nobody know why."

Born sat back, listening. "Goddamn."

"Naw, yo. I ain't feelin that shit." Tareek was quick to let him know that he wasn't in agreement with him. "Shit just don't wash, God. My gut tellin' me this shit is connected. And right or wrong, I'm goin' wit' my gut. That nigga Dark had somethin' to do wit' this."

"How? Them niggas shot themselves," Born reminded him.

Tareek's mind was made up, so he shook off Born's logic. "I don't know, and I ain't askin' no more. As a matter of fact, ain't no more talkin'. As of now, it is what it is between me and the nigga."

"I feel you, God, but we took an oath, and a man's word gotta be good for somethin'. You know?"

"Exactly. That's why I'm comin' to you as a man, and I'm tellin' you I'm outta The Consortium, so the oath no longer applies to me. Niggas don't respect unity and solidarity, God. They don't. Niggas wanna beef and cause confusion. The only way the hardheaded believe is if they feel it, not see it. So from now on, I'm doin' me," Tareek explained.

Born nodded. "I respect that, yo, and I appreciate you comin' to me with this if you out. That means that you and Dark's issues ain't Consortium issues."

They reached out and shook hands.

"And you know that Briggen got beef with The Consortium because he can't get his product from Nick's girl. So there is gonna be some shit there. Shit ain't running like it used to. So God, be wise. With me gone, ain't too many vets left but you," Tareek warned.

Born smiled.

"Remember, God, they came at me first and missed. If they come again, the God will be on point."

"Indeed. So peace, Lord. Be easy."

"Peace."

Dark's phone rang. He checked the caller ID as he drove. It was Quita. He was on his way to handle business, but he decided to answer and set up something for later. He knew he shouldn't still be fucking Baby Boy's girl now that they were doing business, but he felt no loyalty to the young nigga. To Dark, he was just a worker. A pawn. A valuable pawn, but a pawn nonetheless. Besides, Quita's ass was always hot and tight, and the bitch had him turned out on her back door action.

He answered. "What up, li'l mama? I—"

Quita quickly cut him off. "Baby Boy on the phone. He finally got out of the hospital. He in the county."

"Yo, Dark!"

"What's good, li'l homie?" Dark frowned.

"Man, shit fucked up! I got shot and shit! Lucky I had on that vest or I wouldn't be here. I'm just gettin' in the county. They got me for home invasion, attempted murder—man, a buncha shit! I need you to come through for me, big homie," Baby Boy explained.

"Say no mo', maine, I'll put my bondsman on it ASAP," Dark assured him.

"Good lookin', yo."

"You already know," Dark replied. He had already heard about the twins' double suicide. He hadn't known how Baby Boy had pulled it off, but hearing his charges, he quickly figured it out. "You a beast, li'l homie!"

Baby Boy smiled proudly. He was beginning to look up to Dark, not knowing he was gutting Quita on the low.

"Yeah," Baby Boy replied.

"Sit tight, I got you," Dark repeated, then hung up.

"No do—" Baby Boy started to say, but he caught a swift motion out of the corner of his eye.

He looked up just in time to see the razor-sharp jail shank slicing through the air and straight at him. The dude holding it he had never seen before, but they were damn sure about to meet and get downright personal.

The dude saw the home invasion story on the news. He knew the house as soon as he saw it because that was his aunt's house. The twins were his cousins. No one else knew who the Howards were, but he did. When they showed Baby Boy's picture and said he had been taken to the hospital, he knew he'd have his chance to get at him.

Now a week later, Baby Boy came to the dorm and he was ready to move.

He went and got his shank out of the stash in his cell. By the time he got back, Baby Boy had gotten on the phone. He gripped the shank tightly and made his way across the crowded dayroom. Had he come up behind Baby Boy he would've never saw it coming, but because he had to go around one of the octagonal-shaped steel tables, he was exposed.

He lunged at Baby Boy with the blade and only managed to graze his side. He knew he hit some flesh because he could feel the subtle resistance to the thrust. But for the most part, he only ripped Baby Boy's jumper.

"This is for my family, nigga!"

Baby Boy wasn't about to waste energy talking. The dude outweighed him by at least fifty pounds, and his rage added another twenty-five. Baby Boy swung a hard right hook catching the dude in the eye. He shook him but didn't stagger him, but the follow-up jab backed him up enough for Baby Boy to snatch the phone receiver and wring the metal cord out of the phone box on the second try.

Baby Boy grabbed the wire and swung the receiver like a Chinese nunchuck dead into the dude's face, and he came head-on a second time. The corresponding clunks could be heard all over the dorm.

Dude dropped to one knee, snorting and shaking his head like a bull. Baby Boy didn't let up. He connected again . . . and again . . . and again . . . When they finally pulled Baby Boy off, he snapped out of the kill zone he had entered. Dude lay sprawled out on his back. Blood was everywhere. Baby Boy was covered with blood, and dude wasn't moving.

"Oh, shit! Youngin' killed him!" somebody yelled.

Five police dragged Baby Boy away as he looked at the man, thinking he wouldn't see the streets for a long time.

When Janay stepped out of the shadows, Born was ready.

He had just gotten home to his sprawling estate in Highland Park right outside of Detroit. She was waiting on him. But when she came out, the crunch of leaves gave her away. Born spun, gun in hand, and aimed only to find Janay's gun aimed at him. Each had the other covered.

Janay smiled. "Glad to see you on point, nephew," she greeted.

"Always, Auntie." He smiled back because he knew his auntie always went hard.

They hugged warmly, prolonging the hug for a comfort they both knew she needed. Finally, they broke the embrace.

"Where you been? I've been callin' you like crazy. Then when I heard you broke out of the hospital, I really got worried. I sent Kay-Gee to Charlotte to check on you, and he said there was a for sale sign in the yard, so I ain't know what to think!" Born explained in a tone that Janay understood and answered with a mustered smile.

"No . . . I didn't kill myself. I thought about it . . . but it wasn't my time," she replied, still hearing the metallic click of the empty chamber. The sound that had sentenced her to a life of suffering and the world, a season of pain. "But I had my broker sell the house . . . and everything. He should be contacting you to handle everything. Not being on the run. I'm never going back. Ever. Hell, I can't."

Born nodded. "I feel you. So what you gonna do?"

"Kill them all, and then . . . I don't know."

"Well, come on in. You look tired."

"I am, but that's what keeps me going. I just came to tell you what I found out. Not only is Dark *not* behind Crystal's death, but he is behind The Consortium hits," she explained.

"How you know?" Born asked, all ears.

She explained how she tracked down Baby Boy and found out he was working for Dark on the Fat Rich, Twins, and Tommy hits.

Born smiled. "Interesting. Good look, Auntie. But I got somethin' for you too. My man on the force said one of those shooters from the funeral was from New York."

He stopped and let that sink in. He saw recognition form in her eyes. She looked at him.

"Wise. Melky's cousin."

Born nodded. "And the other shooter is a goon for a nigga named Mo'Betta. You ever heard of him?"

"No . . . but he about to hear of me," Janay replied.

"He's been runnin' with Briggen since he came home, and you know Skye and Melky were on Briggen's team," Born said, breaking it all down.

Janay smiled a malicious smile. "Good lookin' out, nephew. Thank you."

"Auntie."

She looked back.

"Just say the word and I'll send a swarm on the niggas," Born vowed.

"You already have, Born . . . you already have."

"Your hand's been exposed, Dark," Sherman told him in the back of the stretch Escalade they were cruising the city in.

Beside Sherman sat Joy, and beside her, Nick. Dark sat across from them, sipping Bacardi.

"I'll take care of it," Dark replied, trying his best to keep his eyes off Joy's sexy lips, bedroom eyes, and curvaceous, luscious legs. Her presence was more than distracting—it was magnetic.

"You'd better. This young boy is a step away from blowing it all. On top of that, he almost beat another inmate to death in the county! He's a loose end that needs to be clipped ASAP!"

"So get him out for me and I'll take care of it. I'll send him to Tennessee and make sure he don't come back."

Sherman nodded, and then downed his drink. "I should be able to do that. I'll tell them he's my informant, and I need him on the streets. I should be able to spring him by noon tomorrow."

"Fo' sho'. Now, can we get down to business?"

"Proceed," Joy said, watching Dark with a bemused expression, like a lioness would watch a mouse. She absolutely loved her position as puppet master.

"I've put in a lot of work for y'all, and I wanna make sure at the end of the day, I don't get what I've been givin' niggas," Dark proposed.

"I assure you, Jerome, you would've never met me if you were . . . expendable. We need a face on the street. Yours. You want to run the city, finish off the rest of The Consortium members and you can have it. We need a new organization. My organization. Sherman will provide the police protection, Nick will provide the product, you will provide the network, and together, we can get paid in full," Joy explained.

"And what will you provide?" Dark smirked, flirting hard.

Joy looked at him with the gaze of a goddess, subtly licked her lips, and answered, "Motivation."

Dark chuckled. "I'm self-motivated."

"Then I guess you don't need me," she shot back with a smirk.

The Escalade came to a stop. Nick opened the door. Dark looked out into the dark night. They were three blocks from where he was parked.

"What's up?" he asked.

"These are your streets, right?" Joy asked. "Then walk them."

Dark's ego was bruised by the way she dismissed him as if he was a common thief. He flexed his jaw muscles but held his tongue and got out.

Briggen swung through Mo'Betta's block in a rented Buick LeSabre. Mo' jumped in and as they pulled off, Mo' handed him a McDonald's bag filled with money.

"Yo, big bruh, no disrespect, but what you givin' me ain't even enough to keep my block fed. I mean, if shit that tight for you—"

Briggen waved him off like it wasn't that serious, even though he knew it was that serious. It was written all over the three-day stubble on his face. It was clear he wasn't the man he used to be in every way . . . except in his own mind.

"Just gimme a coupla days."

"You said that a coupla days ago," Mo'Betta reminded him.

Briggen glared at him. "Yo, what the fuck I just say? This Briggen, nigga. Shit just fucked up right now, a'iight?"

Mo' held his tongue because he knew what Briggen was capable of when it came to getting that money. Besides, he still needed a little more time to pick his brain on his out-of-town routes and customers.

"A few mo' days, then we set shit off, maine! Fuckin' Shan on this Redbone shit tryna hand-feed a nigga. Me! Brig! I coulda bought that bitch when I found her, now this nigga Nick got her head fucked up . . ." His voice trailed off, and he shook his head.

"But you, big bruh, she still yo' wife, right? She probably just in her feelings. I mean, goddamn, buy her some flowers or somethin'," Mo' suggested sarcastically, wishing it were his wife. He'd show Briggen how to break a bitch.

Mo'Betta may've been trying to be funny, but his words sparked an idea.

"Naw, yo. The bitch don't need no flowers. She need to be taught a lesson! She wanna play a man's game, then let's play a man's game. Yo . . . I need you to kidnap the bitch for me," Briggen proposed.

"No doubt," Mo' agreed enthusiastically.

"Don't hurt her or nothin' but scare her up . . . bad."

"How I'ma do that without hurtin' her?" Mo' questioned, wanting to hurt her anyway.

Briggen looked him in the eyes. "Then don't hurt her . . . *too* bad," he said.

Mo'Betta nodded. "Say no mo'."

"Then when she call me and I play Captain Save-a-Ho, I'll show that bitch how much she need me! Then she'll fold!" Briggen laughed.

Mo' laughed too. But while Briggen thought he was laughing with him, Mo'Betta was laughing at him. Because Mo' saw a better route. One that would kill both a vulture and an eagle with one boulder.

Literally.

The West Side of Detroit was Tareek's kingdom. By all accounts, he was one of the biggest dope boys in the city and his team was no joke. He had been prepared for war, so if and when they tried to move on him he'd be ready.

He and a bad-ass light-skinned broad were heading to a club called Ace of Spades, one of Detroit's many strip joints. The broad was putting on lipstick in the visor's vanity mirror when they stopped at the light behind an old Ford Taurus. Behind Tareek was a car full of his goons. He glanced over at the chick getting ready to say something when the trunk of the Taurus popped open and a masked gunman sprang out. Tareek ducked, but the broad wasn't so lucky. The stream of bullets from the automatic rifle the gunman was holding peppered and shattered the windshield, then hit her several times in the head and chest.

By this time, Tareek was already scrambling out the door, staying low. His goons returned fire, while two more shooters jumped out of the backseat of the Taurus with automatic weapons.

Brrrrrraaapp! Brrraaapppp! they spat as gunfire erupted in both directions. Tareek took cover behind a parked car and opened up with his .40 caliber. He was more than prepared.

Several seconds later a white van skidded up and blocked the Taurus in. Three dudes jumped out with their own automatic weapons and began spraying the Taurus. Tareek had lulled them into a trap sandwiched between his goons. The Taurus shooters were sitting ducks. In a matter of moments they were all leaking and twitching on the sidewalk. The shooter's arms dangled from the trunk touching the ground. The only one left alive was the driver.

Mook.

Tareek ran up on him and put the gun to his jaw. "I told you that bitch-ass Dark was behind this shit!" He laughed, looking at Mook.

Mook gritted. "Nigga, do what you gonna do!"

Tareek smacked him with the pistol, then began to pistol-whip him until Mook slumped in the seat. Tareek searched his pockets for his phone. When he found it, he quickly went through it until he saw: *Dk.* He called.

"We good?" Dark answered on the second ring.

"Fuck, no, you clown-ass faggot!" Tareek laughed.

Dark got silent.

"You a dead man, nigga!" Tareek spat, then added, "Your man wanna speak to you."

He put the phone to Mook's ear. "Yo, maine, fuck these—"

Boom! The gun exploded through the phone, and Dark could only imagine. He knew Mook was dead.

"Fuck!" he barked as he paced the floor of his apartment.

If his hand wasn't exposed before, he knew it was now. He had been caught red-handed, breaking the oath. He knew the whole Consortium would come down on him, and his team wasn't deep enough for a war with Tareek, Born, and Kay-Gee. He had already sent Baby Boy down to Tennessee, and then sent Mac back down to take out Baby Boy.

He hit Mac as he paced.

"Yep," Mac answered.

"Where you, maine?"

"A few miles from Oak Ridge."

"Yo, I need you to double back. Mook's gone," Dark told him, pinching the bridge of his nose.

"Gone?" Mac echoed. "What you mean, gone?"

"Fuck you think it mean, yo? He gone!" Dark shot back. "Shit 'bout to get hectic, so what I said about the young boy, dead that. Bring him back too. We 'bout to take these niggas to war!"

Mac looked at the phone as if it sprouted two heads. He knew the situation. Dark had told them about the oath, so if Mook was dead, they knew the oath was broken. There was no way he was coming back to go to war with half of Detroit! Dark was on his own.

"Ay, yo, Dark, you know what they say, yo," Mac remarked.

"Huh?" Dark grunted, his mind a thousand miles away, plotting his strategy.

"Your main man ain't your man. Mook was my man, not you. I'll holla, homie!"

Click!

Dark gripped his phone, then hurled it against the wall in a rage.

"Bitch-ass nigga! You dead too!" Dark huffed, trying not to let his fear mixed with anger get the best of him.

His main soldiers were dead or on the run. The street goons he had he inherited from Cisco, so he couldn't count on their loyalty. He knew if he was going to survive, he had to strike first and strike hard. Even if he had to move as a one-man army.

"Fuck it! I'ma show these niggas I don't need nobody!"

Rudy loved the plan as soon as Mo'Betta brought it to him. "You're a thinker, Mo', I like that," Rudy complimented him as he sat behind his desk.

"Only one problem . . . I don't know how to get in touch with her," Mo'Betta admitted. "All I know is she go by Redbone in the street."

Rudy gave him a cocky smile. "I'm not the best lawyer in the city for nothing. I'll put you in touch. Ain't a nigga in the game I can't get at," Rudy boasted, wanting Mo' to think he was more connected than he was. He didn't mention the fact that he was Nick's lawyer and that was the only reason he could get at Shan.

"Shit, then make it happen, maine!"

"It's done."

Two hours later, Mo'Betta was pulling up to Shan's brand-new candy apple red Maserati sedan Quattroporte. He parked beside it, and when he got out, Michelle and Courtney both got out, gun in hand but casually at their sides. She made sure she had them go with her when the situation called for some extra girl power.

"Whoa, li'l mamas. I come in peace," Mo'Betta joked.

Courtney said, "I gotta pat you down."

He raised his hands and turned his back to Courtney. She took his gun off his waist. "I'll hold on to this," she said.

"No problem," Mo'Betta replied, looking Courtney up and down, licking his lips. "Next time I come through, I'ma be checkin' for you."

She didn't respond, so he got in the passenger seat of Shan's Maserati. Shan was texting when he got in.

"What up, li'l mama? I hear—"

"Redbone," she cut him off. "Not *li'l mama*. Redbone. We good?" she said, looking him in the eyes. She was determined to set the respect level from the door.

Mo' was a little taken aback. He hated for a woman to talk shit to him. He imagined himself backhanding Shan, but he kept his composure.

"My bad, Red. My bad. But like I was sayin', I hear you the one to see."

"The only reason I agreed to meet you is on the strength of Nick. So do me a favor, get to the point."

Damn this bitch think she cold, Mo' thought. *Briggen need to check his bitch.*

"I'm here to make a deal. I work for your husband."

"Yeah. I already know that."

"And, ah, he ain't too happy with how you been treatin' him lately," Mo' informed her.

Shan looked at him and chuckled. "Who are you? Dr. Phil? You wanna talk about Briggen's feelings?"

"He wants me to kidnap you."

She stopped chuckling. He knew she would.

"Okay . . . So kidnap me," she said with a sneer.

"Li'l mama, I mean Red . . . if that had been my intentions, you think I'd be tellin' you? I'm here warnin' you. I'm pourin' you a drink hopin' you'd pour me one too," Mo'Betta explained.

Even though she was good at keeping the poker face, inside, Shan was reeling. *Kidnap me? Briggen? My husband? The death-do-us-part nigga that stood beside me in church?* She couldn't believe her ears.

"Why?" She wanted to feel him out.

Mo' shrugged and replied, "To teach you a lesson. Get you to fall back and put him in the driver's seat again. I was supposed to snatch you up, smack you around, and then ask for a grip. He would come through, save you, and take over . . . plus keep the ransom money," Mo'Betta threw in for good measure.

Shan smiled and nodded. "Wow . . . really?" *He is stooping real low.*

"Really, Red."

"So you bringin' it to me . . . what you tryin' to get out of it?"

"A connect. I'm a go-getter, Red. I just need to know the right people. And like I said, I hear you the right people," he answered.

Shan thought for a moment, then said, "I'ma look into this. If what you say is true, I'ma see you, and if it ain't . . . you'll never see it comin'."

Mo'Betta smiled and opened the door.

"Well, since it's true, I'll be waitin' on your call. I'll holla, *Red*."

Mo'Betta got out and slammed the door, leaving Shan to contemplate her next move.

Briggen knew he was dead wrong for fucking his dead brother's wife, but he couldn't lie. The pussy was fire! Besides, he was on some emotional shit fucking the one bitch he knew Shan would go crazy over if she found out.

He flipped Nyla on her back and cocked her curvy legs up over his shoulders. She stretched out her arms, grabbing fists full of the bedsheets as Briggen got in a push-up position and stood up in the pussy, hitting bottom with every stroke.

"Oh, Brig! Brig! My . . . sp . . . spot, that's my—" she gasped as he stroked her G-spot like an expert, pounding her relentlessly.

Her pussy squirted and creamed his dick, and when she felt him tensing up, ready to come, she squealed, "Come in my mouth, daddy!"

He pulled out of her and snatched the condom off. Nyla wrapped her Meagan Good-looking lips around his dick, then sucked and swallowed every drip of cum out of him as his entire body twitched.

They both lay back, naked and unashamed, the guilt having long ago worn off.

"Damn, baby, you be makin' me feel nasty." She giggled. "You must be trying to turn me out."

Briggen chuckled. "Shit, I could say the same thing about you."

"It's workin'."

His phone rang. It was Shan. He sucked his teeth and let it go to voice mail.

"Let me guess. That triflin' ass bitch of yours. When you gonna learn, Briggen? The bitch done robbed you, left you for dead in jail, and is fucking your friend. I mean like, what the fuck?" Nyla was pissed and in her feelings.

Briggen hated hearing it all laid out like that. It made him feel like a sucker. If she saw it, then he knew the streets did too. So he felt like he had to reply and save face.

"Believe me, the bitch gonna get hers. I gotta play lame so I can rock her to sleep. But once I do, all that about to get straightened out. Then I'll take care of my so-called friend Nick."

Nyla gave him a devilish smirk. "Maybe I could help you with that."

"How so?"

"I've been tryin' to use that nigga to get me close to her, but every single time something comes up. I'm 'bout to cut his ass off for real. But if you need me to do somethin' . . ."

The two snakes in the grass looked at each other eye to eye.

"Baby, believe me. We get that nigga out of the way, then Shan will be on top. Once she is, then I'll take care of her, and *I'll* be on top!" Briggen proposed.

"You mean *we'll* be on top." Nyla winked, leaning up and straddling his hardening dick.

He chuckled. "Handle your business, and I'll handle mine."

"Don't I always?" she purred, sliding his dick back inside and biting down on her bottom lip as she started to ride him.

"Hell, yeah, baby . . . hell, yeah," Briggen groaned.

Chapter Fifteen

Dark was on a rampage.

"Spot 'em, get 'em!" Tareek had put the word out in every hood. He put a brick of cocaine on his head. Anybody see Dark and murder him could collect. Every goon on the street was looking for Dark, and now Dark was looking for them.

Dark jumped out of a cab on the West Side, packing twin .457 Magnums and let loose on every hustler on the block. "Y'all niggas lookin for me? Here I come! Why y'all runnin'? I thought y'all was lookin' for Dark!" He cackled maniacally as he left bodies broken, maimed, and dead.

On the Number Streets he drove by spraying bullets, catching the block by surprise. He stopped, got out with a riot pump shotgun, and started sending slugs that lifted niggas off their feet. He murdered one and hit six more before the return fire drove him back to the car, forcing him to skid away.

On the South Side he walked into a Chinese restaurant, pulled out the twin .457s, and barked, "Y'all know what it is! Get the fuck down!"

All five hustlers lay down on the floor.

"You got it, playa, you got it," one of the men said and received two in the back of the head.

His brains looked like they skidded across the dirty linoleum floor. The other four shut their mouths.

"Who been lookin' for Dark? Muhfuckas say it's a bounty on my head. So which one of you gonna tell Tareek I'm here to collect?" Dark shouted out.

Since the last nigga to speak got his head blown off, nobody said a goddamn thing. For which Dark shot another nigga for not talking. The third nigga got the message real quick.

"I'll tell 'em!" he volunteered.

Dark then shot the fourth and fifth niggas point-blank in the head, painting the floor with their bloody brains. He then looked at the third nigga and spat, "Then run and tell that!" Dark turned and walked out.

He dumped the stolen car and then jumped into his Benz. His phone rang. He checked the caller ID. It was Born. "What?" He answered.

"Yo . . . we get the point."

"I can't fuckin' tell! Y'all niggas wanna put bounties out and shit! Fuck it! I'ma make this city so hot, nobody gonna eat!" Dark growled.

"First off, that ain't us, that's Tareek. And he ain't . . . wit' us any-more."

"How you figure?"

"He . . . left the board. This thing is strictly between y'all. I made him lift the bounty," Born explained.

Dark drove in silence, thinking he respected Born, but as far as he was concerned, he could get it too.

"Yo?"

"I'm here," Dark replied.

"So we good?"

"I'll think about it," Dark answered, then hung up.

He ran his hand over his face. Shit was crazy. He was on the verge of owning the city. Now he was one step from being pushed out. He couldn't trust The Consortium because now they knew it had been him behind the killings. And if he was unable to finish the job, he knew Sherman, Joy, and Nick would probably want him eliminated. Shit had escalated beyond crazy.

He found himself driving to the hospital and parked once he found Lisha's car.

Dark planned on talking to her, but when she came out talking to another nurse with a light bounce in her step and looking happy, he just didn't have the heart to bring his darkness into her life.

He thought about how he got the nickname Dark. How his grandmother always said he had a dark energy about him. She was from Mississippi and was deep into practicing black magic. She said she could feel it radiate off him. He had always liked the fact that he was dark, but now it seemed as if it really meant he was cursed. Dark. Black. Bad luck. *Bullshit.* He pushed it out of his mind.

Dark watched Lisha get in her car and pull off. He followed her. Since she wasn't paying attention, it wasn't hard. He wanted to know where his son lived.

Just in case.

They drove to a quiet tree-lined section of Detroit called Parkland. To him it was like a whole different city. So quiet and peaceful. When Lisha pulled up in front of the house his son was in the driveway playing basketball. Dark looked at him. It was like being dead and the ghost of his soul going back in time, looking at himself.

Being dead.

That's what he might as well have been to his little man.

"What can you possibly offer a child, Dark?" Lisha had asked.

Sitting there, looking at this little man made him come to the realization. "Nothin'," he mumbled. "Nothin'." He drove off.

Sometimes being beautiful can be your worst enemy. That's what Janay had become. The victim of her own beauty as the police put the cuffs on her.

She had been following Mo'Betta and Keeta through the mall. They were hugged up and buying things for the baby. Janay was intent on making the child a bastard before it was even born. She kept a good distance but stayed close enough to hear his voice. Mo'Betta never saw her, but a police officer did.

He remembered seeing the picture of the escaped woman from the psychiatric ward of the hospital. The officer remembered thinking at the time, how can someone so beautiful be crazy? He was awestruck by her flawless black skin and regal posture. So when he saw her in the mall he instantly recognized her. He watched her for a few moments before calling for backup. She may have been beautiful, but he heard what she did to the doctor with that bedpan.

"Excuse me, miss? Miss, could you stop for a minute?" the officer requested.

Janay knew he was talking to her, but she pretended not to hear. Instead, she picked up her pace. He too picked up his and radioed in. "Suspect taking evasive action, now heading north."

Janay knew she was in a bind. She could afford to be arrested but not carrying the gun on her that she had used on several bodies on the West Side. When she turned the corner heading north, there was a garbage can. She pulled out the gun discreetly, using her left hand to underhand it. Shielding the action from the officer behind her, she dumped it in the trash. A second officer approached from the opposite direction.

"Excuse me, Miss," he said politely but firmly, walking directly up to Janay and taking her by the forearm, "you're going to have to come with me."

"For what?" Janay asked as if she didn't know.

"Assault."

Mo' and Keeta heard the commotion and looked back. They saw the two officers escorting Janay but didn't see her face.

"I wonder what that was all about," Keeta questioned.

Mo' shrugged. "Probably a shoplifter," he replied, not knowing his life was the only thing that was almost stolen.

They took Janay back to the psychiatric ward of the hospital, to the same room and the same straps. She stared up at the same ceiling and the memories came flooding back, as if they had been deep-rooted in the energy of the room. Her spirit was so tired she could no longer fight the tears. She felt them running sideways across her temple, ears, and hair, soaking the pillow beneath her head. All she could see was Marquis at various stages in his life. When she first held him. When he first looked into her eyes . . . when he first called her mama.

She totally lost it and began sobbing and screaming out, "Whyyyy?" Over and over and over again.

The door opened and a nurse entered with a doctor close on her heels. "Are you okay, Miss Carter?" the doctor asked, his voice a soothing baritone. She didn't respond because she couldn't. She hated for anyone to see her weak, but there was nothing she could do. At that moment, she had no energy to mask it.

"Nurse, I think Miss Carter is going to need a mild sedative," the soothing voice instructed.

"Yes, Dr. Muhammad."

"Or a sheriff. But I'll take it from here."

Hearing the second male voice made Janay tense up. She knew it well. It was cold, metallic, and nasal. She didn't have to look up because she knew exactly who it was.

"Dr. Bennett, how are you? Is this your patient?"

"Yes," Dr. Bennett replied. "Miss Carter is a very disturbed young woman. She suffered a very traumatic experience, but I'm afraid it triggered something much deeper."

"Well, I just heard her crying out and . . . well, anyway, I'll let you take over from here," Dr. Muhammad replied, and then left.

Once Dr. Muhammad and the nurse left, Dr. Bennett said, "Well . . . Miss Carter, I see you haven't improved."

Janay's sobs began to subside. She turned her head and looked into the face of the doctor she beat to sleep with the bedpan. He was smiling and filling a needle with what she assumed to be a very powerful looking clear liquid, meant to numb her or kill her.

"Yes . . . a *very* disturbed young woman. But I'm going to . . . take care of you," he sneered, plunging the needle painfully into her vein and releasing the drug. Seconds later, she blacked out.

Nyla was amped. It was finally going to happen. Nick had called and told her that Shan had agreed to a threesome. They were at the Renaissance Hotel in downtown Detroit. She was so excited that her pussy got wet. Nyla was finally going to get at Shan. She grabbed her little .32 automatic, tucked it in her clutch, and headed out the door.

As she drove she imagined the look Shan would have on her face when she stuck the .32 to her head. She would make the bitch beg for her life. No. She would make her get down on her knees and beg. But she wouldn't listen to her pleas. Nyla was intent on making her pay for what she had taken from her. She would make her suffer. She even thought about making her lick her pussy, but in the end, she would still die. In her mind, she was thinking like Pac:

I ain't a killa but don't push me

Revenge is the best thing next to getting pussy.

Nyla pulled into the underground parking lot of the hotel and parked. She checked her makeup in her mirror. This was her moment, and she wanted everything to be flawless. She checked the .32 once again, and it was loaded. She stuck it back into her purse and got out. As she rounded her trunk and headed for the door, a dark colored van skidded up in front of her. It almost hit her. Nyla jumped back, ready to spaz out but realized a second too late what was happening. The sliding door flew open and a masked figure stuck a double-barreled shotgun in her face.

"Get yo' ass in here!" the figure demanded, snatching her by the hair and pulling her inside the van before it skidded off.

The van rode not too far away and lurched to a stop. She couldn't see where they were because they had a bag over her head and the cold steel of the double barrel to her face. Nyla was scared shitless. She could see the inside light of the van come on through the fabric of the bag as the passenger door opened, and then closed. Someone had gotten in. She felt them brush past her as they climbed into the back. A moment later the bag was snatched off her head and she found herself face to face with a smiling . . . Shan.

"Surprise! Surprise!" Shan sang out sarcastically and the girl beside her chuckled. "Not the kind of three-way you had in mind, is it? Then again, you had other plans. I'm sure." Shan remarked holding the .32, then tossing it down on the van floor between them.

Nyla didn't hesitate. She lunged for the .32. If she was going to die she was determined to take Shan with her. But when she felt some steel at the back of her head and she hadn't even reached for her gun, common sense kicked in and she froze.

"Damn, Red, this bitch trained to go!" Courtney remarked.

"I told you," Shan replied, looking at Nyla and adding, "I told my girls you were a star. Just on the wrong team!"

Nyla glared at her. "You don't know shit about me, bitch."

"I could've just killed you, Nyla, so the least you can do is hear what I have to say," Shan reasoned.

"Ho, we ain't got shit to talk about!" Nyla spat.

Shan didn't reply. She just eyed Nyla evenly as Nyla glared evilly. "Leave us alone," Shan said.

Michelle looked at her. "You sure?"

Shan nodded. Michelle and Courtney got out. Shan never took her eyes off Nyla. The gun still lay between them. "So you want to kill me? You hate me that much? I don't hate you."

Nyla sat there seething.

"But why? I bet you never even asked yourself that, have you?" Shan questioned.

"*Why?* Bitch, you *fucked* my man, you *wrecked* my home, you *ruined* my marriage, and Forever is dead because of you!" Nyla ranted, and then snatched up the gun and aimed it at Shan.

Shan remained calm. "Forever chose to come after me, remember? Just like he chose to seduce me and not tell me about his lovely wife and beautiful daughter! Now you want to kill me for *his* choices? You kill me, my girls are going to kill you and who will be left to raise her?"

"Fuck the bullshit, Shan!" Nyla spat. "Leave my daughter out of this." But deep down, Nyla knew that Shan was right.

"Then pull the trigger, Nyla, and prove that you are the dumb bitch Forever played you to be! He played you just like niggas been playin' us since we started believing all of their bullshit! And what do we do? Hate and want to kill each other over a nigga worth neither of our time!" Shan spoke from the heart.

Nyla held the gun with both hands.

"Look at you, Nyla . . . you're a beautiful, certified bad bitch. But you can be the baddest bitch in the world and a nigga still gonna give us their ass to kiss. You know why? Because we'll kiss it! Kiss it, lick it, tongue it down just to be loved. But at the end of the day, no matter what we do, they ain't gonna love us back. Not like we deserve to be loved. And not like we love them. And you know this. So you need to do you."

Nyla wavered. "What the hell are you talking about?"

Shan looked her in the eyes. "Bad bitches don't beef with bad bitches. Only insecure bitches do that because they know that if we want a nigga we can take a nigga. But us bad bitches? Why do we gotta beef and war? There's too many tricks for us to ever bump heads," Shan concluded.

Nyla couldn't deny Shan's logic. And it was pissing her off. Men had been lying to her ever since she could remember. Even her mother warned her of the slickness of a man's tongue. But she had figured if she was pretty enough or sexy enough that would change everything. But the prettier she got, the more men lied, so what was the point?

"So I guess you wouldn't be mad if I told you I'd been fucking Briggen since he got out of jail? That I can still feel him in my pussy *right now?*" Nyla smirked.

Shan's first reaction was a red-hot rage. But then she heard her own words in her head and it only validated her point. Although it still hurt, it proved that Briggen wasn't shit.

"Truthfully, that shit is triflin', but it only makes my point. Yeah, I loved Briggen just like you loved Forever, but it's obvious neither one of them loved us or we wouldn't be here talking. I'd still be at that prison and Forever would still be your man," Shan reasoned.

Slowly Nyla lowered the gun. "Why didn't you just kill me? Why go through all of this?" Nyla questioned.

"I mean it when I say, 'because us bad bitches gotta stick together.'" Shan replied, hitting her with their motto.

Nyla chuckled. "I like that."

They shook hands. Nyla glanced at the gun. Now that her rage had disappeared she smiled, then looked at Shan.

"This gun ain't loaded, is it?"

"Hell no!" Shan snickered, adding, "I'm crazy, but I ain't that crazy!"

"Us bad bitches gotta stick together," they said in unison and then they both laughed.

"So where do we go from here?" Nyla questioned.

Shan winked. "Nick. He wants a threesome, right? Well, we gonna give him one he won't forget," Shan replied, and then called him. And soon as he answered, she said, "Nick . . . Baby, I'm sorry but I'm not gonna make it. Something came up . . . I can't speak on the phone. I'll see you back in New York . . . I love you too." She hung up with a giggle.

A few minutes later, Nyla's phone rang. "Nick," she said.

"Send him to voice mail," Shan told her.

On the other end Nick muttered, "Shit." He had the room to himself with nothing to do but to think and watch the champagne fizzle out. His first thoughts went to Shan and how he underestimated her. She was a thinker. Just like her brother, Peanut. She calculated his moves carefully and she carried out his instructions to the letter. *Impressive.* She was playing Briggen big time. Because of an ass whipping, she was bringing him to his knees. Hell, Nick was planning on bringing him to his knees for putting his hands on her. But she assured him that she had a plan and made him promise that he would back off and leave Briggen to her. The last time he checked, Briggen was playing Mr. Mom, his weight in the streets was way down, as well as his respect. Nick shuddered at the thought of being punked by a woman.

Now that Mook was gone it was time for plan B. Back in Oak Ridge, Mac started to put together the plan he and Mook had decided on. He reached out to Ray Ray, an old time hustler who served time in the Feds, because he was the only one he knew that could help lock down Oak Ridge. Mac already had the clientele, all he needed was workers.

"I been waitin' on you to holla at me, maine."

"Shit, you can come through now if you can be here by two." Ray Ray told him.

"Say no mo'," Mac replied, hanging up. Then he and Heather were on their way.

Mac drove his car while Heather drove the rental. She would mule the work back. He checked her in the rearview, smiling to himself. Heather was definitely a ride-or-die chick, down for whatever. He had hit the jackpot when he fell on her balcony. He didn't love her, but he loved her dedication.

He pulled up to Ray Ray's dog farm a little after 2 p.m.. He raised purebred pit bulls. Official bloodline. They were sold to the highest bidder for dogfights or for protection. When they arrived they were greeted by Ray Ray's cousin, Lenny.

He was a tall, slim, baby faced dude, clean shaven, and rocked a Mohawk. He gave Mac a pound when he got out of the car.

"Mac, right?" Lenny questioned.

"Yeah, yo."

"I'm Lenny, Ray Ray's cousin. Ride with me. He told me to bring you on down."

"Fo' sho'."

Mac and Heather jumped in Lenny's Cherokee with Lenny and drove down into the woods past several kennels. Pit bulls in cages watched attentively as they drove by. When they drove deeper into the woods, even with the air conditioner on and windows rolled up, the strong stench filled the air.

"What the fuck is that?" Mac asked, face twisted up.

Lenny chuckled. "Hogs. Ray Ray raise them too. That swine bring good money, they just smell like shit," Lenny explained.

Ray Ray was down in the pigpen wearing rubber boots and throwing buckets of slop into one trough for a group of hogs. He saw Mac and smiled.

"What up, folk? What's good?" Ray Ray greeted. "I would give you dap, but my hands fucked up."

"No problem," Mac replied with relief, looking at the slop all over Ray Ray's hands.

"One mo' group to feed, then we can handle business," Ray Ray told him.

He came out of the hog pen, and then the four of them walked toward one another. Ray Ray eyed Heather in her cut off shorts appraisingly. "Who li'l mama?"

"This my people, Heather."

"How you doin'?" she greeted with her Tennessee twang.

"Oh, you homegrown." Ray Ray chuckled.

Heather giggled. "Born and raised."

They reached the second pen. The hogs looked up eagerly. "Look at 'em. Greedy motherfuckas. Eat any goddamn thing . . . even you," Ray Ray cracked, looking at Mac and snickering.

"Muhfuckas won't eat me. That's why I don't eat swine now."

Ray Ray rested his arms on the pen. "So how much we talkin'?" he asked, getting down to business.

"Ten bricks for starters. I need to get my Tennessee team right. Oak Ridge wide open right now."

Ray Ray nodded. "I heard. A couple of my mans from the joint been tryin' to come through. You might know 'em. You know Shokkah?"

Mac shook his head. "No, maine, I never did a bid."

"Well, maybe you heard of my other man . . . dude held my cousin Lenny here down with a banger . . . cat name Dark."

As soon as Mac heard the name, he knew it was a setup. He tried to go for the gun on his waist, but Lenny put a gun to the back of his head.

"Whoa, maine, be easy," Lenny warned, taking Mac's pistol.

Slowly Mac raised his hands. "Yo, you got it. You got it."

Ray Ray pulled out a gun then stepped to Heather, patting her down and feeling her up at the same time. "You ain't packin' is you, li'l mama?"

"Only what my mama gave me," Heather shot back. Her survival mode kicked in, and she was determined not to go down with the ship.

Ray Ray smirked. "Then you good . . . for now."

He turned to Mac.

"Yo, Ray, man. Whateva the nigga payin' you, man, I'll pay you double!" Mac bargained, trying to sound like he wasn't scared, but he was shook on the inside.

"He ain't payin' me. I told you, he saved my cousin's life. I owe him, and this what he call payback. So it ain't business . . . it's personal," Ray Ray shrugged.

As soon as he finished speaking, Baby Boy stepped out from behind the pigpen with a grin on his face, holding a gun and a phone. He handed the phone to Mac. Mac took it, knowing exactly who it was.

"Yo, Dark. Maine, listen—"

"I'm gonna listen, nigga, listen to yo' bitch ass die!" Dark taunted. "You thought I was a joke? You thought you could play me? If it wasn't for Mook, you woulda been dead, and if Mook was alive, I'd kill his bitch ass too for vouchin' for you! Fuck nigga!"

Mac knew he was at the end of his rope, so he wasn't too proud to beg. "Dark, I know I fucked up. But please, man, gimme one mo' shot, maine. Please. I'ma be one hunned. Just one mo' shot!"

"You want one mo' shot? Put Baby Boy on the phone."

Mac handed the phone to Baby Boy.

"Yo the nigga want one mo' shot. Give it to him and after that, come back up here. I need you."

"Yep," Baby Boy replied. Then, without hesitation, he shot Mac twice in the stomach, once in the knee, and once in the shoulder. "Oh yeah, one mo' shot . . . like you asked," Baby Boy chuckled and shot him in the dick.

Moaning and gasping on the ground, Mac wondered why he was still breathing. It didn't take him long to find out. Ray Ray and Lenny picked him up and began to carry him into the pigpen. With every ounce of strength he had left, he managed to reach for the small pistol in his sock. He fired several shots, with his last one hitting Lenny right in the knee. Lenny yelled out in pain. Ray Ray began kicking him in the face.

"No, maine, please! Just kill me, please!" he pleaded, but all he received was sarcastic laughter as his answer.

"Nigga, man the fuck up!" Baby Boy barked. "You mighta lived like a coward, but you can still die like a man."

Mac was hearing none of it. He was too busy crying like a baby. "Please, I'm sorry! Oh God, please!" he sobbed.

Baby Boy and Ray Ray dropped him in the mud of the pigpen.

"I told you they'd eat anything." Ray Ray chuckled as he walked away.

Mac watched as the pigs closed in, hungry, slobbering, and snorting. He howled as the first pig bit him in the side, ripping out a huge chunk of bloody flesh.

"Nooo! Arrgghh!" he howled and screamed.

Dark could hear him because Baby Boy held out the phone. Mac screamed out in agony as the pigs tore his flesh apart. It was like a scene straight out of the movie *Silence of the Lambs*. Baby Boy shuddered as his body parts flew up in the air. He then put the phone to his ear.

"He done, big bruh. What you want me to do with his bitch?"

"I don't give a fuck. Just get yo' ass up here ASAP."

"Say no mo'," Baby Boy replied, then hung up.

He eyed Heather. She eyed him right back. The lust in his eyes told her he wouldn't kill her.

"I'm not his bitch," she said, never losing eye contact.

"I know you ain't," Baby Boy shot back. "He dead."

"Never was. I'm just tryin' to eat, like everybody else."

"So is them hogs," Lenny yelled out, ready to see her white flesh torn to bits.

She paid him no attention and looked at Baby Boy. "Trust. I'm a rider . . . long as you don't end up like him," Heather remarked.

"Shit, I ain't gonna never end up like him."

"Then you got a rider for life."

Baby Boy smiled. He liked the white girl's style.

"Where that nigga money?" Baby Boy probed.

"In the trunk."

Baby Boy turned to Ray Ray. "About them ten bricks that nigga wanted . . ."

Dr. Muhammad knew something was wrong as soon as he saw him. He looked like a regular janitor. He had the mop bucket, the cleaning supplies, the dirty overalls, and even the slow gait. The only thing he didn't have was the shoes to match. He was wearing brand-new Jordans.

No black janitor would wear his new Jordans to do janitorial work. But he kept it discreet. The man pushed the bucket straight down the hall, keeping his head down, avoiding eye contact. He kept walking until he got to Janay's room. That's when he stopped. Muhammad sped up his pace and approached the man quietly. By the time he entered the room the janitor was approaching Janay's bed and pulling a 9 millimeter equipped with a silencer from the small of his back.

Muhammad called out, "Excuse me!" buying himself a precious half second.

The janitor turned, spinning to his right, which Muhammad anticipated because he was carrying the gun in his right hand. The janitor fired, but Muhammad had already moved to his left. By the time the janitor tried to fire a second shot, Muhammad was on him. He grabbed the wrist holding the gun, then hit him with an elbow to his ribs hard enough to crack two of them. The janitor was knocked windless, his legs buckled under him. Muhammad used the same elbow to deliver a crushing blow to his jaw. The janitor crumbled at his feet, unconscious.

Hardly winded, Muhammad looked at Janay. He could tell she was heavily sedated. But behind the haze her eyes were alert. She had seen the whole thing.

She slowly closed her eyes and turned her head.

No more than a half hour later the hospital was up in arms. Nothing of that magnitude had ever happened like that before. An assassination attempt on a patient. Someone had leaked the news to the press so several reporters were trying to get access to the floor. The police knew someone had tried to kill Janay at the funeral, and now that there had been a second attempt, they were taking no chances. They assigned an officer to guard her room 24/7 and added extra uniforms downstairs. They also questioned Muhammad extensively and suspiciously.

"And after that, I called for security," Muhammad explained calmly for what seemed like the hundredth time.

Sherman nodded as he took notes. "Let me ask you something, Dr. Muhammad. You're ex-Special Forces and military intel. Is there something you're not telling me?"

Muhammad eyed him evenly. "I'm not following you, Detective."

Sherman smirked. "Oh, I think you're following me just fine. I'm asking is there anything I should know about Ms. Carter and the two attempts on her life. I just find it a helluva coincidence that an ex-Special Forces guy just *happened* to be around. So is there anything . . . militarily I should know?"

"Like you said, Detective, *ex*-military. I'm a doctor and a civilian. As for coincidence, believe what you want," Muhammad politely but firmly said, and then stood up. "Now is there anything else, Detective?"

"Yeah, actually there is. In order to get on the Psychiatric Ward you need clearance. Since the perp isn't an employee, any idea who could've gotten him clearance?"

"No," Muhammad lied. Because he had a very good idea who it was, and he intended to find out.

Dr. Bennett sat back watching the news in an agitated state of mind. *What the hell had gone wrong?* No reporter could get on the floor so details were sketchy and scarce. But one thing was for sure, the bitch was still alive. He clicked off the T.V. in disgust and sat back on the couch. His phone rang. He knew who it was. Dr. Bennett answered with a question. "What the hell happened?"

"You tell me," Wise replied. "I thought you said his clearance was official."

"It was!" Bennett said, raising his voice a little too high, then repeated, "It was" in a lower tone. "Your guy must've fucked up."

Wise chuckled. "We'll find out."

"Either way, I want the rest of my money."

"You'll get it," Wise assured him even though he had contemplated paying him back in lead bullets. But he reasoned that if the doctor turned up dead they'd link him to the hit and possibly back to him. Wise figured paying the white boy would be easier, and if anything happened, he could easily get to him later. That's how he had got at him from jump. Wise had heard about Janay's escape on the news. He heard about how she beat the doctor to sleep. So he got in touch with the doctor and offered him fifty grand to help him get at Janay if she ever got caught. The doctor agreed. Janay got caught. The rest is now history. Janay killed his cousin Melky, and now he was determined to return the deed.

"When?" Dr. Bennett asked.

"As agreed," Wise stated. "But find out what happened. I need to know."

Chapter Sixteen

Briggen's plan was unfolding perfectly. He had just gotten the call from Mo'Betta and a panic-stricken Shan.

"Oh my God, baby, I'm so scared! Please don't let them kill me!" Shan had cried into the phone.

It took all of Briggen's discipline not to laugh in her face. "Don't worry, baby, I'ma take care of this, okay? Just do as he say!"

"O-okay, baby, please hurry!"

He had stopped to get some chicken wings on the way. He ate them as he drove while contemplating how he'd soon be back on top. Shan would definitely want to fall back, but somehow he'd convince her to let him be her face, just like she was Nick's face. Once he got right, he'd handle both of their trifling asses.

He followed the GPS to the abandoned house on the West Side. The same house Mo' had gone to kill Sharia. Briggen got out with the hundred grand in a duffle bag. The same hundred grand he had been holding to re-up with Shan.

He came up on the porch and knocked.

"Put your hands up!" Mo' barked through the door.

Just like they planned.

Briggen put his hands up, and Mo'Betta opened the door. Briggen stepped in. Mo' closed the door behind him and took the bag. He patted Briggen down. He was unarmed.

Just like they had planned.

"It better be all here!" Mo' hissed, his gun pointed at Briggen's face.

"It is, maine. Every dime," Briggen replied, feeling like he was in a movie acting out a scene.

Just like they had planned.

"Briggen!" Shan cried out.

He saw her in the chair and rushed over to her. "Are you okay, baby? That nigga didn't hurt you, did he?"

"No," she sobbed, throwing her arms around him and giving him a passionate kiss as she stood up. "But you did."

"What?"

Shan smiled. The crocodile tears seemed to dry instantly. "The Italians call that the kiss of death," she remarked.

Then a shot rang out and his right calf began to burn as the bullet ripped through it.

They hadn't planned for this! But Shan had and it was her movie now.

"Arrgghh, what the fuck?!" Briggen cursed. He looked back at Mo'Betta only to find two more chicks step out of the shadows. Both armed and aiming at him.

Shan stood over him, looking down at the man she once loved, married, had kids with and would've died for. She knew she would always love him but that love could fit inside a memory.

"Nothin' beats a cross but a double cross, huh, Brig?" Shan said.

"What the hell are you talkin' about? They kidnapped you!"

"*You* kidnapped me!" she fired back. "My own fuckin' husband! The father of my children! So at least be a man and admit it!"

Briggen dropped his head. After seeing the tears form in her eyes, he couldn't help but be ashamed. "You're right, ma . . . it was me. I set it up. I . . . I just felt like you were in over your head, and I wanted things back the way they used to be. I'm sorry," Briggen explained.

Shan looked at him, wiped away her tears with the base of her thumb, and replied, "I forgive you, Calvin . . . but I can't forget."

With that, she started for the door. In that moment, Briggen realized a lot more was at stake than just his marriage. "Shan! Where you going? What's up? I said I was sorry!"

She stopped at the door and looked back. "I could never trust you again, Briggen. What if this nigga would've killed me? You could put me in that kind of danger¿ The mother of your children¿ No, Brig . . . In that case, I'm sorry too." The tears streamed down her cheeks.

Shan walked out the door with Michelle consoling her.

"Shan! Shan . . . Shaaannn!" Briggen called out as the two killers closed in.

"Shan gone, nigga. This for Redbone." Mo' snickered and shot him in the stomach.

Briggen crumbled but spat, "Fuck . . . you, nigga."

Mo' laughed. "Oh, before you go . . . somebody want to say good-bye."

Mo' dragged Briggen over to the refrigerator and opened it. It was like opening a crypt. The stench was so overwhelming Courtney puked.

"Goddamn!" she cursed, running for the door. She needed some fresh air.

Mo'Betta snatched Briggen up by the collar and brought him face-to-face with Sharia's corpse. He looked into her rotting eye sockets and at her final expression. He would die looking at the expression that seemed to mock him. Even in death Sharia would get her own form of payback.

Sitting in the car, Shan heard the series of shots that she knew had ended Briggen's life. But she was all cried out. She had shed her last tear for any man. She would miss Briggen, but the man she missed had long been a memory. The streets tore them apart. The man who just died, she had loved with all her heart and soul but he acted as if he didn't know it.

The kids. Her body froze. *What have I done¿* Oh, God, no. She hadn't even considered her children until she thought about Briggen taking his last breath. She started to run back inside, but it was too late. Mo'Betta came out holding the bag of money. The deed was done.

Baby Boy had never fucked a white girl before, but now he knew what all the fuss was about. They were fucking freaks! Heather could take dick anywhere. In her mouth, in her pussy, in her ass, and give it back like a pro. She screamed and squealed like she was straight out of her very own porn flick.

Baby Boy had her facedown ass up in the hotel room while she held her ass cheeks open, looking over her shoulder with that *fuck me* look. He slid his dick in and out of her tight puckered asshole.

"Ooh, that dick feels so good! Fuck yo' ass, Baby Boy, gimme all that dick," she cooed.

He grabbed her ponytail, pulling her head back and started slapping her ass while he fucked her. "You a nasty bitch, ain't you? You love this big, black, dick, don't you?"

"Oh yes, daddy, yes! I'm a nasty white bitch!"

He smacked her ass until it was beet red. She backed that ass up like a wild stallion, which only made her come harder and Baby Boy could hold it no longer. He came deep in her ass, pulled out, and then lay down to catch his breath.

Heather got up, came back with a wet rag, and washed his dick. She was ready to slide it in her mouth before he said, "Whoa, li'l mama! Goddamn! Let a nigga get a breather."

She giggled, lying down beside him. "Then don't fuck me so good and have me horny for more."

Heather could tell Baby Boy was more of a street nigga than Mac or Mook, so she decided to play her cards right, figuring it would lock her in with him and prove that she could be loyal.

"I wanna tell you something," she began.

"What?"

She leaned up on her elbow and looked him in the eyes. "Don't trust Dark. He ain't who you think he is."

Baby Boy looked at her frowned up. "What you mean?"

"He sent Mac to kill you. You got locked up, didn't you? Whateva you did to get locked up, Dark told Mac and exposed his hand. I don't know what that means, but I'm sure you do. So I gotta be telling you the truth, or else how would I know?" she reasoned.

Baby Boy couldn't deny it, but he couldn't believe it either. He had begun to look up to Dark almost like a big brother. So to hear he was marked for death made his rage twice as deadly.

"Mac told me. He told me everything. He told me that he and Mook were planning on breaking off from Dark, but when Mook got killed, Mac decided to move on his own. I'm not lying, Baby Boy. I like you, and I want you to know I got your back," Heather explained, spilling her guts and stroking his ego and his dick at the same time.

Baby Boy shook his head. There was no loyalty in the game, but that was cool with him. He would show them he could get cold too.

"Soooo . . . can I get some more dick now?" Heather smiled, his hard dick growing harder in her hand.

He grabbed a handful of her hair and guided her wet, waiting mouth back where it belonged.

"Good morning, Doctor Bennett and Nurse Rice," Muhammad greeted as he entered the break room.

They both returned his greeting, then Nurse Rice walked out. While Dr. Bennett fixed his coffee, Muhammad locked the door. Dr. Bennett heard it lock and looked around.

"Doctor Muhammad, what—"

Muhammad walked up on Bennett and towered over him. Bennett was five feet nine and barely one eighty while Muhammad was 6-feet four and a solid two ninety. The look on his face read—dead serious.

"Who are you working for?" Muhammad seethed.

"I have no idea—" was all he got out before Muhammad gripped him around the throat and pinned him against the wall. Bennett tried to dash the hot coffee on him, but Muhammad grabbed his elbow at a pressure point and the cup fell from his hand.

"Arrgghh!" Bennett howled as Muhammad kept the pressure on his elbow and throat.

"Listen, cracka, I don't like racist muhfuckas. I'm ex-Special Forces, and I'm pissed the fuck off! You could not be in a worse situation! Now tell me who you are working for or I will break your goddamn neck!" Muhammad hissed.

Bennett's mind screamed, "Tell him! This nigga is crazy!" So he listened to his mind.

"I-I don't know his name! He-he approached me. I swear to God! I don't know who he is!" Bennett blabbed.

Muhammad released him. He knew if he turned Bennett over to the police the people behind the hit attempt would disappear. He didn't want that to happen. He wanted to know who was trying to kill Janay. He had looked her up and read all about her. His heart went out to the sister and her devastating losses. But looking at her and recalling the day he heard her cry out made him want to protect her. And now he had to protect her because he had failed before.

He looked into Bennett's face watching as the color slowly returned to it. "I won't turn you in on one condition. You make me the doctor of record for her," Muhammad demanded.

Bennett hurriedly agreed. "I-I'll do it today."

"You'll do it now, and if you or anyone else comes anywhere near her, I'll kill you, Bennett, and I'll enjoy every minute of it. Are we clear?" Muhammad hissed.

"Yes, yes—we're clear."

"Now do it."

Bennett rushed from the room to carry out his orders.

Forty-five minutes later Dr. Muhammad walked into Janay's room with her chart. The officer was in the room and Janay was sitting up in the bed, arguing with him. She was still strapped to the bed by her ankles.

"I don't care who said it. I don't need fuckin' police protection!" Janay barked.

"I'm sorry, Miss Carter, that's not up to you or me," the officer explained calmly. "I'm just doing my job."

"Well, go do it somewhere else!"

"What's the problem?" Muhammad asked Janay.

"Who are you?" she questioned, looking him up and down with disgust. *With your Morris Chestnut looking ass.*

Muhammad suppressed a smirk. He liked her sass. "Your doctor, ah, Dr. Akbar Muhammad."

"What happened to the other doctor?" she asked suspiciously.

"He's no longer assigned to you."

"Well, somebody needs to tell the police that I don't need protection. It's contributing to my stress levels."

"But, Miss Carter, there have been two attempts on your life. One right in this hospital. The hospital and the police are worried about a third one," Muhammad explained.

Janay didn't say anything, but he could tell she had been too sedated to fully comprehend or recall what had happened.

"Regardless, I don't need protection. In fact, I don't need to be in this hospital. So if—" Muhammad cut her off politely but firmly. "Miss Carter, a lot has happened, but I will do what I can to clear this up. Officer, your services are no longer needed."

"But I'm—"

"No! I'm her doctor, and if your presence is stressing my patient, then I have the final say," Muhammad said authoritatively, but winked at the officer, adding, "I will talk to the hospital."

The officer, catching on, nodded. "Just as long as my ass is covered."

"It is," Muhammad assured him, and the officer walked out. Muhammad turned to Janay. "And as for you, whether or not you belong in the hospital is up to me. Cooperate and I can make an informed assessment. If you don't, I can't until you do."

He nodded curtly and walked out. Dr. Muhammad went out into the hall and he approached the officer. "Listen, do not let her see you. No matter what, stay out here. I know you have a job to do, but so do I. Let's work together and both of our jobs will be easier, okay?" Muhammad proposed.

"No problem."

Muhammad started to walk away.

"Excuse me. I heard you were a S.E.A.L.," the officer remarked.

"Yes sir. Third Tactical Unit, First lieutenant."

"Me too. I was First lieutenant as well. Pleasure to work with you, Sir." The officer saluted.

Muhammad smiled and returned the salute.

When Janay woke up, Muhammad was sitting in the chair near her bed reading a book. "What are you doing here?" she asked, feeling vulnerable because a stranger was watching her sleep.

"Well, you didn't want police protection, so I have to watch you."

"Don't you have other patients?"

"I did, but they died." Muhammad shrugged. "Hopefully I'll have better luck with you."

Janay chuckled in spite of herself. "That wasn't funny."

"I can't tell." Muhammad smirked. "So . . . are you ready to talk?"

"No, I'm not," she replied with a challenging tone, letting him know it would take more than a laugh to get her to open up.

"Okay," he said, returning to his book.

She expected more of a resistance. His nonchalantness threw her off. Still, his presence was comforting and she drifted back to sleep.

"You saved my life," Janay told him when she awoke an hour later.

After sleeping off the last of the heavy sedatives her head began to clear and she began to remember. She remembered the soothing voice just on the other side of her cries and she recognized it as Muhammad's. Then she remembered seeing the two men struggling by her bed, and one of the other men slumping to the ground. The man that looked into her eyes was Muhammad.

He put down his book and nodded, maintaining eye contact.

"Thank you," she added.

"You're welcome. Do you . . . can you remember the other man's face? Have you ever seen him before?"

Janay shook her head. "No."

"No, you don't know him, or no, you won't tell me?"

Janay mustered a slight smile. "No. I don't know him."

"Do you know who tried to kill you?"

"No," she replied.

It was his turn to smile. "Whenever you lie, think about the truth and never divert your gaze," he schooled her. "But I understand. You look like a woman that wants to handle her own affairs. But everybody needs somebody sometime."

She didn't respond.

"Miss Carter, I cannot release you unless you give me something. Convince me. And if you lie to me, do a better job," he said.

"You can't keep me indefinitely," she shot back. But there was a tinge of uncertainty in her tone.

"If you're a threat to yourself or others, yes, we can get a court to commit you to our care."

She rolled her eyes and looked away.

"But I wouldn't do that to you. I just need you to give me something," Muhammad remarked.

He waited a few moments. "Now . . . do you know why you're here?"

She slowly looked at him, and then nodded.

"Can you tell me why?"

"They killed . . . my son."

It was a start.

Chapter Seventeen

The Fairlane Town Center in Dearborn, Michigan, was flooded with people. Every station in town was talking about it. The *American Idol* tryouts had come to Detroit. Everybody and their momma who even *thought* they could sing had come out looking for that chance to become a star. Quandra was one of those people.

"Ohhh, girl, I'm so happy for you!" Quita gushed. She loved her little sister to death. But she had often worried about her. All she did was go to school, watch T.V. and suck her thumb. At one time she thought Quandra may have been mildly retarded, but she wasn't. She was just a star waiting to happen.

"Aren't you nervous?" Quita asked.

"No," was Quandra's simple reply. She didn't even take her thumb out of her mouth.

"Say hi to J-Lo for me," Quita requested.

When Quandra's number was called the whole host of hood rats Quita brought erupted with cheers.

"Go get 'em, girl!"

"Quandra, do your thang!"

"We love you, li'l sis!"

Quandra entered the audition area in the middle of the mall and walked straight to the small mock stage and looked into the faces of Jennifer Lopez, Keith Urban, and Harry Connick, Jr.

"Awww, she is absolutely adorable," J-Lo cooed. "What's your name, sweetie?"

"Quandra," she answered, thumb still in her mouth.

"Speak up, sweetie, and take your thumb out of your mouth," Harry advised her.

Quandra shook her head. J-Lo chuckled. "Are you nervous?"

"No. I'm going to win," Quandra answered, as if what she said was already a fact.

"How are you going to do that with your thumb in your mouth?" Keith Urban asked her.

Quandra cracked a smile. As soon as she slid her thumb out of her mouth, she blew the first note of the Jackson Five's "Who's Loving You." The wail she created with just those words might as well have spelled win because that's what she did to the hearts of the three judges and the millions of Americans watching. By the time she whined, warbled, and blew through the words, *I had you*, J-Lo was in tears, Harry was in awe, and Keith was on his feet.

"Please-please!" Keith called out, resting his hand on the desk for balance. "Sweetie, if you sing any more I may just . . . explode! *My God!* I don't *need* to hear anymore! You're going to Hollywood!"

"What just happened?" Harry asked.

"Oh my God! Hollywood? Baby, you're going to heaven!" J-Lo squealed.

Quandra put her thumb back in her mouth and walked off the stage. She already knew what the other two judges would say.

"Now *that's* confidence," Keith remarked.

When Quandra emerged from the audition area and approached Ryan Seacrest, Quita, and the Hood Rat cheerleaders, (Dena, Holly, and Talaya) she pulled her thumb out of her mouth long enough to say, "We goin' to Hollywood!"

Quita and company started screaming and jumping around like they had won the lottery. She hugged and kissed Quandra, tears streaming down her face.

"Oh my God, I can't believe it! I can't believe it!"

They were celebrating so much she didn't even hear her phone ringing. Baby Boy had called three times before she heard it ring. "Hello!"

"Fuck you mean hello? Fuck is you doin'?"

"She won! Baby, she won! Quandra won!"

Baby Boy smiled. Even though he was in war mode, Quandra was like a little sister to him, so he took a moment to share in her happiness.

"Yeah, yo, *that's* what's up. But I told you to be on point! I'm in the parking lot! I told you shit is serious!"

"Okay!"

"Bring yo' ass on, Quita!"

"I said okay!" she huffed, hung up and added, "Mannish ass!"

Quita, Quandra, and the entourage came out to where Baby Boy told her he was parked. As soon as Quita saw Heather in the passenger seat of the rental she turned to Baby Boy and asked, "Baby Boy, who this white bitch, and what is she doin' in my seat?"

Baby Boy looked at Heather. "Get in the back," he instructed her, which Heather did with no hesitation because she knew her position.

Baby Boy turned back to Quita, walking her a few feet away out of earshot of everyone.

"Yo, Quita, I know you still be fuckin' with Dark, so don't lie to me." Baby Boy wanted to hear her say it.

"Sometimes," Quita admitted sheepishly, quickly adding, "But only when you be gone and I be lonely."

Baby Boy dismissed her excuse. He already knew Quita's problem. He was more hot with Dark. *How could he be still fucking Quita?* It only confirmed what Heather told him. *The nigga couldn't be trusted.*

"A'iight, look, call that nigga tonight. Tell him you lonely, and—"

"No, Baby Boy, I wanna be wit' you tonight." She pouted. "You can bring the white girl. I don't care."

"Naw, it ain't that. I just want you to get the nigga over there," Baby Boy explained, giving her that look she understood so well.

Realization blossomed in her eyes. "Oooh, okay, no problem." She shrugged. "When?"

"I'll call you. Just be on point, Quita. I ain't playin'!"

"I will. I promise. I love you! We goin' to Hollywood!" she sang.

"I love you too, baby girl, and we already in Hollywood. You my star!"

Quita was the one person who could do no wrong in his eyes. It was fucked up that she would still fuck Dark, but sometimes you can give a person everything, and still, they will never change.

Shan took Mo'Betta to Ruth's Chris Steak House out in Sommerset to meet Born. When they arrived he was already seated facing the door. As they approached she could see in his approving smile that her entrance had the desired effect. She was wearing a tan Louis Vuitton suit, business but sensual.

When she reached the table, Born rose like a gentleman to pull out her chair and greet her with a kiss on the cheek. He was wearing Creed, a scent she didn't really care for, but it smelled delicious on him. Before they sat, she introduced the men.

"Born, this is Mo'Betta. Mo', this is Born."

They gave each other dap, sizing each other up casually, and then they all sat down.

"Yo, I heard about Briggen. I'm sorry to hear about that," Born remarked, offering his condolences.

"He'll be missed," Shan replied.

Born could tell Shan was far from in mourning, so it wasn't hard to put two and two together. *It's a dirty game* he thought.

"Actually, that's what I wanted to talk to you about. Briggen's spot on The Consortium," Shan said.

"What about it?"

"I want to sponsor Mo'Betta to fill it," Shan answered, getting right to the point.

"I see you don't waste time," Born remarked, looking Shan in the eyes to make sure she got his point.

She returned his gaze letting him know she did. "Life's too short. My motto is carpe diem. I'm thinkin' about getting it as a tattoo."

"Seize the day," he said, translating the Latin. He turned to Mo'. "So, you're Mo'Betta, huh? I heard a lot about you . . . not all good." Born was straight-up.

"Everybody's got haters. If you don't, you ain't doing something right," Mo' shot back cockily.

"Naw, yo, I don't listen to haters. My circle consists of Gods and wise men, so when they speak, I listen. So I'ma ask you . . . one time . . . Where is Wise? And what's your beef with Janay?" Born questioned calmly, but there was no mistaking his tone.

Neither Mo'Betta nor Shan knew Born had a car full of shooters in the parking lot, waiting for the signal to light Mo's ass up as soon as he stepped foot out the door.

Mo'Betta frowned up. "Yo, maine, I don't know what you talkin' about, and I definitely don't like the way you're bringin' it to me."

"Your man Tech got killed, right? He got killed at Crystal's wake, right? I already know he was one of your goons so don't play with my intelligence. I walked in the door neutral. Don't make me walk out and pick a side," Born warned.

The two men eye-danced intensely, neither wanting to back down. Both young and wild, so their egos and testosterone levels were heavily permeating the air.

Shan had no idea what was going on. She was extremely nervous but did a good job of concealing it. She turned to Mo'Betta and said, "This ain't about pride. It's about money. Answer the question."

He looked at her. He hated for a woman to tell him what to do, but he knew he needed her so he relented. "Like I said, I don't know any Wise. But at the wake . . . the nigga Dark had my cousin Rob killed, so I came for him. This Janay broad, I don't know her either," Mo'Betta explained.

Born nodded, understanding what had happened. Wise and Mo' had just picked the same time to hit Janay and Dark. Just like that, Mo's life had been spared, and he didn't even know it.

"Well . . . you know Dark is on The Consortium too," Born remarked even though technically he wasn't. "And we don't allow beef between members. That's the purpose of The Consortium. And like Red just said, it's about money . . . not pride. If your cousin was in the game, then he already knew what he signed up for. This game plays for keeps," Born jeweled Mo'Betta.

Mo' nodded. "Fo' sho'."

"So you think you ready for the big leagues?" Born challenged.

"The question is, is the big leagues ready for me?" Mo' shot back arrogantly.

Born smirked. "We'll see," he answered, then turned to Shan. "Red, you know we have to have Mo'Betta checked out, and then we can put it to the vote. As for me, I don't have a problem with him comin' in as long as he plays by the rules."

"Believe me, he will," Shan replied.

"Yo, Red, just like you, I can speak for myself," Mo' informed Shan, looking Born in the eye. "I can respect the rules but ain't no nigga gonna play me."

Born nodded, and they all stood up. Born gave Red a parting kiss on the cheek.

"I'm not a fan of Creed, but it smells good on you," she flirted.

"It'll smell better on you," he winked, making her giggle at the hint.

As she walked away Born asked, "Where were you thinkin' about getting that tattoo?"

She smiled over her shoulder. "It's more fun if you guess."

Once they were outside, her whole demeanor changed and she spazzed out on Mo'Betta.

"Mo', what the fuck was he talking about? And why didn't you tell me you had beef with Dark?"

"That ain't have nothin' to do wit' you," Mo'Betta answered.

Shan stopped and tried to get in his face, but he was much taller than her. "No! *You* got it twisted! *You* work for *me!* My beef is yours, not the other way around! Never let me walk into a situation with my eyes wide shut behind your bullshit again! Are we clear?"

Mo'Betta had never come so close to smacking the shit out of Shan. She sensed it and stepped in even closer, taunting him. Her eyes daring him.

"I asked . . . Are. We. Clear?"

Mo'Betta told himself the time would come when he would put Shan in her place and enjoy every minute of it. It was that thought that helped him smile and reply, "Crystal."

"Then we understand each other. Call me and I'll have that ready for you," she said heading to her car chirping her alarm.

She called Nyla. "So are we a go?" Shan asked.

"Of course. The nigga ran wit' it. He'll never see it coming," Nyla snickered.

"People never see the obvious until it's too late," Shan remarked. The two coconspirators shared a laugh.

Dark sat outside Lisha's crib like he had been doing a lot lately. It was the only way he could get a glimpse of his son. He would watch him play basketball in the driveway until it got dark. He wanted to tell him to work on his wrist strength and not try to be fancy. Get the basics down pat first. He wanted to play one-on-one with him, hear him laugh and call him daddy. Watching his son away from the craziness of the streets was beginning to change Dark's perspective on priorities. He wasn't ready to leave the game, but he was ready to take a step in that direction.

Lisha pulled up in the driveway like she did at 4:15p.m. every day. Dark got out of the car carrying a duffle bag.

"Hey, Ma! Watch this!" Damian called out as he shot a three-pointer and made it.

"Hey, Lisha!"

The voice startled Lisha because she knew who it was. Picking up on his mother's apprehension, Damian sprinted to his mother's side as if unaware of his inability to protect her. Dark smiled proudly at his attempt to protect his mother.

"Damian, go in the house," Lisha told him.

"Ma, who is that?"

"Damian! What I say?"

Damian looked at Dark. In the back of his mind, Dark could tell Damian was forming an idea of who he was. Reluctantly, he did what his mother said. When he was gone Lisha spat, "Jerome, I know you didn't follow me!"

"Not today," Dark replied. "I . . . umm . . . I've known where you live for a while."

"What do you want, Jerome?" she asked, crossing her arms across her chest defensively but willing to hear him out.

"Yo . . . I'm just . . . I wanted to see my shorty."

"Well, you've seen him, so—"

"It ain't right what you doin', Lisha. A man has a right to see his child," Dark reminded her.

"Not if it's going to put the child in harm's way. What if Damian would've been with you when you got shot? What if someone would've been following you when you were following me? Then what? Y'all niggas always talkin' about your rights, but what about your *duties?*" Lisha asked him.

Dark could only drop his head.

"Yo . . . I ain't come to argue. I came to say . . . I was thinkin' about coppin' this brand-new Benz S550. I was gonna sit that bitch on 22's and shit."

"Whoop-de-fuckin'-do," Lisha remarked sarcastically.

"But I thought my shorty's future was more important," he remarked, tossing the duffle bag at her feet. "It's two hundred grand. It's the least I could do."

Lisha looked at the bag in amazement.

"I ain't perfect, Lisha, but, goddamn, neither are you. You can change but I can't? You talk about duty, but you ain't even tryin' to give a nigga a chance! This shit work both ways," Dark spat, then began to walk away. He turned and added, "And tell D to work on his wrist strength. It'll help with his jumper!"

Dark got in the car leaving Lisha with her jaw dropped.

As he pulled away his phone rang. He checked the caller ID. It was Quita. "Yo."

"I wanna fuck."

Dark smirked. He loved the way Quita got straight to the point. Besides, he had stress he needed to work off, and her tight, wet asshole was just the remedy.

"So fuck."

"I wanna fuck you. I love the way that phat dick fill this asshole, mmm," Quita cooed, and released a seductive moan.

Dark was getting hard just listening. "I'm sayin' . . . where you at?"

"Home," she moaned like she was about to come.

"Gimme like twenty minutes."

"Oh, daddy, hurry. This ass on fire," Quita sang.

"Just keep it hot, li'l mama, I'm comin'," he chuckled, then hung up. "Freak!"

Baby Boy was definitely ready to move on Dark, but he wasn't sleeping on him either. He knew the dude was no joke, so he wasn't taking any chances. He got at the one dude he knew wanted Dark even worse than he did. Mo'Betta.

They were both from the West Side and knew of each other although they had done little more than acknowledge each other in passing. But Baby Boy was known for his hammer game, and Mo'Betta was known for getting that gwap. It was only a matter of time before their paths crossed, whether in beef or collaboration. Dark gave them a reason to collaborate.

Baby Boy knew Mo'Betta had been behind the shootout at Crystal's funeral. Mo's shooter that got killed was from Baby Boy's projects, and he knew the kid worked for Mo'. Now it was time to put that knowledge to work. Baby Boy reached out to Mo'Betta, and Mo' agreed to meet.

"So the bait already set?" Mo' asked as they stood, both leaning on the driver's side door of their cars.

"Indeed. My people should be callin' the nigga as we speak," Baby Boy assured him.

Mo'Betta nodded. He knew Baby Boy was a soldier, but still he wondered, so he asked, "Why you givin' me this nigga head on a platter?"

Baby Boy spat, "Fuck that nigga, maine! He tried to leave me for dead down in Oak Ridge. But he don't know I know. Now it's time to serve justice."

Once Mo'Betta heard the words *Oak Ridge* he knew Baby Boy was telling the truth.

"True, indeed. I feel the same goddamn way. But what up, though? What you tryin' to do after this?"

"Shit, it's whateva wit' me. I got a little somethin' bubblin' outta town. Why, what's good?" Baby Boy wanted to know. Mo'Betta had piqued his curiosity.

Mo' smirked. "Trust me. With Dark outta the way, I'ma be the man to see in the 'D', and I'ma need some strong soldiers, especially when I get on with The Consortium."

"That's all good, homie. But from here on out, a nigga's soldierin' days is over," Baby Boy announced proudly. "I'm promotin' myself and pledging my allegiance to Born."

"I respect that, homie. Well then, let's say both hands wash the face."

"Say no mo'."

They dapped. Baby Boy's phone rang. "Yeah."

"He on his way, baby."

"Cool." He hung up. "It's a go," Baby Boy told Mo'. They moved out to get in position.

Dark pulled up to Quita's apartment building. He got out keeping his eyes peeled and hand close to his waist. As he crossed the street he heard, "Big bruh!"

He turned quickly and saw Baby Boy approaching. His guilt momentarily blinded him to the coincidence. When Baby Boy caught up with him he gave Dark a gangsta hug.

"What up, li'l bruh? I was comin' to check if you was back!"

"Fo' sho'. I tried to call you, but you ain't answer," Baby Boy replied.

"Shit been hectic, maine. A lot of shit on my mind."

"Yeah? Me too," Baby Boy spat pulling out his pistol and aiming at Dark.

Dark's reflexes were on point. He knew he didn't have enough time to pull his pistol, so he opted to slap Baby Boy's gun away, then pull out his piece. Baby Boy watched with anxiety as the pistol flew from his hand and Dark caught him with an elbow that brought blood from his nose.

"Bitch-ass nigga! You thought you could play wit' me?" Dark laughed at him.

"Oh, so you think shit is funny? Yo, my niggas!" Baby Boy called out. As soon as he did, Mo' and his two shooters crept out of their positions in the shadows and ran down on Dark from two directions. By the time Dark had realized what he walked into, he felt twin burners to both his temples that froze him in place.

"Sneeze, nigga!" Mo'Betta dared him, taking Dark's gun off his waist.

Baby Boy jumped up and punched Dark dead in his face, staggering him. He then followed up with a barrage of punches that dropped him to the ground. The four men collectively stomped the so-called King of the Streets onto the street, releasing the pent-up rage they all felt, for different reasons. While Dark lay unconscious, a van appeared, and they scooped him up, and then dumped him inside.

Nick was finally about to see his fantasy come true. Tiny and Shan in a ménage à trois.

He was amped. He had even taken some Ecstasy and Viagra. Not that he really felt like he needed it, but he wanted to make sure he enjoyed every minute of the threesome.

He had had ménages before, but not with two bad broads. He felt like he had talked them into it. It just proved the strength of his game.

Nyla was feeling Shan. She had opened her eyes to true game. Too many women let men manipulate their minds, and when the shit hit the fan, instead of getting mad at the man, they take it out on the female. It didn't make any sense, and Nyla appreciated Shan for pointing that out. It still hurt to have lost Forever, but he had made the decisions Nyla had mistakenly held Shan responsible, when the truth was, his death was only the consequences of his own actions.

But now they were about to run the scam on Nick. The plan was, they would get him all aroused while getting their drink on. But his drink would contain something extra to put him to sleep. Then they would film him having sex with two men and blackmail him for the money.

"Ohhh, girl, you are fuckin' cruel!" Nyla snickered when Shan broke it down.

"He said he wanted a ménage, right?" Shan laughed.

Courtney and Michelle wired the place up, placing black boxes along the walls in almost every room.

"Cameras," Nyla squealed. She figured they could make a fortune. She didn't want to do Nick like this, but the motto was, 'us bad bitches gotta stick together.'

When Nick knocked at Nyla's door, she answered it wearing only a thong and a sheer nightie. The Viagra and Ecstasy that he popped sprang into action immediately. He closed the door behind him and snatched Nyla's little ass up. She giggled and hit him.

"Calm down, big daddy, you act like this is your first rodeo," she said.

"Shit, you wish. If it was a league for this shit, I would be MVP. Believe that." Nick was really feeling himself.

"Awww, talk that shit', big daddy."

He was amped. He couldn't wait and immediately called Shan.

"Don't worry, baby, I'm on my way," she told him. "Put Nyla on the phone."

Nick frowned. "Who's Nyla?"

Hearing her real name, Nyla frowned too. Nick extended the phone. She took it.

"Sorry, girl, but . . . uhh . . . we had to make it look like an accident. *People never see the obvious until it's too late.*"

"An acci—" Nyla started to say, and then it hit her like a ton of bricks. The black boxes. *Cameras,* they had said when she asked.

Nyla frowned when she recalled Shan saying those same words before. *This bitch set me up. Once a snake always a snake.*

In actuality, Shan was just down the street sitting in a parked car with Courtney and Michelle. Shan lifted the remote control and extended the antenna. She hit the switch and Nyla's whole house went up in a big fiery *boom!* The series of explosives detonated room by room. Each explosion building on the last until the house and half of the house on either side were burning down.

"Technology is a mother," Shan said, because with one press of a button she was now the number-one boss bitch in the 'D'.

"Yes, Steve, authorities are being very tight-lipped about the explosion that rocked this community a few hours ago. They have drawn the interest of federal forensics," the Latino reporter said, standing in front of the smoldering remains of Nyla's small English brick home. "A source close to the investigation did say that there's a possibility a terrorist cell had shielded themselves in Detroit and somehow their explosives had mistakenly detonated. Also, we do know that two people were discovered inside the house. My sources confirmed that one of the victims was reputed drug kingpin Nicholas Powell. No word yet on who the other person was. Terrorist *and* drugs? Drugs? Yes. But terrorist in Detroit? Stay tuned for more details."

Janay watched the news from her hospital bed. She knew by the surrounding houses that that was her cousin Nyla's house. But why didn't they mention her name? Did that mean she was alive? What about Tameerah? Was that even her in the house with Nick? She could only speculate, but what she did know was who was behind the whole thing. She smiled. It had been a perfect plan, one she should've seen long ago.

"Janay."

Hearing the soothing voice brought her out of her zone as it always did. She looked into the face of the man she was slowly becoming very comfortable with.

"You look as if you knew those people," Muhammad remarked.

She nodded.

"Are you going to be all right?" he asked, taking her hand.

"Am I?" she replied, giving his hand a squeeze.

He smiled. "Yes . . . I think you will be."

The ropes were so tight they had cut off the circulation in his hands and feet. He couldn't feel them at all. If he didn't know better he'd think they had cut them off. After everything else they had done to him, being numb was a welcomed blessing. His face was swollen from the beating, and he slumped in the chair they had tied him to. He knew he would die. They wouldn't be dumb enough to let him go, but he still prided himself on taking it like a G.

Soon he heard footsteps coming down the stairs and realized he had lost track of time. How long had he been there? Hours? Days? Weeks? It didn't matter because he knew it was over. In fact, he welcomed it.

When he saw the man approach it all made sense.

"You!" he grunted, hating to acknowledge he had lost.

The man chuckled. "Surprised? Not surprised? I gotta admit, I still can't read you. But I won, and that's all that matters, huh?" the man gloated.

"Nigga, suck my dick. Do what you came to do. Get this shit over with because I got some bad bitches in hell waiting for me," he spat.

"In due time, my nigga, I wanna savor this moment," the man answered, walking around him, circling him like predators do to wounded prey. "You know it's over, right? The Consortium is done. Now I run this show . . . solo. Briggen's dead. Nick's dead. Now you."

The man stopped in front of him and looked him in the eyes. Despite the beating he still had that fire in his eyes.

"You wanna know how I did it, don't you?"

"Fuck you," Dark spat.

"Well, I'ma tell you anyway, cause the shit is just so fuckin' gangsta you gonna love it! See, you thought you were workin' for Sherman the whole time, but you were really workin' for me!" He laughed. "And the best part was The List. Even Sherman thought it was real. He thought it was a list of motherfuckas that could blackmail him, but it was really a hit list I made up so Sherman would clear the streets for me. Self-preservation is the first law of nature. Make a man think it's in his self-interest and he'll do whateva you say!"

Dark shook his head. The man was right. The plan had been diabolical. "And the shootout? You set that up, huh?"

He smiled. "What better way to take the heat off yourself by puttin' a hit on yourself? I knew to hit Six-Nine but you saved Crystal. That was her lucky day. No biggie. It was only a matter of time before I hit you all."

"But, but Joy and—"

"Mines."

"Duffy?"

Born laughed. "I got big plans for that nigga. I'm sending him all the way to the top. He has a strong shot at the presidency."

"You ain't no god, nigga . . . You the devil!" Dark scoffed. "If I could clap I would give your ass a round of applause . . . I'ma die a legend," Dark taunted.

Born got in his face and responded, "Nigga, I thought you knew the science. The devil is a god too! Checkmate, nigga! And for the record, your run was short. You had no loyalty, no team, and you needed a bitch to put you on. So in my eyes, you gonna die the lame that you are."

Born laughed and stepped back as Mo'Betta and Baby Boy came into the room carrying baseball bats.

"So now you know. It was me. You were just my puppet. But now it's time to cut the strings. Yo, boys, have fun, but burn it down when you finish," Born instructed as he left the room.

"Fo' sho'," Mo'Betta nodded.

He had been the one who Born contacted. Once Mo'Betta let Rudy know he had Dark, several minutes later, Born had called him. Mo'Betta felt like he was being followed ever since his meeting with Born and his call only confirmed it. He knew Born would be a powerful ally against Shan, so he was ready to try to slide up under Born like he slid up under Briggen.

Mo' put his new plan in the back of his mind and turned his attention to Dark. He swung the bat hard into his kneecap, making Dark grit his teeth against the howl that threatened to erupt.

"Still don't wanna holla, huh?" Mo' snickered. "Don't matter, nigga, I'm still gonna enjoy watching you die. This for Rob!" He gritted, swinging the bat into Dark's face, shattering his nose and breaking several teeth.

Baby Boy followed up with a blow to the forehead that cracked Dark's skull. The blows began to rain down on him, knocking him and the chair over. The first few were mind-numbing pain. But as they beat the life out of him, with each blow he felt less and less. He had had a good run—the type of run that couldn't last. But he knew the streets of Detroit would never forget him. The majority of his mission was accomplished. A hood legend. His mom would have to be proud of him now.

Right before he blacked out forever, his last thought was of Damian shooting the basketball. He mumbled, "Wrist strength, shorty . . . work on your wrist strength."

Born walked out of the warehouse and headed for the stretch Phantom awaiting him. His plan had been perfect, but it wasn't done yet. He wanted much more than just the streets of Detroit, and he had the next level plan to obtain it. Besides, he had a secret weapon. Her.

"Hello, big daddy," Joy greeted as he climbed into the car.

She threw one curvaceous sexy leg over him while she kissed him passionately.

"Peace, love. How you? Did you take care of that?"

She smiled that cat-eyed smile that reminded him of a lioness after being fed. "Don't I always? Sherman won't be a problem."

Born nodded. "Everything went as planned, except, Nick. I didn't see Shan coming," Born admitted. "Shorty is definitely smart."

Joy giggled. "Don't worry, daddy, let me take care of Shan. I'll show her what a true boss bitch is."

Born poured them both a glass of Armand de Brignac, then held up his glass. "To the future, love."

"To the future," she toasted, and they downed their drinks together.

Acknowledgements

All praise is forever due to the Creator. Book #13! Yah Yah, love you much. Don't know what I'd do without you. The Staff. Never seen such dedicated folks ever. Love you all. You know who you are, Hasana (wahidaclark.org), Sherry, Al-Nisa, Mr. Barry, Kalimah, Sabir, Jabaar, Kisha, Hadiyah, Lindsey, Amin and Dwayne. You guys are in a league of your own. Slim and Baby, thank you for allowing me to do me and opening new doors. Cash Money Content Staff, Marc Gerald, Molly Derse who gets a special thank you for this bomb-diggity title: Blood Sweat & Payback (the hardest working little lady in publishing), Donna Torrence, Dawnalisa Johnson, Kia Selby, Vickie Charles. The behind the scenes Team at Simon & Schuster, thank you. To my editorial Team, you guys Rock!! You guys make my job very challenging and you push me to the limit! We got another *New York Times* Best Seller on our hands! Maxine Thompson (the backstory police), LJ Wilson, you Rock! Keisha Caldwell, thank you. Nuance Art, you are awesome!! I am so proud of you! Another bangin' cover. Thank you for being my right hand man, creative consultant and traveling partner. Big Fifty from Detroit, much love! Last but not least my the Browns, my moms Berta and Dad, my little Brother Melvin and Jabree, Aunt Marva who tries to get to every book signing in New York, Aunt Ginger, my agent, the pitbull in a skirt, Claudia Menza. The WCP authors, you guys rock but remember books don't sell themselves.

Once again, this one goes out to my readers!!! As always, I aim to please!! Let's goooooo!

2014 is the year for the Official Queen of Street Literature!

Watch for me!

Follow me on twitter and instagram @wahidaclark

BLOOD, SWEAT & **PAYBACK**
Reading Group Discussion Questions

1. Did you enjoy the fourth book in the Payback Series? Why or why not? Which characters did you like or dislike?

2. Janay's character seemed to have made a sudden spiritual transformation, but the moment her faith was truly tested and she lost the one thing she loved more than life itself, she turned right back to the life of crime. Seeing how her grief caused her to turn away, can anyone truly be saved as long as they are in the flesh?

3. Nyla, as well as the rest of the characters were set on vengeance against one another. How important is forgiveness to you? Or do you consider payback more fulfilling for the heart and soul? Please explain.

4. The Twins gave their lives for their family. How much does your family mean to you? Would you offer yourself as a sacrifice? Why or why not?

5. Tareek told Born The Consortium members didn't respect unity and solidarity. Is this also true of this present generation? Should members of any group engaged in illegal activity expect its members to have rules and regulations? Explain.

6. Nyla blamed Shan for the destruction of her marriage to Forever. Why do you think women often blame the "other woman" for their man's or husband's infidelity? What would you do if you discovered your husband or man was cheating?

7. Lisha discussed Dark's absence in their son Damien's life because of the danger his lifestyle posed to her and their son. Lisha stated

how men argue about their rights, but avoid their duties. What is the difference between a father's rights and a father's duties?

8. What is your opinion of Shan allowing her children's father and her husband, Briggen, to be killed? Do you agree with her decision? Why or why not?

9. Do you agree or disagree with the following line from the story? Explain. ". . . but sometimes you can give a person everything, and still, they will never change."

10. What are your thoughts on Baby Boy and Quita's relationship?

11. "Everybody's got haters. If you don't, you ain't doing something right." How true to life is this statement for you?

12. Shan and Briggen argued about who should be out getting the money. In a marriage does it matter which party is the bread winner? Explain.

13. Do you agree or disagree with the following statement? Why or why not?

    "Where has it gotten us? In my country of Sudan, the European give us Bibles, the Arab gives us Koran, but they get our resources as we get famine, war, and genocide. So, if we are to judge a tree by its fruit, what kind of seed are we planting?"

14. Do you think it's greed or a will to survive when hustlers decide they need to make just "one more run." What are your thoughts on this ideology as it applies to the character Briggen?

15. After reading the following statement, do you think society places very little value on black life in America? Do you think previous cases such as Emmett Till, Rodney King, James Byrd Jr., and Trevon Martin, prove this theory.

    They couldn't identify him, so they weren't a threat. Besides, they were white. One dead nigga was one thing, but two dead white people changed the game.

TWO SNEAK PEEKS OF
THUGS PART 7

WHY TWO?
I need you to vote on which way I should take the story.

If you like **Version One**
Text me at 973-671-1609 and type #VersionOne

If you like **Version Two**
Text me at 973-671-1609 and type #VersionTwo

Thugs Part 7
Chapter One
Of Version One

"To family."

"To family!"

Trae toasted, and they all toasted back, clicking their champagne flutes. They were all there together again, the whole family back where it all started . . . New York, New York.

Trae and Tasha had to relocate because of the situation with the Li Organization. Although Mr. Li had gotten Trae out of all of his charges, he had given Trae an ultimatum: *get out of California or face massive retaliation*. Trae chose to leave, but he knew it wouldn't be the last he heard of Mr. Li or his daughter Charli. Therefore, he found himself obsessed with putting together a master plan to end his problem once and for all and to get paid doing it. So if he succeeded, the rewards would be great.

Faheem and Jaz moved back to Jersey because of the hit Jaz had done on Oni. The situation had gotten too hot, especially with Oni's brother, Ronnie, a police officer who promised to get at Faheem. Not to mention the fact that Steele and the East Atlanta Gresham Boys were beefing causing the body count to reach an all-time high. Steele was accusing Faheem of Oni's death. The ATL was no longer the place for him and Jaz to be.

The tension between Kaylin and Angel was at an all-time high because Kaylin was the main co-conspirator in Trae's master plan of taking the game to the next level.

The Ritz Carlton ballroom was packed for Lil' E's album release party, and everyone was all smiles as the diamonds glistened and the champagne flowed.

"Yo, I can't believe I'm back at the same spot where I proposed to my baby." Trae leaned over and kissed Tasha on the cheek. She turned away with an attitude. "This is also the same spot where I threw this nigga's birthday party." Trae was referring to Kaylin as he looked around, obviously getting nostalgic. "How you pull this off?" He turned to Kaylin.

"I almost didn't. This youngin' named B-Murder got his people running it. They on that King shit big time. The only way I pulled it off was to share my credentials with him. The nigga had the nerve to do a due diligence check on me. Can you believe that shit?" Kaylin replied.

"You bullshittin'," Trae snapped. "How a Blood gonna be running the muthafuckin' Ritz Carlton? I ain't never heard of no shit like that."

Faheem shook his head. "Shit, he ain't lying. Them muthafuckas taking over from here all the way to Trenton. Wait until you see how they got that little ass city sewed up. I thought Atlanta was bad."

"Yeah well, now that we back in town. King or no King, you either get down or lay

down," Trae spat, giving Faheem a pound.

Tasha looked at Trae out of the corner of her eyes. She hated to see him jumping back in the game with both feet. She sensed he was doing it to spite her. She couldn't quite put her finger on why.

"I gotta go to the bathroom," Tasha said, putting her glass down and standing up.

Sensing her vibe, Jaz, Kyra, and Angel got up to go with her.

"Make sure you find your way right back," Trae told her, with just a slice of menace in his tone.

Tasha ignored him as she and the ladies walked away. Trae eyed her until she disappeared into the crowd.

"Yo, fam', what up with you and Tasha? Y'all ain't said next to nothing to each other all night," Kaylin questioned.

"I'm good," Trae responded, sipping his champagne.

"Man, no you ain't," Kaylin told him. "What's up?"

Trae smiled. "Why you all up in mines, dawg?"

"Nigga, spill it!" Kaylin ordered. "You know we gotta keep the home front intact."

"You know I know that shit. But I'm picking up some vibes from her about this pregnancy. I think she wants to tell me something."

Kaylin became quiet as if lost in thought. A few people came over to their table to congratulate him, show him love, and just show some respect. Some of them also showed Trae love as well. As soon as they were gone he said, "Man, I know you ain't saying what I think you're saying. Go ahead with that bullshit."

"I'm serious, yo. I feel it. I tried to ignore it, but it ain't going nowhere."

"Feel what?" Faheem asked, feeling out of the loop.

"That the baby she carrying ain't his," Kaylin schooled him.

"Then whose is it?" Faheem regretted the words as soon as they came out. "Oh, fuck! My bad, son."

"Ain't no thing. It is what it is. I just gotta deal with it, that's all. I'm good."

"And how do you plan on doing that?"

"I said I'm good," Trae told Kaylin sharply.

Kaylin shrugged it off. "Okay, you good. As long as you good, fam', I'm good."

Wanting to change the subject, Faheem poured himself more champagne and said, "Trae, I'm definitely feelin' the plan, but the Dons . . . if shit get crazy, they'd be risking an all-out war with Li. You sure it's worth being the cause of that shit?"

"'No doubt," Trae answered. "I've been on the inside, so I know Li's weakness. Believe me, we do this right, the Dons will see multimillions real fast."

"And if we don't pull it off, it's our asses," Faheem added.

"Ain't no plan B. So you either with it or you ain't," Trae reminded him, with a look in his eyes that said he would do whatever it took to win.

Kaylin watched Trae as he spoke. He knew Trae and he had to admit, Trae hadn't been the same since he came home. Really, since he started fucking with the Oriental bitch. It was like he had something to prove, and Lord have mercy on whoever got in the way.

They walked into the elaborate ladies room only to find two girls leaned against the wall, tonguing each other down. One girl had her leg cocked up around the other girl's waist while the other chick played in her pussy. Even when Tasha, Angel, and Jaz walked in, they didn't let up.

Tasha cleared her throat hard. "Goddamn!" Tasha huffed. "I mean really? We in a hotel. Go upstairs and check into your fuckin' room."

The two girls got the message, untangled themselves and walked out. The more aggressive one eyed Angel lustfully as they left.

"Why you hatin'? You and Trae used to get y'all freak on anywhere and everywhere," Jaz reminded her as she turned to the mirror, fixing her hair.

"Please! That shit is taking over the world, and when it's done like that, it is not cute. I'm just sayin'," Tasha commented.

"What's up with you and Trae, Tasha? Y'all are like frigid tonight. We are supposed to be celebrating," Angel asked.

Tasha kept up her sassy façade for as long as she could, but alone with her girls she was able to let her guard down.

"Girl, I know, and it got me fucked up. I don't know what's going on anymore."

"Hell, me either. We all going through the same shit. And I'm not feeling it. We were supposed to be done with this street shit a long time ago," Angel said.

"Yeah, but it's like . . . I don't know . . . I try to talk to him to get at least an inkling of what's going on, but it's like I'm not getting through, you know," Tasha answered, fighting back tears.

"Believe me, ma, I feel your pain. Faheem been on his hot and cold shit ever since that shit went down in Georgia," Jaz added.

"No. For me, it's deeper than that," Tasha said hesitantly.

"Deeper? What do you mean?" Angel asked.

Tasha hugged herself and took a deep breath. "Remember I told you I took the DNA test?"

Angel gasped and covered her mouth because she knew what Tasha was about to

say.

A tear fell from Tasha's eye as she nodded. Kyra caught on, and she grabbed her chest saying, "Oh my God! Tasha, please don't tell me that you are carrying Kyron's baby?"

Hearing her problem out loud made it too much for Tasha. She burst into tears. Angel rushed to embrace her. Once the tears stopped, Angel had to ask, "But I thought you told Trae it was his?"

"I did. I had to. I felt as if he wouldn't forgive me this time. I don't want to lose him, Angel. I swear I don't know what to do. If I have this baby, and it comes out looking like Kyron, Trae will leave me. But if I have an abortion, he'll know that I lied to him," Tasha cried.

Kyra gasped. "Abortion? You damn near ready to deliver, Tasha."

This time when she cried, both Angel and Jaz embraced her in a three-way hug. They knew Trae and Tasha had been through a lot, but they all had their doubts that the marriage could survive her having another man's child.

End of **Version One**
Text me at 973-671-1609 and type #VersionOne
If this is your favorite!

Thugs Part 7
Chapter One
Version Two

Trae

I thought that a change of venue would fix everything, but I was wrong. The problems we ran from ran to us, and then fucked up all our commitments. Family, trust and love were damn near destroyed by the temptations that we both surrendered to. We wanted out of the game but the game was not done with us. I guess the old saying, *there is no getting out* must be true because no matter how hard we tried we just can't get out.

I woke up and looked at Tasha lying peacefully in our bed. Unable to sleep I walked around the house trying to put together a plan to get our lives and love back on track. Peeking in on the twins and Caliph brought good feelings but the reality that I was back where I started from, back in my New York apartment, back in the city that brought me so much wealth and so much pain tugged relentlessly at my heart. Being in that cell brought out the animal in me. The beast I tried to rid myself of had taken over and mercy was not an option. Here I am back in the game with an enemy looking over my shoulder that I need to terminate.

I sat on the couch, lit a blunt and with each pull I embodied the old Trae. The Trae that needed the kill more than air itself. My fate was decided the day I was born. I was born a true leader and anything that dared to threaten my throne would be destroyed.

Tasha

I had barely picked my head off the pillow and the feelings of regret filled my stomach. I looked over at Trae's empty spot and the memory of the things that are missing in our life flooded my mind. I wanted to cry but I was so sick and tired of the tears. The only thing left for me to do was to start over. I questioned myself about why I fell in love with Trae. What was it about him that rendered me incapable of being in control of my life? And why was I still married to him?

At this point, it seemed as if the only thing that was real between us was our children. He is so happy that I am giving him a daughter that he can hardly contain himself. I gave him a copy of the DNA results just to put his mind at ease so that we can put all that bullshit behind us. However nothing seems to be working. I don't know if it is being in New York, the pregnancy or what, but we both fucked up everything that we cherished and now we are just surviving together. Is it worth it or should we just let go?

As I walked to the bathroom I reflected on last night. My husband's touch and the look in his eyes when he's holding me, warms me and is irreplaceable. But the cold stare that peers out from his soul chills me to the bone. This is not the Trae that I know and love, this is the Trae I almost lost to death and prison and by each waking hour he is turning into a beast. The blood on his hands was changing him and to be true to myself it was changing me.

Angel

It's only been a few months since Kaylin and I were looking death in the face. So much has changed in all our lives. Tasha and Trae are back in the city and it brings me both joy and pain. And having Trae back home puts Kaylin in a whole different mindset. I know one thing; I have invested too much in my family and our business to let shit slip from my grasp because of his loyalty to his family.

When I walked into the studio this morning I was overcome by the feeling of emptiness. Not only was Kaylin not in our bed when I went to sleep, he was not in it when I woke up. Then to walk into the place that he calls his second home and not see a trace of his presence let me know one thing. He was back in.

I walked into my office, took a seat and contemplated my next move. At this stage in our lives I thought that we were done with this petty street shit. Me and Kaylin were definitely going to have a long talk. I said it before and I thought everyone understood that regardless of how much I loved having my girls around me what I wasn't going to let happen was letting their bullshit fuck up what me and Kaylin have built.

The longer I sat and thought about it the angrier I became. I picked up the phone and dialed Kaylin. This was a conversation I needed to have sooner than later.

Kaylin

I rolled over in the bed and grabbed the phone that had been ringing back to back for the last five minutes. I knew it was Red but shit I had just laid down and was in no mood to listen to her spazz out. I knew if I didn't answer now I would have to deal with her rants later.

"Hey baby what's up?"

"I see you found your way home," she stated.

I could feel the heat from the other end. "Yeah, I'm home. You need something?" I asked turning over onto my back.

"Yes, I need to know when you are coming into the office. We have a lot to go over."

"I'm not sure. I gotta get some rest then I'll roll up there later." I turned over and tucked the pillow under my head.

"Kaylin what are *we* doing?"

"What do you mean?"

"Look, I can't do this. Ever since Trae has been back in the city you been on that bullshit, late nights and early mornings. Not to mention you have not been in the office in three days. So my question is what are we doing?"

"Red, we can talk about this when I get up there. Let me get some sleep. I need to clear my head."

"You know what? Get all the sleep you need. I had a decision to make and you made it very easy."

When the phone disconnected I looked at it to make sure I didn't just dream that shit. I called her right back and got no answer. When I rang the front desk the secretary said she had just jumped on the elevator. *What the fuck is she up to?* I tossed the phone onto the night stand. I started to throw on some clothes and head up there but then I thought, *fuck that.* I'm the boss in this muthafucka and her spoiled ass been calling shots long enough. I settled into my warm spot and drifted off.

Jaz

Back in New Jersey, I thought to myself shaking my head as I ironed Kaeerah's clothes for school. Faheem was fully recovered physically but the mental scars I was sure would never heal. Our relationship was getting better but there was a hole in his spirit that I knew my love could never fill. I looked over at him sitting at the table talking to our little princess and even though a smile took over his face, I knew there was pain and hate in his heart.

Once I got Kaeerah off to school I sat next to Faheem and began to lay down what I called in my mind *the law*.

"Baby, we need to talk."

"What's up?" he said as he reached for the remote and lowered the volume on the television.

"I know we just got settled, but I don't think I can stay here in Jersey. I fought too hard to get out of here and the last thing I want is to raise our daughter here." I looked at his face in an attempt to gage his mood.

"So what are you trying to say?" he turned staring me dead in my eyes. A lump formed in my throat as I tried to rephrase my request.

"I want to leave. And I want you to let me go," I said as tears welled up in my eyes.

"What the fuck do you mean? You want me to let you go?" Faheem looked as confused as I was.

"I am miserable here and I feel like I am about to lose myself. And I don't want to be around while you are back in the streets. I know you can understand that." And as the words left my lips warm tears flowed down my cheeks.

"Let you go? How am I supposed to do that? How can I keep you safe if you way across the country somewhere? Jaz, you can ride with me for a few months and what I got to handle will be handled." He said with all the sincerity his voice could muster then placed his soft lips to mine.

"I don't have to go far, Faheem. And how can you keep us safe if you all in the streets? And a couple of months? Do you hear yourself?"

"Do you hear yourself?" He got up on me again and kissed me. He pulled back and he gave me what seemed to be a warning. "Letting you go is not an option. You will stay right here." He kissed me gently then pulled back, got up and walked towards the bedroom.

An eerie feeling flooded my body as his words floated through my mind. He had just confirmed my worst fears and I needed to put my plan into motion and quick.

Kyra

I rubbed my stomach tenderly as if each second was going to be my last. I was still having good and bad days. My memory was still fading in and out and the dizziness seemed to be coming more frequently. Being away from Rick was killing me and at times I felt so defeated. I had lost my past, hated my present and was so unsure about my future. Even though he made frequent trips to see me it was not the same as having him here with me. My emotions and hormones were running rampant. I stood there watching Trae asleep on the Laz-E-Boy. He had on a wife beater, sweat pants and his feet were bare. He took Marvin away from me and Aisha. I couldn't get that out of my mind.

Trae

I laid back in my favorite chair acting as if I was asleep. Tasha was on her knees sucking my dick as if she was mad at me or is if I was making her. It wasn't even all of that. We needed to talk. We needed to start to get things right somehow. I reached over and turned on the light.

"So, why do I deserve a blowjob? You want me to do you?" I looked down and to my surprise, Kyra slid my dick from out of her mouth and looked up at me. "What the fuck? Kyra? What the fuck are you doing?" I pushed her away from me, stuffing my dick back into my pants. I felt violated. "Tasha will fuckin' kill you. I will kill you. What the fuck is wrong with you?"

She stood up looking at me all crazy as if what I was asking her was an insult. "I think it's time for you to go. Pack your shit. You got's to go. Aisha can stay, but you have to go."

"Trae, no."

"Trae, no. What? What is y'all up to?" Tasha stepped into the living room.

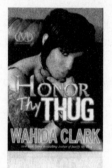

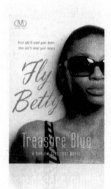

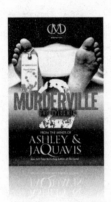

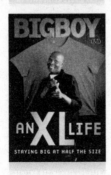

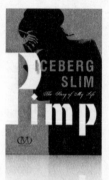

OFFICIAL QUEEN OF STREET LITERATURE

WAHIDA CLARK
NEW YORK TIMES BESTSELLING AUTHOR

FOR BOOKINGS CONTACT: BOOKINGS@WCLARKPUBLISHING.COM
New York Times Bestselling Arthor - The First Lady of Cash Money Content!

WCLARKPUBLISHING.com